THE
AGENT

The Agent

ISBN 978-1-7327747-7-3

Cover & Illustration: Alex Roberts, AJR Designs
Book Design: Jim Shubin, BookAlchemist.net

THE
AGENT

MARSHA ROBERTS

Easy Riter Press

ONE

"ONE MILLION, TWO HUNDRED FIFTY thousand dollars." The lightly accented voice confirmed that the sum had been transferred into her account today. Victoria Clifford thanked him and clicked her phone shut. For just a moment, she let herself enjoy the sweep of elation. Damn, it felt good. A net worth of nearly US$10 million. And all on her own power.

She grabbed her Louis Vuitton and headed out the door. The little toe on her left foot throbbed with each step, like an ice pick chipping away, sending a shooting spasm straight to her temple. Those alligator pumps—she was going to have them stretched. Maybe she should go back and change. No, they were perfect with her new ivory dress; it would be a crime not to wear them. Anyway, there wasn't time to change. She shifted the pain to the part of her brain that didn't feel it and walked down the driveway, heels clicking happily, like everything was fine.

The smooth leather seat of her convertible was warm from the sun. She tilted the rear-view mirror for a quick check. Not bad at all. True, she wasn't mistaken for a model anymore, but that was okay. *Better have wits if you don't have beauty,* her father used to say. Victoria prided herself on having both. Image was everything. Even in the bright morning glare, hers was pretty impeccable. Genes, some would say ... she's got great genes. Some of it was genes, sure, but most of it was just damn hard work and discipline.

Her cool, jade eyes skimmed over her face in the mirror, in particular examining her nose for any evidence of this morning's celebratory sniff. Satisfied, she put her sunglasses on, started the car and headed for the Sausalito office of Barnaby Wells Realty.

Could it get any better than this? Top-producing real estate agent in Marin County, California, for three years running, plus a side job that earned her millions. Of course, it wasn't technically a job.

She pulled onto Napa Street toward the office, replaying this morning's phone call again in her head. Nothing beat the thrill of a secret life—unless it was having two or three. Better than sex or coke. And just as addictive.

The office was crazy busy, even for a Monday. This year would surely go down as one of the biggest boom years ever in San Francisco Bay Area real estate history. At eight in the morning the reception lounge already bulged with waiting clients. The main office area was like a trading floor ... phones ringing, staff rushing, voices loud over the din.

Josh jumped up to meet her. She couldn't help but smile; those boyish Italian types always got to her. "New client wants to talk with you about a listing on Sunset in Tiburon. Those go for around five or six mil, don't they? Here's the contact info." He spoke in a rapid clip and grinned as he handed her the paper.

She scanned the sheet, taking in the basic details about the property and its owners, then saw the small yellow Post-it at the bottom. *Can't wait to see you tomorrow nite,* it said.

She looked up to see him slide a wink at her.

"Got to go!" As he dashed past her, she caught a trace of his cologne and a warm wave shot through her. To think some women settled for just one man.

She turned back to the spec sheet. The owners were Charles and Maribeth Simmons. She called the number and made arrangements with Maribeth to see the house the next day. Then Victoria fell into the routine of returning calls and researching listings. A few hours later, she caught sight of her watch and was shocked to see that it was almost one. Her weekly appointment—the one she never missed—was in twenty minutes.

She grabbed her things and made for the door. "I'm off for a few hours," she told the receptionist. "Not sure if I'll be back today. I'll have my cell in case anyone needs to reach me."

It took only a few minutes to pick up lunch. She carried the low-fat, blueberry-yogurt smoothie outside, sipping in the thick sweetness slowly, rolling it over her tongue, savoring every drop. Next door was Phyllis' Burgers. The smell of grilling meat went straight to her salivary glands. Now that was what she really wanted ... a burger ... charred on the outside, a little oozy on the inside ... tart, melted cheddar topping it off. No lettuce, no tomatoes, no mustard, no ketchup, nothing to fetter the exquisite taste. Just a chunky, luscious burger, cheese spilling over the sides and a toasted bun—no, not a bun, a toasted sourdough baguette, yes, a sourdough baguette. Maybe just today to celebrate the deposit. After all, she deserved it. Over a million dollars, for God's sake. Come on—if not today, then when? The thought played in her head, messing with it.

No fucking way. Don't give in. Breathe in through your mouth—stop smelling it! One small slip and you'll be a size 16 again—your seams splitting with blubber and self-disgust. *Fatso, get your butt out here and help me with the lawn. It'll help work off some of that flab,* she heard her father say.

She speeded up and passed Phyllis'. No, the smoothie would do just fine, thank you. She caught a glimpse of her figure in a storefront window. It was worth it. No one would ever guess that she used to be a fat kid. She had to be careful, though—more than careful. Vigilant. Watch every morsel. Otherwise she'd be right back there—a blob. *You fat shit, there's no fucking way you're having that burger.*

She arrived at Tatiana's sipping the last of her smoothie.

"Hey, gorgeous, how are you doing?" Tim, the receptionist, kissed her on both cheeks. "You are looking fabulous. New boyfriend? Come on, you can tell me."

"No. Still single. Don't you have anyone for me, Timmy?"

"Honey, I hang out with the wrong crowd for that, but you don't need any help—you're not fooling me!" He led her into the private room reserved for facials. "Can I get you a glass of wine?"

"Some Sauvignon Blanc would be heavenly, thanks! Just half a glass, though. I'm gaining weight."

"What? You are not! I see those skinny little ribs sticking out!"

"No, really, Timmy. I'm up a half-pound since yesterday and I've hardly eaten anything!"

"Listen, the only part of you that's heavy is that plus-sized inner critic. Now you just get comfy. I'll be right back with the wine."

He closed the door and Victoria kicked off her shoes. Her aching toe, now raw with a blister, nestled into the lush carpet, savoring the sweet pleasure of release. She got undressed, wrapped the white terry towel around her chest and pulled her hair into a ponytail. She was just letting her muscles sink into the soft reclining chair when Tatiana bustled in.

"Victoria, darling, so good to see you. You look

marvelous, as usual," Tatiana said in her thick, Ukrainian accent.

Tim brought in the glass of wine and set it down next to her. "See you later, hon." He closed the door gently behind him.

"Now you just relax and we make you even more beautiful." Tatiana reached for the first of the creams to be applied to her face.

Victoria took a long, smooth sip of wine and lay back in the chair. She let the piped-in harp music float into her mind, unwinding it—turning it off high alert—just for now. She let her nerves succumb to Tatiana's supple, sturdy hands as she smoothed and stroked her face and neck. She felt herself falling into a trance. Over a million deposited today and maybe the prospect of another million or two in three or four months. Her thoughts turned to the Simmons house. It sounded promising. There was something about it. It was too soon to tell, of course, but she just had a hunch. And her hunches were usually right.

She wasn't actually psychic, like her Aunt Vera, but every now and then she had a definite sense of what was to come. It wasn't really a feeling, but more like a sensation ... like she was perceiving the world in another frequency. It had happened when she saw Maribeth Simmons' name, as though she had known it all along. Like it was already part of her life, or her history. When she got these flashes, the future and present blended together into one unit of time, so that it was difficult to tell which events had already happened and which were yet to come.

If, indeed, Maribeth was to be next, Victoria couldn't wait to get started. It meant she would get to see Theo soon. Her heart gave a little skip. They would pull it off again, just as they had when they were kids. The stakes were much bigger now, and the risks way higher, and the thrill—the thrill was in a whole different sphere.

Unlike their scams as kids, though, this was not one they could do all on their own. At least so far, they hadn't figured out how. There was one part only their Aunt Vera could play.

The perfect crime. Five times now without a hitch. And entirely her own creation. A delicious smile formed under the moisturizing cream. She started to replay each of the cons in her head. Soon she was dozing, each breath a delicate sigh.

There was a gentle tapping on her shoulder. "Darling, it is finished," Tatiana whispered.

Victoria forced herself out of her reverie. It took her a moment to collect the words to thank Tatiana. Fighting grogginess and a sense of stupor, she managed to get dressed and reapply her makeup, then made her way to the reception desk.

"Wow! Ravishing!" Tim gave her the once-over. "Honey, if I wasn't such a queen, I'd pounce on you in a minute." He grinned. "Need any products today?"

"Thanks! Yeah, actually, I do. A three-ounce jar of the rejuvenator."

"Here it is. With the facial, that will be $200," he said.

She looked around quickly to make sure no one was close by, then handed him her credit card and three hundred-dollar bills. "Here you go."

He pocketed the cash and processed the credit payment, keeping up the breezy banter without breaking stride. "Thanks, honey. Now you take care and have some fun. You work too hard!" He kissed her on both cheeks.

Back in her car, she reached into her purse for the cream. In the jar were two neatly folded bindles of cocaine. Good for a couple of weeks.

Yes, there was nothing like a few good secrets to keep life interesting, and the more the better. She thought about all the little secrets she had going, then turned her attention to the big one.

TWO

THE DRIVEWAY OF 227 SUNSET wove through a small grove for several yards before ending in front of a three-car garage. Victoria stepped out of her car and took in the setting. Even after living in Marin for over a decade, the spectacular natural beauty of the place still blew her away. Massive redwoods fronted the property, giving it a stately curtain of privacy. She looked carefully at the house. It was a traditional, two-story, white-brick Tudor, with a large bow-shaped picture window on the right of the front door—eat-in kitchen area, she guessed. The second floor featured a turreted window on each of the two front corners with a wide balcony in between, flanked by French doors.

The land appeared to slope downward behind the house and garage. She imagined this probably afforded a spectacular view of Angel Island, the bay and San Francisco beyond. Definitely a great property. The house style was a bit staid for some tastes, but barring any major disasters inside, it should be an easy sell.

The front walk wound through a lavender garden before leading to the entrance. Victoria drew the scent into her lungs and savored the calming effect. Just as she was about to press the buzzer, the door opened and Maribeth Simmons greeted her.

"Victoria, I'm Maribeth. It's good to meet you." The blonde woman extended her hand and shook Victoria's warmly.

Victoria sized up her new client quickly. Maribeth Simmons was an attractive woman—not stunning or beautiful, but nice-looking in a wholesome sort of way. In her mid-thirties, Victoria guessed. She was slightly shorter than Victoria and a few sizes larger. Standing in the doorway with very little makeup and wearing a simple pale-blue sweater set, khaki slacks and brown loafers, Maribeth reminded Victoria of a young Martha Stewart.

"Come on in," Maribeth said. "Would you like some iced tea? Coffee?"

"No, thanks, maybe later. Why don't you show me the house?"

As Maribeth began the tour, Victoria launched into her standard background questions. "Why are you selling?"

Her new client paused for a second before answering. "My husband was reassigned back to St. Louis with his company." Victoria found out that both Simmons were originally from Missouri. The husband had been transferred to the Bay Area about a year ago.

"Wow! Short assignment," Victoria said.

"Yes, unfortunately."

The house had the same air as its owner—pleasant, conservative and in need of a bit of spark and updating. The living room was large, with floor-to-ceiling windows that faced the bay. But rather than being positioned to take full advantage of the view, the matching taupe sofa and love seat sat blandly in the corner of the room with a drab, maple coffee table in front of them. Two armchairs upholstered in a muted flowered pattern completed the conversation cluster.

As if to make up for the plainness of the furniture, multicolored dried-flower arrangements and glass containers of potpourri were everywhere. If Maribeth had looked closely at Victoria, she would have seen her nose twitch visibly in disapproval.

"What a stunning view," Victoria said, finding a compliment she could deliver truthfully. They moved into the adjoining dining room, which also looked out on the bay, but was just as boringly furnished. At least the kitchen was more cheerful, with its cherry-dotted curtains—a throwback to the 1950s. Still, it was a large room. White wood cabinets provided ample storage and there was enough counter space to accommodate a small bakery. For a buyer with a discerning eye, it could be ideal.

Victoria kept up an easy chatter as they mounted the stairs to the second floor. She was already strategizing about how to bring up the subject of staging. It was a potentially delicate topic. Some clients were happy to have an expert rearrange their furniture, cull out extraneous items and bring in some new pieces to make their property more marketable. Others took great pride in what they believed to be their decorating ability and were offended when the idea of staging was raised. Victoria wondered what Maribeth's reaction would be. In this case, though, she had to take the risk. Showing the house in its current state was out of the question. And she had seen only half of it.

In the center of the second floor was the master bedroom. This was the room, it turned out, with the long balcony running along almost the full length of the front of the house. Victoria commented on the room's spacious size and brightness and went to check out the closets. She got to the entrance of the walk-in closet and stopped short. One entire half of the closet was bare; the other was filled with what were obviously Maribeth's clothes.

"Oh, so your husband has already moved to St. Louis?"

"Yes, he has."

Something in Maribeth's voice told Victoria not to pursue this line of conversation further for the time being. But a small seed of excitement began to take root.

"There are five other bedrooms up here," Maribeth said.

"Plus a family room." They went on to look at the second and third bedrooms, which featured the turreted windows Victoria had seen from the outside. While architecturally interesting, they looked like unused guest rooms, each with the requisite bed, nightstands and dresser, but totally devoid of personality. The next bedroom, at the back of the house, had an unbeatable bay view, which was almost totally obscured by packing boxes stacked nearly to the ceiling. Next was the "family room," which had become Maribeth's craft room. A massive table stood in the center of the room. At one end were various trays with assorted beads of every size and color. The other end had a patchwork of different sized pieces of felt, each with a partially completed necklace, bracelet or pair of earrings on it. A few finished jewelry items lay at the center of the table.

Victoria was immediately drawn to a nearly finished necklace with a sequence of luminous turquoise and coral stones. She walked over to it. In the middle of the string was an unusual piece that looked like an antique Asian pendant. It was flat and round, a couple of inches in diameter and about an inch thick. It appeared to be made of bronze. The image of a Buddha was at the center, surrounded by Chinese characters. It looked like the piece might originally have been a locket, but its seams were now welded on all sides with no evidence of a clasp.

"This is exquisite, Maribeth."

Maribeth smiled. The first genuine smile since her arrival, Victoria noted.

"You're very creative," Victoria said.

"Not really. I copy designs from beading and jewelry magazines. I do it just to pass the time."

"It takes a lot of skill to make these, even if they aren't original designs." Victoria picked up an amber and copper necklace and matching bracelet, admiring them. "You should give yourself more credit." Even though she had barely met the woman, she had a feeling that this advice could be applied to many areas of Maribeth's life.

They moved on to the last bedroom, which was set up as an office—one that apparently wasn't used much. The desk was almost bare, save for a computer and a pad of paper. The bookcases were a series of gaping, empty rectangles.

In fact, except for the master-bedroom suite and the kitchen, the entire house showed few signs of life. It reminded Victoria of a furniture store, a collection of room displays with perfectly matching pieces and a splash of accessories—orderly and appropriate, but soulless. The home gave no clue about the personalities of its owners. In spite of the killer views and attractive architecture, the house was cold and lifeless.

"It's a great property," Victoria said as she followed Maribeth down the stairs. "Too bad you weren't able to spend much time in it."

Maribeth led the way back to the living room; she was holding her hand to her forehead, Victoria noticed.

"Maybe I'll take you up on that iced tea now." Victoria followed her into the room. "And we can talk about the asking price and how you'd like to handle availability of the house for viewing. Unless, of course, you'd like to include your husband in the discussion, too. If so, we could call him, or wait until he's back in town. ..."

Maribeth's hand was over her eyes and now her head sank forward. Victoria walked around to face her and saw that she was crying silently. "Are you okay? Is this a bad time? I can come back another day." She avoided looking directly at Maribeth.

"No, I've got to do this; we might as well get it over with." She sounded calm in spite of her obvious distress.

"I'm sorry ... you really don't want to sell the house, do you?"

Maribeth took a deep breath and let it out slowly. "It's a lot more than that, I'm afraid. Do you mind sitting down for a few minutes while I throw some water on my face and get us some iced tea?"

Victoria sat on the colorless sofa and thought about her new client, a small thrill taking root. Her instincts had already told her something was off before the crying. Not a single article of the husband's clothing in the closet, an empty office, and now that she thought about it, she didn't recall seeing a single photograph anywhere. Perfect!

Her client came back into the living room carrying a tray with a pitcher, two glasses and a plate of cookies. "I'm so sorry I lost it. I guess the fact that the house is going up for sale finally sank in."

"Really, Maribeth, I can come back some other time."

"No. Look, I should probably tell you. I'll have to tell you at some point anyway." Maribeth's gaze darted around the room, finally resting directly on Victoria. "My husband didn't get transferred to St. Louis. He left me." Victoria could see new tears beginning to pool in her eyes.

"Oh, I'm so sorry." Victoria put down her glass. What had been just a speck of excitement now blossomed. She frowned and pursed her lips to stop a smirk from forming.

Maribeth was gripping one hand in the other. "He went

back to St. Louis to be with someone else. He left me here to sell the house." The words came out haltingly. Victoria was pretty sure it was the first time she had said them out loud.

"He not only left you, but stuck you with having to sell the house?"

"It's not quite as bad as it sounds." Her lips tried to smile, but settled back into a thin line. "He felt really guilty about cheating on me and then dumping me, so we agreed that I could keep all the profit from the house if I stayed to sell it— plus half of our assets, of course."

"How long have you been married?"

"Seven years. The thing is, I had no clue he was fooling around. Unbelievable, right? I feel like an idiot. I even thought we had a great marriage. He was so good to me, so supportive. You know, until now, I could never understand how some women claimed they were shocked when they found out their husbands were having an affair. I figured I would know right away. I would just sense it, you know, like radar. But I didn't. I feel like a dumb housewife in some cheesy soap opera—seven-year itch and all. It couldn't be more trite." She caught herself. "I'm sorry, laying all of this on you. You don't even know me, and here I am spilling my guts."

"Don't worry: I can understand how awful this must be for you. I take it you don't have kids?"

Maribeth's face seemed to grow heavier for a moment. "No, we don't. I wanted to, but Charlie wasn't sure, so we decided to wait for a while. That's one reason we got this huge house to begin with. We thought … well, at least I thought … that we'd have kids. But we never did, and I guess it's a good thing we didn't. I can't imagine going through this with kids—it's enough of a nightmare as it is.

"Look, I'm sorry for taking up your time with all this," Maribeth went on. "The truth is, I don't have many people I can talk to. I don't have any family left and I haven't made any real friends here yet, so when the subject came up, I guess the dam just broke."

"I don't mind at all," Victoria reassured her. "I feel so badly for you. And especially if there's no one here who can help you through this. How about any people you work with? Aren't you close to anyone there?"

Maribeth started a laugh and shook her head. "No, that's another part of this stupid story. When Charlie got transferred here, I left a job I loved in St. Louis. It was such a once-in-a-lifetime opportunity for him to come here, setting up a new subsidiary. They offered him an excellent package, lots of stock options, and so on. It seemed to make sense for me to quit my little job and make a move that could pay off for us substantially from a financial standpoint.

"So, I've spent most of the last year getting us settled here. I was just starting to look for a job—I sent out my resumé to some headhunters—when Charlie announced he was in love with someone else. So, here I am with no friends, no job, no husband, no life, just a house to sell and the prospect of having to start from scratch. I'm sorry; I keep dumping all this on you. Would you like more iced tea? How about some cookies? You haven't touched any of them."

"No, thanks. I'm fine. So, what was your job in St. Louis?"

"I was a features editor for the *St. Louis Post Dispatch*."

"Wow! A writer, huh?"

"No. An editor. There's a big difference. Those who can, write—those who can't, edit." She gave a small laugh.

"In any case, I'm sure there's a big market for editors here. You won't have any problems getting a job—if you want to work, that is."

"Being an editor in St. Louis is one thing. San Francisco is another thing altogether. I don't know if I could actually get a job here. To tell you the truth, I don't know what I want. I don't know if I really want to stay here. I've been thinking about going back to Kansas City, where I'm from."

Maribeth shook her head. "Okay, that's it. You've heard enough of my problems. Can't I talk you into another glass of tea, or wine, maybe?"

"Actually, I have to run," Victoria said, looking at her watch. The eagerness was rising in her throat, threatening to make its way into her voice. She concentrated on sounding businesslike. "But we do have to finalize the paperwork for the sale. I'm thinking we should put it on the market for $5.3. What do you think?"

"$5.3 million? We just bought it a year ago for $4 million."

"The market has been crazy here. Properties have been appreciating thirty percent annually—or more. It's definitely a seller's market. You're hitting it at a great time."

"Well, at least that'll be one thing that's going right. Sure, let's put it on for $5.3 million. You're the expert."

"Okay, great. I'll have everything drawn up for your signature right away. How about getting together tomorrow or Thursday to go over the papers for the house, and then I'll take you to lunch?"

"Tomorrow's fine. I want to get this over with as soon as possible."

"Okay. Eleven o'clock at my office? Then we'll do lunch. By the way, Charlie did give you power of attorney for the house sale, right?"

"Yes. He made sure all the details were covered; filed a quitclaim deed and everything. Eleven sounds great." Maribeth led Victoria to the front door and took her hand into both of hers. "Thanks for listening. I'll try not to be such a basket case next time."

"Hey, don't worry about it. We'll get through this together. I'll do everything I can to make the house sale as easy as possible for you. And by the way, it's a great house. You won't have any trouble selling it."

As the door closed behind her, Victoria allowed herself a wide smile. "Yes!" she said under her breath. The lavender, which had calmed her on the way in, was now invigorating. She glanced back at the house before getting in her car. "Absolutely perfect!" she said—out loud this time.

It was one o'clock in the morning in Geneva. Too late—or too early—to call Theo. Damn! She wanted to tell him right away. But it would have to wait.

Besides, she had to get ready for Josh.

THREE

THERE WAS A KNOCK AT VERA PETERLIN'S DOOR. She looked up as her assistant, Cynthia, led in her new client. "This is Carolina Crespi." Cynthia closed the door, leaving them alone in Vera's office.

"Welcome, Carolina." Vera went over to her and shook her hand. Carolina was a petite woman, in her early thirties, Vera guessed, and attractive in an understated way. Her polished brown hair was wound in a neat bun, drawing attention to her most prominent feature—wide, dark eyes that seemed to shine from within.

"Why don't you sit down over here?" Vera gestured to one of the two ultra-suede armchairs on either side of a black lacquer table and took the other seat herself.

Carolina surveyed the room, then knit her brows as she looked straight at Vera. "You're Vera?"

"Yes. You sound surprised."

"It's just that I didn't picture you, or your office, like this."

"Let me guess. You were expecting waist-length hair and Indian batik?" Vera grinned.

"Well, yes, sorry, something like that," she apologized. "But you look like a business executive or something."

Vera was proud of her looks. In her mid-fifties, she carried her age well. Today, she had swept up her hair in an elegant chignon, which highlighted her broad, even features.

"Yes, I consider myself a business professional."

"And your office is so interesting. May I look around?"

"Of course."

Carolina stood up and walked over to Vera's desk—a slab of amoeba-shaped glass bolted to three steel legs. She ran her hand over the curved, aluminum phone that stood like a piece of sculpture, then walked over to the other end of the desk where a Baccarat crystal ball perched on a delicate silver stand. Several small, three-dimensional stars dangled within.

"A crystal ball. That's funny!"

"One can't take one's work too seriously."

Her client made her way to the bookcase and picked up a large volume that lay face up on the middle shelf. She squinted at the cover. "What's this?"

"It's about Bohinj, a particularly beautiful area in Slovenia where I am from."

"Oh, that's your accent. I thought it was German. Sorry. I didn't mean ... your accent ..."

"Don't worry, no offense taken."

Carolina walked over to the wall opposite the bookcase. She studied the rows of framed black-and-white photographs that lined the wall. "Wow! Willie Brown, Peter Coyote, Diane Feinstein, Bonnie Raitt. Are all these people your clients?"

"Yes, actually, they are. I have been very lucky to develop quite a following among local celebrities here in the Bay Area."

Carolina returned to her armchair. "Your office is so different from what I expected."

"You expected patchouli oil, incense and heavy drapes?"

"Drapes would be a mortal sin!" Carolina said, staring out the expanse of windows that faced Mount Tam.

"Mortal sin! I haven't heard that for a long time. You're Catholic. I used to be a Catholic once, too."

"Not practicing anymore, but I guess the jargon is hard-wired in my brain." Carolina shrugged. "About your office, though, I just expected something more psychic-like."

"As I said, I consider myself a businesswoman and this is a business office, no different than if I were an attorney or CPA. To tell you the truth, it has always been interesting to me that most psychics don't apply their powers to business situations, just to personal ones. I consider myself a combination financial advisor, therapist, career counselor and management consultant. I'm very good at what I do. And since I'm good, people come to me for advice as they would to any expert in those fields. And they pay me well. If someone truly has the gift of seeing the future, why would they waste their time at county fairs? Why wouldn't they put their talents to work where they could really make an impact and a good income?"

"Yes. I guess that makes a lot of sense. I never thought of it that way." Carolina settled into her chair opposite Vera.

"How did you hear about me?" Vera asked.

"A colleague at work recommended you. He said you were the best."

"That's very kind of him." Vera paused. "Now, why don't you tell me why you're here?"

"It's about my job. I'm not sure what to do. I'd like your advice."

Vera closed her eyes and took three deep breaths. For several seconds she said nothing, but her eyes fluttered under her lids. Then she began to speak. "Looks like you're in high finance, venture capital, mergers and acquisitions, something like that?"

"Yes! I'm in corporate development."

"And I see a lab, beakers. Is it a pharmaceutical company?"

"Wow! How did you know? Biotech, actually. Coro Biosciences."

"Let's see what the cards say." Vera reached for the open mahogany box at the center of the table and extracted a well-worn Tarot deck. She shuffled the cards, cut them a few times and laid out three in a row from the top of the deck. She studied them carefully.

"The first card is 'change.' Things have changed for you at work. It used to be one sort of environment, and now it is quite the opposite. Let's see if I can be more specific."

Vera stared at the second card for a few seconds. "This card tells me it is a negative change. The environment is full of negative forces, people who are negative, people whom you don't like."

Turning her attention to the third card, Vera smiled a bit. "And the third card is 'rebirth,' meaning a new life, in this case referring to your career. This tells me you will be leaving your current work environment and going to a new one. Is that correct?"

Carolina had moved to the edge of her seat. She stared at Vera, her eyes wide. "Oh my God—that's right! Well, at least the first part. It is a very negative environment for me right now, that's for sure. And like you said, it wasn't always that way. A lot of the people I used to work with, who were really great, are now gone. New management's taken over and I just don't like working with them. I feel like the odd man out. They've brought in a lot of their own people and their work style is very different from mine—and how the company used to be. They're cutthroat, arrogant, competitive. I hate working there. I feel like I just don't belong."

"But you haven't left …"

"Right. I haven't left because I have quite a big financial stake in the company. I got a lot of stock options when I joined. And I'll lose them if I leave. But you say you see me changing jobs?"

Vera examined the cards again. "Yes, you'll definitely be working in a new place and it looks like you'll be much happier, as well, like when you first joined your current company. In fact, I think you will find that a few of the people who were your colleagues when you first joined Coro, and whom you liked, work at this new place."

"What's the new company?"

Vera shut her eyes for a full minute, and then shook her head. "No. I'm sorry, I can't see a name."

"But what about all the stock options I'd give up? I don't know how I can leave from a financial standpoint; I'd just be throwing a lot of money away. Shouldn't I stick around for a while longer, so more options will vest?"

Vera returned to her reverie. Again, her eyes moved from side to side under her lids. "I actually see you leaving with a substantial amount of money. You are happy with the arrangement. It seems like even though you don't like the management there now, or the environment, management needs you because you're a key player. You are good at what you do and you are in the middle of a couple of very important transactions that will bring considerable revenue to the company. Is that right?"

Carolina leaned even further forward. "Yes! That's right! I'm working on two major deals. If they work out, it'll mean huge revenues for Coro."

For a few moments Vera sat motionless. Then she began. "I see a series of scenes. You are meeting with a man in an office. You are telling him that you are leaving. He is quite surprised and upset." A long pause. "He is trying to convince you not to leave. He offers you a higher salary." She moved her head almost imperceptibly from side to side. "You refuse." Another pause. "Then he asks you to stay for at least a couple more weeks, until these ..." she searched for the words, "important deals you're working on close." She frowned for a moment. "Again, you refuse." Another pause. "Then he tells you he will ... what is he saying?" She tilted her head to one side, closed her lids, squinting. "The company will vest all of your ... options. That's it. They will vest all of your options if you agree to stay until the transactions are completed."

"You can actually see things happening like that, step by step? That's amazing! If it really turned out that way, that would be great!"

"Yes. Wait. There's one more thing," Vera said. "A British accent. The person speaking with you has a British accent." Her eyes opened, and she fixed them on Carolina. "Does that mean anything to you?"

"Yes, yes it does!" Carolina nodded eagerly. "My boss is British. That's incredible. I can't believe you know all this! Are you really sure this will happen?"

"I am almost always right, my dear. In this case, I saw the scene very clearly and the voices were unmistakable. Also, the rebirth card corroborated what I saw and heard. I am quite certain this will happen."

"Wow! Thanks. That gives me a lot to think about."

They went on to discuss the details of how Carolina should handle her departure from her job.

When the session ended, Vera escorted her out and wished her well. She closed the door behind her and walked over to her desk. An uneasy feeling was edging its way into her consciousness. Something about this new client. She wasn't sure what. She opened her drawer and saw the message light blinking on her red cell phone.

"Teta Vera, it's me." It was her nephew Theodore. Both he and Victoria still called her "teta," the Slovenian for "auntie," as they had when they were children. "Nothing new here." Theodore sounded calm and relaxed. "Just calling to say hi and see if anything's in the works yet. I'll call you later."

She smiled when she heard his voice, then winced at the last part of his message, "anything in the works." Sweet Theodore. At least he had been sweet when he was a child. Victoria, too. Until something changed. If only they could be a normal family, getting together for birthdays and holidays. Vera picked up the phone and entered a number.

"Miles Fuller, please." She opened a drawer and reached for a cigarette, then thought better of it and slammed the drawer shut. It was at times like these that she found it hardest to cut down on the habit. Instead, she chewed on the inside of her cheek and paced back and forth, waiting for Miles to come on the phone.

"Vera! Good to hear from you. What's up?" Miles' British accent greeted her.

"I believe the situation with Carolina will be resolved to your satisfaction."

"That's great news! So, she'll depart without a fight?"

"She will resign."

"You're joking. We won't have to terminate her? How did you manage that?"

"That's what you're paying me for. I always try to over-deliver."

"You're brilliant, no doubt about it. Thanks ever so much."

"Just one thing, though. You'll have to let her options vest. Tell her you need her to stay for another couple weeks or so, to finish up the deals she's working on, and you'll give her the options in return. I know it will be a direct hit to earnings, but I thought it would be a small price to pay."

"Bloody hell, I'd give them to her tomorrow if I thought they would make her go away."

"No, Miles. Play it cool. She has to think this is her idea, and that you're resistant. So, don't offer it up right away. Spend some time negotiating."

"Right—got it! I just can't wait to get rid of her, so we can finally get some work done around here. Thanks ever so much for making this easy on us."

Vera pointed out that the arrangement also benefitted Carolina. She would net close to a half-million dollars from her vested options and she would be spared the emotional anguish of a court case. What's more, her self-confidence would be intact—maybe even bolstered—because she would be leaving an unpleasant situation, having negotiated a generous exit package, at that. The way Vera saw it, everyone won.

"Well, I don't really give two hoots about her confidence; it already exceeds her competence, as far as I'm concerned. I'm just happy to be rid of her."

"A solution where everyone wins is always the best outcome, Miles. And yes, you will be rid of her, as you say, in fairly short order."

"Brilliant!" said Miles. "I'll ring you when we work out her exit. Thanks ever so much. You are truly a miracle worker!"

"I'm glad you're pleased with my work." Vera smiled to herself. "One more thing, Miles," she said. "Is it true you are all a bunch of arrogant, back-stabbing jerks?"

Miles laughed. "Absolutely! And bloody proud of it!"

Vera chuckled, too, then stopped. There was something in his laugh—a faint, unusual rumble. To confirm her suspicions, she pushed on. "But then again, all you Brits are that way. It's a national trait, isn't it?"

He chortled again. This time she was certain. She interrupted him. "Miles, I'd like you to do something for me." Her tone was serious.

"For you, my dear, anything! What would you like?"

"Look, I'm sorry to spring this on you, but it's important. I don't want to scare you, but I feel like I have to tell you."

"Scare me? Not much that scares this old geezer these days. What is it, my dear?"

"Miles, please see a doctor. I think there's a problem with your lungs. And if you go right away—and I do mean right away—it won't be too late. It's still at an early stage, but it can progress quickly."

There was dead silence on the other end of the line.

"Miles? I'm sorry if I've frightened you. You know, sometimes I see these things, and I can't just ignore them. If there's anything at all I can do to head off something like this, I feel it's my responsibility to do it, especially for someone I've known as long as you."

Finally, a subdued Miles spoke slowly. "My father died of lung cancer when he was about my age. I never smoked, so I thought I was safe. But if you say I should have it checked out, I will certainly do it." His voice was shaky now. "Vera, for God's sake, don't apologize. I can't thank you enough."

"Just go right away, Miles. Please." She replaced the handset and felt a sense of satisfaction. He would be treated, she knew. And he would live a normal lifespan, she knew.

Her gift, as she liked to think of it, was a mixed blessing. Yes, she got to help a lot of people with both business and personal challenges. But sometimes there were things she wished she didn't see, problems she wasn't able to resolve.

She remembered the first time she had felt it, not knowing what "it" was. She'd been nine years old. Her grandfather had come to stay with them for a couple of weeks. One day, as she was sitting at the dining-room table talking with him, his image—life-sized and identically dressed—left his body and walked away through the wall of the room. "Where are you going, Nono?" she had asked; it was that real to her. The following morning, he died of a heart attack.

As she got older, Vera began to understand that she was psychic. She knew that there would be times when she would see terrible truths that she could do nothing about. But once she truly understood her power, she made a vow to herself that she would use it to help people in any way she could. And she did. With one exception.

FOUR

Victoria drove up the sharply winding road that led to a row of luxury townhouses perched at the top. She could have afforded a property four times the size of this one, on its own large acreage, but she didn't want people to know she was that wealthy. Her place was an average size for Marin County, with two bedrooms, a study and a large living/dining area. While not over the top from a square-footage standpoint, virtually every room had a 180-degree view of the Sausalito harbor and San Francisco in the distance.

She went into the study and picked up her voicemail, then started to get ready. Josh would be there in an hour. The shower's hot spray massaged her shoulders, relaxing her for the evening ahead. The scent of the lavender gel took her back to the Simmons house. The property had come up on the very same day that her deposit from the last project was confirmed. That had to be a lucky sign.

So far, every detail about the Simmons house and circumstances was adding up just right. It would be their next project. She was sure of it. And tonight she could celebrate the end of one perfect crime and the beginning of the next. Though Josh wouldn't know it, of course.

She selected a satin halter-top in the same shade of green as her eyes. She slipped her finger past the blouse's deep V-neckline and rubbed in a few drops of made-to-order French perfume. The lights in her bedroom were dimmed. Eight Diptique candles lined the large picture window, filling the room with the subtle, exotic scent of myrrh. The comforter was turned down, exposing ultrasoft, white Frette linens. She stood at the door and admired the effect. Perfect.

Next, she moved to the living room, her favorite place in the house. It looked like a page from an avant-garde architectural magazine: Italian furniture accented with a splattering of Asian antiques, large potted palms clustered in corners, naïve art from Africa and South America. Pillows in all colors and sizes were strewn on sofas, armchairs and even the floor.

A bottle of Sancerre chilled in an ice bucket on the glass cocktail table, a block of truffle pâté at its side. The voice of a new French blues singer floated lustily in the air. Victoria was slicing a baguette when the doorbell rang.

"Wow, you look luscious," Josh said, his lively eyes taking her in. In the old movies, they'd call them "bedroom eyes," she recalled. He closed the door behind him and put his arm around her. After a long, deep kiss, he pulled back. "Great to finally be alone together. Has it been only a week? My God, it feels like a month, at least!"

Her fingers played with his curls. "Yes, one week, but a very long one." She grinned, thinking for the hundredth time how adorable he was. He was only twenty-eight, and looked even younger. What she loved most about him was his exuberance. He took such sheer joy in life. He was never "fine"; he was "fantastic." An event was never "fun"; it was "a blast." Food was never "delicious"; it was "incredible." Admittedly, the lows were equally exaggerated, but luckily, there were few of them.

He put both arms around her and pulled her to him tightly, kissing her again, this time longer and deeper. She felt a little light-headed. Even after six months, he still had that effect on her. Like electricity. Of course, a good part of it was because he was married. She grinned to herself. It was really just another sport. A game. Like hockey, in which she had excelled in high school.

There was nothing like it. Nothing like slipping that hockey stick in front of the opponent, snapping away the ball and swooshing it into the goal. Except now it was men. That was the prize ... solid proof that she was better, smarter, prettier, sexier.

A fat shit like you will never amount to anything, she heard her father's voice. *You'd better find a guy who'll take care of you ... if you can manage to nab one. And you know they don't go for flabby girls, don't you?*

After a couple of minutes, she pushed Josh away playfully. "Now, slow down a bit. Let's relax and have some wine first." She took his hand and led him into the living room.

Josh pretended to sulk. "Oh, all right, all right, if you want to be civilized about it. But do you know how excruciating it is to see you every day and force myself not to stare at you all the time?"

"Aww ..."

"Seriously, you're all I think about. When we're in the office, I just want to get you alone in the conference room and lock the door. I work like crazy just to distract myself. I don't know if you've noticed, but my sales have been incredible in the last few months. If only Barnaby Wells knew the real reason!"

"Well, maybe we should try that conference-room thing

sometime. Around midnight when no one's around?"
Victoria poured the Sancerre. "Seriously, though, maybe we
could try to see each other more often? I would like that."

"I don't think I can swing it," Josh frowned. He reached
for a glass and took a long gulp. "I'm afraid she may already
be suspicious."

"What? Why do you think so?"

"I can't put my finger on it, but she acts funny when I
tell her I have a client meeting at night. She's always up
waiting for me when I come home. And I could swear she
sniffs my clothes."

"You're just paranoid. There's no way she could know."

"Well," Josh took another swig. "I have zero desire to
sleep with her and I'm not good at faking it."

"Tell her you've got a lot going on at work, which is
true," she giggled.

Josh rolled his eyes and helped himself to some pâté.
"Yeah, I'll try that." He had another couple sips of wine. "You
know, until lately, she thought I was sexy as hell. That was
at least one way I measured up. Otherwise, she pretty much
runs the show. When we met, we were both in college. We
were equal. After graduation, I even supported us while she
worked on her MBA. Then she got it, and everything turned
upside down. Now she has a big corporate job, making five
times what I make. I don't even know what the hell she does,
really. And like I said, the one thing I was really good at …"
He finished off his glass and Victoria poured him another.

"Sorry, I'm rambling. This is the last thing you want to
hear about or that I should be wasting our time together
talking about. I'm sure you're right. It's probably just my
imagination."

He reached for her hand. "What I'm not imagining is
how incredible you look, and how I don't want to be civilized
a minute longer." ˙

At six o'clock sharp the next morning, Victoria got up for her twice-weekly aerobics class. She was making the bed hastily when she noticed a streak of dark blue peeking out from under the comforter. She pulled it out; it was Josh's tie.

Back at work after class, she slipped the tie into a manila folder and walked over to Josh's desk. "I think this is yours," she said handing it to him casually.

He grinned and took it from her. "Thanks. I was looking for it when I got home."

She returned to her desk and called Maribeth.

"Oh, I'm so glad it's you," said Maribeth. "I was just about to call you. Look, I want to apologize for yesterday. I just wasn't myself. Or maybe I was too much myself. But anyway, I shouldn't have subjected you to my downer of a mood. You were there to discuss the house, and I just launched into—"

"Please stop apologizing," Victoria interrupted her. "It was absolutely no problem. I'm glad I was there to listen. I'm just calling to confirm our eleven o'clock meeting this morning to discuss the listing. And then, if you're free, I'd like to take you to lunch."

"Definitely. I'll be there. Lunch would be fun! I'm leaving now to meet with my attorney about the settlement. I'll come right over afterward, which should be right around eleven. Again, I'm really sorry ..."

Victoria cut her off. "I told you. Stop apologizing. Bye now. See you soon!" She hung up. This one will be a piece of cake, she thought.

FIVE

THEO'S SNEAKERS POUNDED THE MUDDY TRAIL along Lake Geneva. The sun was just starting to set; he could start to see the outline of his breath. For the last three years, he had begun and ended almost every day this way, running, usually around the lake, elsewhere if he was out of town. The rhythmic drumming. Thump, thump. Thump, thump. His feet. His heart. His chest. It was one of the few ways he could clear his mind, blot everything out and fight the insomnia that plagued him every night. Keep going. Keep going. Be strong. Over-come. Keep going. Far-ther. Fa-ster. Run through it.

Drenched, he arrived at the entrance of the luxury condo building where he lived. He propped one foot up on the wall and lunged, stretching his muscles, and then switched to the other foot. He jogged up the stairs to the lobby and waited for the elevator, sweat still dripping from his body and his breath coming in shallow rasps. When the door opened, a leggy brunette bolted out and almost ran in to him.

"Oh, Theo, so sorry!" She blushed and then quickly recovered. "How are you? Seems like I haven't seen you around much lately."

"Fine, thanks; just busy, you know." He hurried into the elevator, inserted his key card and pushed the button for the penthouse.

"Maybe we can get together for a drink or something?" she said, tilting her head and brushing her bangs to the side.

"Yeah, sure," he said just before the doors closed. "Piss off!" he said after they shut.

He ran his fingers through his sopping hair and tried to mop the sweat from his eyes. God, he must look and smell like hell. Yet that didn't stop her.

If only they'd leave him alone. He did nothing to encourage them. Sure, he knew he was handsome. But Vic kept telling him it wasn't his classic Slavic good looks that made women want him. It was his kind face. "Your face has this permanent expression on it that always says, 'I'm so glad to see you,'" she would say.

That was a joke. There was hardly anyone he was ever glad to see, except Vic, of course. And he didn't get to see her nearly enough. Since Isabella had left him three years ago, he wasn't the least bit interested in a relationship. There was no way he was going to open himself up, start thinking about a future with someone, only to have the rug pulled smoothly and deceptively right from under him. So he was on autopilot: eating, sleeping, running. He purposely avoided women, except when Vic called him in on a project. And then it was his job.

All those women who were after him now should have seen him three years ago. What would they have thought of his kind face then—unwashed and unshaven for weeks, reeking of alcohol and sweat?

If Vic hadn't shown up in the nick of time, before he had gone totally bonkers, he'd still be there, holed up in his apartment. He was pretty much recovered now, he thought, and felt pretty good about himself. But the unsteadiness, he knew, was still there, just below the surface, in remission, like a hidden tumor just waiting for some woman to get close enough to uncover it and have it metastasize all over his carefully controlled life.

The elevator doors opened directly onto the foyer of his apartment. He always felt a wave of peace when entering it. This was the way he liked it, far from the madding crowd, tranquil and elegant. The main living/dining area of the penthouse was essentially one huge space with no inner walls, except for one around the powder room. A long hallway at the far end led to the master-bedroom suite.

The furniture was ultra-modern and almost entirely white, in cool contrast to the dark gray concrete floors. The place would have been stark were it not for the large, abstract oil paintings that covered virtually all the available wall space. As if in apology for the monochromatic tones of the rest of the apartment, the artwork was a riot of color, with no hue unrepresented.

As always, his eyes went immediately to the expanse of window along the long stretch of the living area. Lake Geneva, with towering mountains in the distance, was teal-colored in the evening light. The view never failed to lift his spirits. Those mountains somehow filled in the pieces of him that were missing, making him whole. They seemed to promise some higher purpose, a future worth waiting for.

Theo made himself a drink and was taking it over to his study area when his red cell phone rang. He looked at it and smiled. "Hey, you!"

"Hey, what are you up to, handsome?" Victoria said.

"Just sitting here night and day by the phone. Waiting for you to call."

"Hah! Good boy!"

They chatted for a few minutes, catching each other up on their lives. Then Victoria cut to the chase. "Listen, I think we've got our next prospect. Fits the profile perfectly. The only thing I have to confirm is exactly how much she's worth, but I'm virtually certain it's fine. I thought I should give you a heads-up, so you can start making plans. I'll let Teta Vera know, too, of course. You'll have to be here in a few weeks."

"Okay. Sounds good. I'll get on it ASAP." Theo hesitated a moment. "Say, I don't mean to be picky, but does this one at least have all her own teeth and not need a walker yet?"

Victoria giggled. "Cut it out. You're exaggerating just a bit. The last one was only in her mid-fifties."

"Could have fooled me. Between the Metamucil, Mentadent and arthritis ointment, there was barely room for the adult diapers in her luggage."

"You're a brat. I promise, this one's more up your alley— definitely has potential."

"Uh-oh, potential. I know what that means. A 'nice personality.'"

"Well, let's just say that like her house, she needs a little staging."

"Like a facelift and gastric bypass?"

"Stop it. No, just the Clifford touch—Vickidore's," she said, referring to the joint name they'd used for themselves as children.

"I'm just giving you a hard time. You know I trust you. I'll get right on it and start the paperwork going."

"And I'll let you know when I've confirmed the financial piece. I'm so glad I'll get to see you soon!"

"Me, too."

"I've got to go now. Love you lots."

Love you, too," he said softly.

What would have happened to him without Vic? She had quite simply saved his life. And then she had given it a purpose. Her scheme not only kept him occupied, but also made him a lot richer than he ever would have been as a D-list actor, if he could have even achieved that status. Professional acting was out of the question anyway after Isabella. He couldn't have stomached the constant interaction with people. This way, he had solitude, but also the opportunity to play a role from time to time, have some fun, make a lot of money, and best of all, see Vic.

Thank God for her. Maybe someday he'd be able to reciprocate, though he doubted it. It wasn't that he hadn't always been there for her in the past. She had leaned on him, as he had on her, many times since they were kids. But now she was so self-sufficient that he couldn't envision her ever needing him in that way anymore. But, he reminded himself, by playing his part in her projects, he was, in fact, giving her something she needed. Something she couldn't do herself.

After a quick shower, he dressed and picked up his red cell phone again. "Johann, hello, it's Franz," using the alias Johann knew him by. "I need papers again. You know, the usual—three sets, all American, driver's license, credit card, etcetera." He listened to the response. "Superb! Ring me when it's done."

SIX

VICTORIA LOOKED UP FROM HER COMPUTER to see Maribeth standing in front of her. A page from L. L. Bean, she thought. Another twin sweater set—pink this time, with navy blue slacks and the same brown loafers she'd had on yesterday. Her hair was pulled back in a ponytail, probably the same way she'd worn it in high school.

The pink shell undulated with a little, blubber-like roll around her waist. Victoria hid a shudder. On the positive side, it looked like her new client had taken a bit more time with her appearance. Her eyelids showed signs of pale-blue shadow and she wore blush, though a tad too much. The same makeup she'd worn in high school, too, Victoria was willing to bet.

Maribeth had a long way to go before she would be ready for Theo, Victoria realized. A complete makeover was probably not in the cards, based on Maribeth's conservative background and the fact that time was short. But a few, key changes could be managed before he came on the scene.

Taking some files from her desk, she led Maribeth into a small conference room. They sat across from each other with a thick stack of papers between them. On top lay a Mont Blanc pen, engraved with "Barnaby Wells."

"How was your meeting with the attorney?" Victoria started to open the files.

"Fine. It's going really well. Thank goodness it isn't turning out to be one of those horrible fights some people have."

Yeah, they always start out that way, Victoria thought. "Glad to hear it. Okay, let's talk about the house." Victoria got down to the business of discussing the listing price. She showed Maribeth comps of similarly sized homes sold recently in her neighborhood. "The market's pretty hot right now, and summer's always a good time to sell. So, I think the $5.3 million we talked about yesterday is the right number. It should go pretty quickly at that price. Are you still okay with that?"

"Sure, that would be wonderful! And the quicker the better, as far as I'm concerned."

"Okay, good. I've had all the papers drawn up at that price. I've got to warn you, this is quite a signing exercise, thanks to all the laws." Victoria spent the next twenty minutes taking Maribeth through the various disclosures and agreements and getting the required signatures.

The final document requiring a signature was a sensitive one. Victoria told Maribeth that she was recommending that they not include the property on the Multiple Listing Service, at least at first. The relatively high asking price put the house in a bracket where networking it among realtors who typically dealt with exclusive properties would be the best way to go. If they listed it on MLS, Victoria explained, Maribeth would be bothered by all sorts of riffraff wanting to see the house at all hours of the day and night: nosy neighbors, petty thieves who visited open homes only to see how much they could fit in their purses and backpacks, and in general, people who had nothing better to do with their time than see how the other half lived.

If they went with an exclusive listing, only those who were truly interested and financially qualified would be able to see the house. And their realtors would have to contact Victoria first, so Maribeth wouldn't be getting dozens of calls asking if she could leave the house on a moment's notice so it could be shown.

"Gee, I don't know about that," Maribeth said. "Look, I really want the house to sell fast. That's the most important thing to me, even if I don't make quite as much money on it. So, I think we should list it on MLS to give it the widest exposure possible."

Victoria could feel her stomach tense. It had to be an exclusive listing; otherwise she had no control over one of the most crucial elements—the timing of offers. "Maribeth, trust me on this one. Your house will sell fast, *and* you'll get your price."

Maribeth was playing with her necklace. "No, really, I want to get rid of it right away. Let's just list it."

Victoria felt a spasm in her stomach. "Okay, no problem." But it was a problem. Victoria was already figuring out how to get around it. She had a plan. Risky, but the only way. Then she moved on to another touchy subject.

Pulling out what looked like a checklist, she spoke matter-of-factly, as though it was part of the normal proceedings. "I always recommend staging the house to show it off to its best advantage." She looked down at the paper, pretending to be examining the form.

"Staging? You mean taking out all our things and putting in new furniture?"

Victoria was prepared for this. "No, no, we wouldn't take out all of your furniture. We'd probably leave a lot of it in;

you have very nice things. We'd just get an interior decorator to maybe move things around a bit, bring in some accessories, artwork, that sort of thing. Of course, some of your things will have to go into storage, but probably not a lot."

"Well, okay, I guess, if you think it'll help," Maribeth sounded uncertain. "I know I don't know much about decorating."

"Trust me, Maribeth; this has nothing to do with your personal taste. We do this all the time for the houses we sell. The idea is to make the home as universally appealing as possible."

"All right. Let's do it." She sounded only slightly more enthusiastic. "I want to get rid of all my furniture anyway once the house sells. Too many memories."

"Okay. I'll arrange for Suki to come in the next few days. She's phenomenal, the best stager in Marin. By the way, it's better if you aren't home while she's doing her thing. It can be pretty disruptive." Victoria went on to discuss installing a lock box and other details of making the property available for viewing.

When they were finished, they drove a few blocks away to Victoria's favorite Sausalito restaurant. It was an unusually warm day for May, so the top was down, sending their hair flying in the salty breeze. They settled at an outdoor table on the deck overlooking the bay and ordered drinks, a margarita for Maribeth and Sauvignon Blanc for Victoria.

Their table had a brilliantly clear view of the Golden Gate Bridge and downtown San Francisco. Dozens of sailboats skimmed over the water, seeming to barely touch its surface. Others close to shore bobbed from side to side, rooted to their anchors.

Maribeth leaned back in her chair and closed her eyes, tilting her head up toward the sun. "It's so gorgeous out here today that for a second I forgot how miserable I am." She rolled her head slowly, as though absorbing as many of the warm rays as she could. "You know, it's funny, but in all the time Charlie and I lived here, we never had lunch or dinner on the water. In fact, now that I think about it, we didn't go out much at all. I do like to cook, and Charlie was always traveling." She smiled wryly. "I thought it was business travel. What an idiot."

"Maribeth, I don't know you very well at all, but it seems to me that you're much too hard on yourself. From what I've heard, most wives don't find out about the other woman until their husbands have been having affairs for months, even years. So, it's not that unusual to be blindsided like you were."

"Yes, well, my case is a little different. I haven't quite told you the whole story." Maribeth stared out at the boats, avoiding Victoria's eyes. "Let's order another drink."

When the drinks arrived, Maribeth took a couple of deep draws from her straw, then looked directly at Victoria. "It wasn't another woman. It was a man."

Victoria almost choked on her wine. Now *this* was an unexpected turn. But a good one, she quickly calculated, something that could work in their favor. "Wow! And you never suspected?" The words were out before she had a chance to stop them. She regretted them instantly. The wine, no doubt. *Slow down before you make more mistakes, you imbecile.*

Predictably, her question set Maribeth off on a string of self-recriminations. "See what I mean? How could I not know my husband was gay after being married to him for all that time? How could I miss *that*? Weren't there any clues? Didn't I notice he wasn't that interested in me sexually? Didn't I wonder why not?" She dove into her drink again. "No, I didn't notice. No, I didn't wonder. Because there were no clues as far as I could tell. Our sex life wasn't exactly what you see on cable, but then again, we had been married for a while and I figured that was normal. Who knows what normal is, anyway?" She took a deep gulp of her margarita. "Here I am going over all the seedy details of my personal problems with you again. I agree. I'm an idiot for not knowing what was going on."

"Look, Maribeth, I'm so sorry. That's not what I meant."

"Don't be silly. Of course, I should have known. Tell anyone my story and they'll wonder how I could possibly *not* have known. I myself can't figure out how I didn't see it. I mean there must have been some signals, right?"

"Do you know the other man?"

"Yes, he was right in front of my eyes. Phillip, Charlie's best friend … single, cute, never married. We'd have him over to dinner all the time in St. Louis. We'd go to ball games together, go to the movies; he was like one of the family." Maribeth caught herself. "Scratch the 'like.' He and Charlie would play golf together and go fishing on weekends, at least that was the story.

"When we got transferred here, I guess Charlie tried to break it off with Phillip. That's what he told me, anyway. But he just couldn't. He wasn't sleeping; his blood pressure shot up and he started drinking more. I thought it was the pressure of the job. He complained a lot about the deadlines, the fact that his new boss was driving him too hard. Then his travel schedule picked up and he'd be here for a few days, gone for a few days.

"Finally, one night when he had finished a whole bottle of wine by himself, he told me. He couldn't stop crying. Said he hated himself for hurting me. Said he still loved me, but not in the same way he loved Phillip. Said he just couldn't pretend anymore; it was eating him up. He kept apologizing over and over again.

"And I ... I was in shock. I felt like my insides had frozen. I couldn't breathe. I must have just stared at him with my mouth open for hours. Well, maybe minutes, but it felt like hours. The weird thing is, the whole time he was telling me about it—and while it was dawning on me what it meant—I had this urge to hold him and tell him everything was going to be all right, that somehow we could work it out. But I couldn't talk or move. It was like my brain and body were totally paralyzed. I'm not sure how it ended. I think we both fell asleep from exhaustion.

"The next morning when I woke up, he was packing his bags. That's when words finally came to me. When I think about it now, what I said sounds so cliché, the things people always say in these situations, but I guess there's a reason everyone always says them, huh?" Maribeth gave a wry laugh.

"I asked him to stay, to give us another chance, or at the very least to talk about it some more and see if we couldn't find another solution. Charlie said there was no point. He had been through it all in his head a thousand times to see if he could find another way out, and there was none—except suicide, which he told me he had thought about briefly.

"I guess that scared me even more, so I just shut up. I got dressed, went over and hugged him really hard, just held him and held him, both of us sobbing. I said goodbye, got in the car and left." Tears were streaming down Maribeth's face. She excused herself to go to the restroom.

The waiter placed a plate of seared tuna salad in front of Victoria and a bowl of seafood pasta at Maribeth's place. Victoria looked at Maribeth's plate and flinched. Chunky noodles were almost totally submerged in the thick cream sauce that glistened with little rivulets of grease. She squelched her disgust and gave a sympathetic smile as

Maribeth returned to the table. "Lunch is here! And pasta is great comfort food," she said.

As they began eating, Victoria tried to maneuver the conversation to lighter topics, but Maribeth kept coming back to her failed marriage. Since she clearly wanted to talk about it, Victoria decided to probe an aspect that particularly interested her.

"So, your meeting with your attorney went well? Charlie's agreed to split everything fifty-fifty like he said, plus give you the proceeds from the house?"

Maribeth was happy to share the details. "Yes, it's really simple. We're splitting our savings and checking accounts, plus a couple of bond funds we have. Also, Charlie has agreed to pay me alimony unless I remarry. So, it's actually more than fifty-fifty. I don't really need the alimony, anyway, since my half of our assets amounts to ..." For a moment Victoria thought that Maribeth was actually going to give her a figure, but she ended with, "Quite a lot. Plus, I'll have the profit from the house."

Victoria broached the next part carefully. "It's really none of my business, I know, but didn't you say Charlie got a lot of stock options from his company when he transferred here? And what about his 401k and retirement accounts?"

"I'm sure my attorney included that."

"Again, I don't want to intrude," Victoria pressed, "but I've seen too many cases where wives settle for nowhere near their share when a couple splits. For one thing, they want it to be an amicable parting; they don't want to cause any waves. And for another, sometimes they don't have the full picture of what they, as a couple, are worth."

"I do want it to be a civilized divorce. But I'm also sure that Sam is handling it all fairly so that I really am getting half of everything."

"Sam. Is that your attorney?"

"Yes, Sam Wheeler, from Crosby and Laughton, in the Embarcadero. Have you heard of him, or the firm?"

"No, I haven't, but that doesn't mean anything necessarily. And Charlie is using a lawyer in St. Louis?"

"No. We're both using Sam. Actually, Sam is a friend of ours. He went to college with Charlie and lived in St. Louis for a while before moving out here to join that law firm."

There it was. The opening she was waiting for. She tiptoed up to it and stepped tentatively over the threshold. "Maribeth, this isn't any of my business, but what you said kind of worries me."

"Huh? Why?"

"Oh, sorry I brought it up. I don't really know you well enough or your situation."

Maribeth stopped twirling her pasta. "What? Tell me!"

"No. I overstepped my bounds. Let's talk about something else."

Maribeth put her fork down. "Just tell me. What worries you?"

"Look, I don't want to upset you even more, but as a friend, I have to say that what you've told me about your attorney sounds fishy." She was gambling that Maribeth already considered her a friend. "First of all, it sounds to me like Sam's real loyalty is with Charlie, not you. I mean, you may have gotten together socially with him from time to time as a couple, but when push comes to shove, he's known Charlie a lot longer than he's known you. It's Charlie he's going to be supporting in this, not you.

"Also, I think you should get an independent appraisal of your joint assets, just to make sure that all of your financial holdings are included in the divvying-up process. I don't mean to question Charlie's motives," she tried to sound sincere, "but how do you know for sure that there weren't other accounts or other funds that he may not have told you about?"

Maribeth was attacking her pasta again, a little more forcefully than before. "Charlie wouldn't do that to me. He was so upset about leaving me. He went overboard in saying I could have all the money from the house sale. He wouldn't try to cheat me out of the rest. I trust him."

"Maribeth, again, no offense to Charlie." Victoria aimed directly for the raw nerve. "But he did manage to have a long-term, serious relationship without your ever knowing about it. So how can you be sure he's not doing the same with the financial stuff?"

"I'm telling you; Charlie wouldn't do that." Maribeth was starting to sound annoyed, as much as she could allow herself to sound annoyed. Victoria guessed that Maribeth was so afraid of offending people that she rarely let her negative emotions show. What sounded like mild impatience was probably plain anger. Time to switch the subject.

Victoria dropped Maribeth off at her car at Barnaby Wells. She told her she'd call to coordinate a time when Suki could see the house and schedule a convenient date when the staging could begin.

Back at home, Victoria removed her red cell phone from her desk and called her Aunt Vera.

SEVEN

"TETA VERA, IT'S VIC."

"Vicky, are you well?" There was concern in her aunt's voice. Even though they both lived in Marin, the two very rarely saw each other and spoke by phone only when necessary. So, a call generally meant one of two things. Either there was some sort of emergency or a project was underway.

"Yes, I'm fine, thanks. And you?"

"I am very well, *mičkena*," Vera said, using one of the pet names she had called Victoria since she was a young child. In those days, it made Victoria furious to be called "little one." "I am not little anymore!" she would insist, stomping her feet. Even then she had wanted to be an adult, in charge and in control.

"I take it the project you told me about is now going to happen?" The tone of disapproval hung between them after the question was out.

Nothing, though, could squelch Victoria's euphoria. "Yes. This one's perfect. Wait 'til you meet her. She's a piece of cake."

"By that you mean that she is an innocent, respectable woman who is going through a difficult period in her life?" The sarcasm dripped off of each word.

"Teta, don't be like that. The good news is Theo is making arrangements to come. He will be here in a couple of weeks. You're happy about that, right?"

"Victoria, please don't speak to me like I am a senile old lady who lives only for the few moments when she can see her family. You and I both know what this is really about. And you and I both know that I don't approve."

Victoria certainly knew that her aunt was anything but old and senile. In fact, she had great respect for the fact that Vera had come to America with a lot of ambition and little else and had managed to make a name for herself as a savvy businesswoman and advisor. She was only in her fifties now and would probably be in her professional prime for at least a couple more decades. On the few occasions when Victoria was really honest with herself, she thought about how Vera had built her professional career and reputation from scratch, while Victoria's own financial success was largely illegitimately earned. But then she would catch herself. It took just as much smarts, perseverance and gumption to achieve what she, Victoria, had achieved—more, maybe, considering what she had to overcome.

"What is her name?" her aunt was asking her.

"Maribeth Simmons. She fits the profile totally. No, more than that, she *is* the profile." Victoria went on to give Vera the details of Maribeth's situation. She rattled through the next few steps of the plan, then started to sign off with, "This one will be easy, I guarantee it. I'll let you know when we'll meet with Theo. Love you!"

But Vera cut in before she could hang up. "I love you, too, *mičkena*. But really, do we have to do this again? Don't you and Theo have enough by now? Or isn't it about the money anymore?"

Victoria steeled herself. Her aunt's judgmental attitude was becoming more and more annoying. "Look, Teta Vera, just this one more time, and that's it. I promise—this is the last time. I want to make sure Theo has enough, so we don't have to worry about him anymore. You know he can't make it on his own." She knew exactly where to aim and went straight for it.

"And I am happy to help him financially for the rest of his life. I have told you both that before."

"You know that won't work, Teta Vera. You know that would zap whatever self-confidence Theo has managed to scrape together. He has to feel like he's earned his money, not just had it handed to him."

Vera gave a forced laugh. "Earned? That's an interesting choice of words."

Victoria played her trump card, the one that had always brought these debates to an end in the past. "You promised Mama." She could hear the huff of breath on the other end of the line.

"I promised your mother that I would look after the two of you, but I'm sure this isn't what she foresaw. In fact, if I really had your best interests in mind, I would never have gone along with all this in the first place, let alone so many times."

Victoria could picture her aunt's spine become rigid as she fired the words from her lips.

"Look, this is the last time, I promise. Please help; we can't do it without you." Damn, how she hated having to depend on someone.

"We'll see," Vera said acidly and then hung up.

"Thank God," Victoria said to the dead phone, knowing they were good for one more time.

EIGHT

VICTORIA DROVE BY THE FRONT of the Simmons house, pulled over to the side of the road and dialed Maribeth's home number. No answer. Good, she was at the dentist, as planned. Victoria now had the house to herself for a full hour and a half before meeting Maribeth at the spa. She had told Maribeth that Suki, the designer who was scheduled to stage the house, would be arriving at nine. But that wasn't going to happen. It would turn out that Suki had been unavoidably delayed, and they would have to reschedule her visit for the following week.

Victoria eased up the driveway and parked. The scent of lavender greeted her again as she headed up the walk to the door. Strange how so much human turmoil could exist in such a peaceful setting. Yet, exteriors often lied. She thought of the neatly trimmed green lawn that stretched out from the porch of her childhood home. And the sweet rose bushes that lined the walk leading to the door. No one would have guessed what went on inside there either.

She entered the Simmons house and was once again struck by its blandness. It could have been almost anyone's home, without being anyone's in particular.

She began her search in the master bedroom. The nightstand held printouts of some of Charlie's emails, presumably sent after he'd moved out. One email seemed to be a reply to Maribeth's emails, asking him to come back and give their marriage another try. His response explained that he had already moved into Phillip's house in Ladue. Victoria reached into her large tote and pulled out the thick Day-Timer she always carried with her. She started jotting down notes.

On the dresser was an antique jewelry box. She rummaged through its contents and in one of the bottom compartments found a wedding ring. She looked at the engraving inside the ring and scribbled in her book. Before leaving the master bedroom, she couldn't resist taking another look at the walk-in closet.

She threaded through Maribeth's clothes and shook her head: shapeless skirts; twin sweater sets mostly in pastel shades; pleated trousers, some even with elastic waistbands. And shoes ... she was amazed that there were only 10 pairs. Stocky pumps in basic black, brown, and beige, and loafers in black and beige. She must be wearing the brown ones again today. Plus, two identical pairs of what Maribeth would probably call "dressy" sling-backs, one in black patent leather and the other in a dull tan. Two pairs of flip-flops completed the selection. Even women who were just scraping by had more shoes than this. Victoria herself used to get the latest styles from second-hand shops after her father left them. No doubt that as soon as Maribeth's hair and makeup were taken care of, her wardrobe had to be the next priority.

Victoria bypassed the guest rooms and craft workshop, figuring there wasn't much there that was of interest to her.

Just as she was entering the office, she heard her cell phone buzzing in her tote. She glanced at the screen. It was Maribeth. It was nine forty-five. Maribeth was supposed to be at the dentist; why would she be calling now? She clicked the phone open with her right hand and gnawed on the little finger of her left hand. "Hello?"

"Hi, Victoria, it's Maribeth. Listen, my appointment was canceled. The dentist called in sick this morning. I guess they tried to reach me, but I never got the message. So, I'm on my way back in to Marin. I'm actually just getting off the highway at my exit now. I know Suki's doing the staging and I'm not supposed to be around, but I forgot my credit card at home and just need to dash in and get it. Anyway, I wondered if you wanted to get together for a cup of coffee before we go to the spa, since I got back from the city early."

For three full seconds Victoria froze, unable to force her mind into action. Finally, thoughts fought their way in. She snapped her head to the window, expecting to see Maribeth's car already there. Ordering calm into her voice, she said. "No, sorry, that won't work, Maribeth, I have a client appointment in a few minutes. In fact, I'm on my way to it right now, so I have to go. Sorry, got to run. See you at eleven!"

She ran down the hall and bolted down the stairs. As she got to the last step, her heel caught a groove in the wood and she slipped, landing on her hip and careening into the side table in the entryway. A flowered ceramic vase rocked from side to side, then crashed onto the floor in front of her, its white silk roses resting over its broken remains.

"Jesus fucking Christ!" she said out loud. Maribeth would be walking through the front door at any moment and find her sprawled there. Her hip throbbed, but she sprang up, ignoring it. She could walk, thank God! But the vase, no time for that; she'd have to figure out an explanation later. Quickly, she ran to the front door, shut it behind her and reset the lock box. Or tried to. The code wouldn't work. The lock hung there, jaw open, like an upside-down grin. She scoured the street and saw no signs of a car. Turning to the box again, she played with the code, but it wouldn't work. Fuck it. Time's up.

Victoria left the unsecured box dangling from the doorknob and raced to her car. She backed out of the driveway, put the car into first gear and lurched forward onto the road, away from the direction Maribeth would be arriving from. As she crested the top of the hill, she glanced back to see Maribeth's car heading into the driveway. When she turned to face the road again, a huge, brown mass loomed directly in front of her. She jammed her foot on the brake and the car slammed to a stop. The deer stared at her, then bolted into a driveway.

Victoria pulled over to the side of the road and turned the ignition off. Her heart thudded in her chest. She looked at herself in the rearview mirror and noticed that she was sweating. Not perspiring—sweating. Big, round globules rolled down her forehead and gleamed on her upper lip. Her armpits were moist; dark patches were beginning to form on her blouse. She wiped her face with a tissue.

That was too close. *You sloppy piece of shit.* Her gray cell phone was ringing again. It was Maribeth. She was very upset.

"Victoria, I know you're going to a meeting. I'm sorry to bother you, but this is really urgent. It's very disturbing, actually. When I got home just now, the lock box was open. Anyone could have come by and opened the door. How could the box be open? Suki is supposed to be here doing the staging, right?"

"Right. You mean the lock box is open and Suki's not there? I can't imagine what happened. I'll call her right away. I'm so sorry about this, Maribeth."

"That's not all. The vase that was by the door is broken.

There are pieces everywhere!"

"What? Oh my God! I'm so sorry, Maribeth. Is anything missing, as far as you know?"

"No, I don't think so. Everything else looks normal. I checked my jewelry and it's fine, thank goodness. But what do you think happened? Should I call the police?"

Victoria forced herself to sound calm. "No, not yet. Let me see what I can find out."

"Are you sure? I mean, if someone broke in, I should report it."

"Yes, of course, but first let me check to see if it was Suki, though I can't imagine that she would have broken something or left without locking up. But let me just check with her. I'll call you right away."

"Okay, but do call me right back." Maribeth seemed to realize she was being pushier than usual and pulled back. "Victoria, thanks so much. I'm really sorry to bug you, but I was so shocked when I saw the lock box and then the vase. I thought that maybe a burglar—"

Victoria broke in. "No, you're absolutely right. I'm glad you called. This is serious. I promise you I'll look into it right now."

Victoria hung up. She took another tissue and touched her forehead again. Her hand was trembling. *I am falling apart. I'm going to blow this and get caught. What the fuck is wrong with me? My nerves are shot. They can't buckle like this. You're getting soft. Just a flabby softie.*

Toughen up, you little shit. Don't be such a wimp. She could hear her father, on her eleventh birthday. The morning had started in a quiet, not celebratory, way. But quiet was something she had come to appreciate more and more in those days. She would take quiet anytime over … the opposite. She'd been wearing a brightly printed dress that was as cheerful as she wished she felt. Her father and brother joined her at the breakfast table, each lost in his own thoughts. Her mother turned from the oven, holding a towering stack of pancakes, topped by eleven glowing candles. She beamed as she started to sing, emphasizing each syllable for exaggerated dramatic effect. "Haaaa-peeeeee birrrrth-daaaaaay ... tooooo youuuuu." She placed the pancakes down in front of Victoria, put her arm around her and kissed her on the cheek. A whiff, a scent, L'Air du Temps wafted from her memory. "Happy birthday, honey!"

Theo had grinned happily, exposing the new gap in his front teeth. "Happy birthday, Vic!"

As if caught by surprise, her father had looked nervously at her mother, then nodded to his daughter. "Happy birthday, Victoria."

"The pancakes, Vic! Serve the pancakes!" her brother encouraged.

"Theodore, settle down. You'll get them soon enough," her father said curtly.

"But Father—"

"I said, be quiet."

"Darling, it's okay. Vicky can start dishing them out," her mother said.

"That's right, contradict me in front of the children. I try to enforce discipline and you undo it as fast as you can."

"Darling, I was just ..." but her father slid his chair away from the table and marched out of the room before her mother could finish.

Trying to keep her composure, her mother brushed her hair aside from her forehead. "You two go ahead and start. Your father and I will be back in a second."

But they weren't. Victoria and Theo ate their pancakes in silence, listening to the escalating fight between their parents in the bedroom down the hall. It started with shouting back and forth, then they heard only their father yelling—and then, only their mother, sobbing.

They both went to Victoria's room, where Victoria pulled out Theo's favorite book of bedtime stories and read him "Peter Pan." Their mother didn't emerge from her bedroom that day, but their father did. In the afternoon, he knocked on Victoria's door. "Time to go to the Turners," he said from the other side. The family had been invited to their parents' best friends' house for an early dinner to celebrate Victoria's birthday. "Get your brother ready and let's go."

"What about Mother?" Victoria asked.

"She doesn't feel well. She won't be coming."

"But I don't want to go if Mother's not going," Victoria said through the door.

The door swung open and her father glared at her. "We are going without her. Now get ready."

As they drove across town to the Turners, Victoria sat next to her father without speaking. She pictured her mother alone in the bedroom and wondered how many days it would be this time before she came out. Sadness pulled at her like an anchor, rooting her further and further into her seat, her head bent so far forward that the tears dropped neatly into her lap without touching her cheeks.

Her father glanced over at her. "What the hell is the matter with you?"

Victoria didn't—couldn't—answer. Misery clogged her throat, a big painful ball, barely allowing her to breathe. And she was scared. Scared of what her father would do when he saw her crying.

He pulled the car quickly to the side of the road, jamming on the brakes so hard that Theo lurched forward, hitting his head on the seat back in front of him. Her father turned to her and leaned forward so that his face was only inches from hers. She could see the red rising in his cheeks and feel his breath on her face.

His eyes narrowed as he looked at her. "You stop crying right now. Stop feeling sorry for yourself, you little shit. We are going to see the Turners in ten minutes and you're going to act like everything's hunky dory. Got it? Your eyes had better be dry and you'd better be all smiles and chipper like your chubby little normal self, you hear? If you feel bad, just think of all the ice cream and cake you're going to eat. That should cheer you up."

He turned to restart the car and she felt for the Kleenex in her pocket. Unraveling it, she snuck a peek at her brother. Tears welled in his eyes, but he didn't let them drop. "I love you," he mouthed.

She didn't have the rejuvenator jar then, but she did now. Opening it, she carefully deposited the white powder on her compact makeup mirror. With a credit card, she worked the small mound into a fine, thin line. Glancing around quickly to ensure no one was around, she rolled up the $100 bill she kept for just such occasions and sniffed in the happiness she deserved.

NINE

VICTORIA PULLED INTO THE SPA parking lot. Maribeth was already there. She rushed over to Victoria immediately. "I got your text that there was no need to get the police involved. So, what *did* happen? Was it Suki?"

"It's okay, Maribeth. Well, it's not okay, but it wasn't a robber. I called Suki as soon as I got off the phone with you. She was at the hospital. She was so sorry about what happened. She said she had gone to your house to start the staging, but then got an emergency call from her daughter's school. Her daughter had had a seizure. Suki said she just panicked. She ran out of the house and tripped in the hall, knocking the vase over. She couldn't get the lock box to work, probably because she was in shock. She said she had started to phone me, to let me know, but then a call from a doctor came through and she took it. She got wrapped up in dealing with doctors and trying to figure out what happened to cause the seizure, if there would be side effects, all those things, and forgot to call me. Again, she said to tell you she was very sorry—and that she'd replace the vase, of course.

"Look, I know you're upset, Maribeth. I would be, too. But really, it's a fluke. It won't happen again."

Maribeth looked relieved. "Yeah, okay, I guess it was an accident. Thank goodness it wasn't a break-in. That would have been more than I could take right now."

Victoria put her arm on Maribeth's shoulder. "Let's go in and concentrate on relaxing for the next few hours. I think we could both use it." She led the way to the reception desk. Her hip was pulsing with pain from the fall. It was a struggle to keep from limping. Served her right. She deserved it. Every bit of it. It would be a reminder to be more careful.

Timmy looked up and gave her his usual effusive welcome. "Vicky, honey, so great to see you!" He jumped up from his chair and gave her a hug. "I'm so glad you're giving yourself a nice long treat here today. You are positively overworked and overstressed. Not that you look it, of course. You look marvelous. But you can't fool Timmy, I know you too well." He looked over at Maribeth. "And who is your friend? I don't believe we've met?"

Victoria's face melted into a warm smile. Timmy's presence alone calmed her down. "Timmy, this is my friend Maribeth. Maribeth, this is Timmy. Timmy is the spa's secret weapon. He can make you relax and feel wonderful just by talking to you."

Timmy put his arm around Maribeth. "Welcome, honey, you've come to the right place. When you leave here, you'll feel like a new woman, I promise." He winked at Victoria and led the two to their first set of treatment rooms. They each started with a facial, then were served a light lunch while they waited for their deep-tissue massages. After the massages, they had manicures and pedicures. Then they were directed to side-by-side hairdressing stations. Jonas had been doing Victoria's hair for the last couple of years, so he started right in, appraising the length, playing with the part.

Maribeth's stylist, Stephan, eyed his new client. "So, what do you have in mind?"

"Oh, a trim, I think," Maribeth said. "And my roots are getting dark, so I probably need to have them touched up. Same color as now."

"Hmmmm, okay," he said without enthusiasm. He looked uncertainly at Victoria.

Maribeth caught it. "Why? Do you think I should have something else done?"

"Well, if you're set on this look …" He looked at Victoria again.

"I've been wearing my hair like this forever. A long time ago, I went to a stylist in St. Louis and they told me this was the best style and color for my features and hair type."

"Exactly," Stephan said.

"What do you mean?" Maribeth looked slightly offended.

"Can I be honest with you?"

"Well, sure."

"Victoria, can I tell it to her straight, or do I have to be polite?"

"Tell it to her straight, but be polite."

"Okay. Look, honey, this style and color went out with the eighties. Maybe it's all the rage in St. Louis, but that alone should tell you something."

Maribeth studied herself in the mirror, turning her head from one side to the other. "So, what would you recommend?" The words ventured out cautiously.

"All one color is boring and looks fake. I think we should put lowlights in your natural color, which is light brown, right? Then, we can put in some blonde highlights to give it depth, but not this brassy blonde. Something more subtle and believable. As for the cut, this pageboy isn't doing anything for you, except blaring out 'middle-aged, midwestern housewife,' so something with a few layers around your face and in back—a little tousled. It would make you look a lot sexier."

"Sexier? I don't want to look sexy."

"Oh, yes you do!" Victoria interjected.

"Why? Charlie's gone and there's no chance of getting him back."

"So your guy left you, huh?" Genuine concern replaced Stephan's flippant tone. "That definitely sucks, honey. How long ago did he leave?"

"Two months ago," Maribeth murmured into her lap.

"Two months isn't a very long time. You're sure he's not coming back?" Stephan asked gently.

"No," Maribeth shook her head, looking like she might start to cry.

"You know what?" Stephan said. "You need a new look. Not for anyone else. Just for you. I want you to feel wonderful about yourself when you look in the mirror and right now, it looks to me like you feel lousy about yourself. You are one gorgeous lady, but you're hiding it. Let me do my thing and I guarantee you, you'll love it. Victoria can vouch for me, can't you, Vicky?"

"Absolutely. He's the best, Maribeth. Next to Jonas, of course."

"Yeah, you should have seen Victoria before we got ahold of her," Jonas joked. "She looked like she came off a farm in Kentucky, straight bangs and eyebrows thick as a corn field!"

Maribeth agreed to let Stephan do his hair makeover. Two hours later, she was glowing at her reflection in the salon mirror. She had a bouncy, sassy cut in a warm nougat shade, highlighted with pale wheat. "Gosh, I look like a different person," she said.

"No, you look like *you*," Stephan corrected her. "You were a different person before, someone still stuck in St. Louis, Misery, in the eighties, someone who was dumped by a guy and dumping on herself."

Victoria walked in while Stephan was speaking. "You should be a shrink, Stephan," she said. "But no, then the world would lose one of its finest stylists. Maribeth, you look incredible! Sexy is right!"

Maribeth blushed and smiled. "Oh my gosh, thanks so much, Stephan."

"The way to thank me is to come back here every six weeks so we can maintain your knockout status!"

"I promise!"

Victoria hurried Maribeth to her makeup appointment. They were greeted at the station by Luella, the spa's resident makeup artist.

"Tell me what makeup you usually use," Luella asked.

"Not very much," Maribeth said. "Just light-blue eye shadow and some blush and a pink lip gloss."

Luella's eyebrows moved slightly.

"What's wrong?" Maribeth asked.

"Nothing, dear, it's just that I bet you've been wearing that stuff for almost twenty years."

"Well, yes ..."

"You need something more sophisticated now. Will you permit me to try something different?"

"Sure." Maribeth didn't sound very convinced.

"Don't worry. Luella knows what she's doing," Victoria reassured her. "She's been in the business for over twenty-five years."

"Okay, but I don't want to look too made up."

Luella began applying an ointment to Maribeth's face. "Don't worry, dear."

A half-hour later, Victoria watched Maribeth examine herself in the mirror. There was a brightness in her eyes and a flush to her cheeks that didn't come from Luella's expert hands.

"I really like it!" Maribeth said softly. "It's so natural." And indeed, it was. Her skin tone was evened out and dashes of subtle peach brightened her cheekbones. The smoky taupe on her eyelids, fringed by darkened lashes, made her eyes seem an even more vibrant blue. To complete the picture, Luella filled in Maribeth's lips with a rosy mauve lipstick. The effect was classic and understated, but current at the same time.

"It looks like me, only much better," Maribeth said. "It's not as 'girly.' More adult. Thanks so much, Luella! I definitely want to buy everything you put on me. Hopefully, I'll remember what to do with it."

"If not, you just come by and ask me. Anytime." Luella filled a bag with Maribeth's purchases and handed it to her. "Just promise me you'll throw away the old stuff!" were Luella's parting words.

"You really do look fantastic, Maribeth," Victoria said as they headed out.

Maribeth grabbed Victoria's hand. "I don't know how to thank you. You know, I never paid that much attention to my looks. I mean, I always looked decent, but to tell you the truth, I thought all that hype about hair and makeup was superficial, like people who spent a lot of time on it were trying to be someone they weren't, like there were a lot more important things in life than what color lipstick to wear. And there are, of course. But it's amazing how different I feel." She stopped for a moment and nodded to herself. "You know what it is? It's hope. I know it sounds ridiculous, but for the first time in months, I feel like the future might actually be something to look forward to. I mean, a girl with this hair isn't just going to sit around and feel sorry for herself for the rest of her life."

"Exactly!" Victoria said. *I'm not such a nasty person after all*, she thought.

When they got to Timmy's desk, he was effusive as ever. "Vicky, darling, you look totally relaxed. You're just glowing, honey! And what happened to that midwestern gal you brought in here? All I see is this smokin' chick with the saucy hair." Both women laughed.

He turned to Maribeth and put his hand on her shoulder. "Now, honey, you have to go out and buy a hot outfit to go with the new you! I'm sure Vicky can help you pick something out."

"That will have to be some other time. We have a date right now," said Victoria.

"A date? We do?"

"Yes, drinks to celebrate our relaxing day and to toast how fabulous you look," Victoria said, studying Maribeth's outfit. She was wearing one of her sweater sets, in navy blue, along with her standard khakis and loafers. "Take off your cardigan," she said.

"Why? It's chilly outside."

"Please, just try it, okay?"

Maribeth removed her outer sweater and stood in front of Victoria and Timmy in her sleeveless shell. Victoria spun her around, looking at her back. The shell had a round collar in front, and a fairly deep V-neck in back. "Take off your shell, and wear it with the back in front," Victoria instructed.

"But it's too low. I'll be cold."

"Honey, this isn't Alaska. You'll be fine!" Timmy assured her.

"You can wear the other sweater over it until we get where we're going," said Victoria. "Now go ahead; let's see how it looks."

Maribeth went into the ladies' room and reappeared wearing the shell backwards as Victoria had suggested. The neckline rested attractively on her breasts, exposing a couple of inches of cleavage. "This is too low for me," said Maribeth, putting her hand up to her chest.

"Oh, no, honey, you have great little titties. You should show them off!" said Timmy. "Here, I have another idea," he added. There was a jewelry display to the side of the reception desk. The spa sold hand-made pieces by local artists. Timmy selected a gold-chain necklace with a bottle-green bead in the shape of a small bell dangling from the middle. He fastened it around Maribeth's neck, adjusting the length so the bell rested at the top of her cleavage. "You can ring my bell-ell-ell," he sang. Then he picked up a pair of dangle earrings in the same shade and hooked them into her ears.

"I don't know," Maribeth said, frowning at herself in the mirror. "I don't usually wear low-cut tops, or much jewelry, for that matter."

He stepped back "You look perfectly juicy!"

Maribeth's hand went up to her mouth. "Oh, good grief! I don't want *that*. I don't want to look like a tramp."

"Honey, you don't look anything but classy. But that Miss St. Louis 1982 look isn't workin' for you anymore. Tell her, Vicky."

"Timmy's right, Maribeth," agreed Victoria. "Your clothes are nice, but they don't do much for you. They could do with a little spicing up."

Maribeth shrugged. "Well, okay. You were right about the hair and makeup; you're probably right about this, too." She put the cardigan over the shell and buttoned it up. "Just until we get to where we're going," she assured them.

"Okay, okay. Now, let's go show you off. Like I said, we have a date!" Victoria said.

Timmy kissed them goodbye and they headed out to their respective cars.

Victoria lowered her window and yelled out to Maribeth. "Follow me. We're going to Tiburon!"

Twenty minutes later, they were at the Fogscape bar. It was packed with the Marin after-work crowd—mostly in their thirties and forties, all dressed casually, not a suit to be seen. The place was in full happy-hour mode. A pulsing, euro-techno beat welcomed them as they entered. The air was thick with beer, wine, chips and laughter. They had to jostle their way to the bartender and wave to get his attention.

"I propose a toast," said Victoria when they got their drinks. "To the future!" She clinked her glass against Maribeth's.

"To the future!" Maribeth's newly polished nails gleamed against her glass.

"And what are you ladies celebrating, if I may ask?" The man was tall, with a shock of red hair and a sprinkling of freckles. He angled himself between them.

"Oh ... new beginnings," Victoria said, grinning. Just then, one of her cell phones rang; she glanced at it and excused herself. When she returned in ten minutes, Maribeth and the redhead were laughing.

"What did I miss?" Victoria asked.

"I was just flirting heavily," the redhead said. He turned to Maribeth. "Unfortunately, I have to leave, but I'd love to help you celebrate next time you're here. My name's Kevin, by the way. I come here all the time after work. Hopefully, we'll meet up again." He clinked his empty glass against hers.

"Wow! Maybe I should have stayed away longer," Victoria said when he was out of earshot.

"No, I'm glad you came back. He was just joking." Maribeth blushed.

"I don't think so. I saw the way he looked at you. He was definitely interested." Victoria's phone rang again. It was Josh. This time, she took the call right away, moving across the room to find a quieter spot. "Sorry, no, I can't make it tomorrow night. How about Saturday?"

She heard his hesitation on the other end of the line. "Saturday, you know, she and I usually go out to dinner."

"Oh, sure, I understand. I guess Monday then," she said, making sure he caught the disappointment in her voice. In the few moments of silence that followed, she could almost hear the inner debate going on in his mind.

Finally, he said what she hoped she would hear. "Well, maybe I can swing Saturday. Yeah, I'm sure I can. I'll tell her I have a client dinner or something. Let's do it. Seven o'clock?"

"Seven's perfect!"

"You drive me crazy. See you!"

"Now that's a huge smile. Who was *that?*" Maribeth had come over to her and was grinning.

"My secret lover."

"Secret? Who is he?"

"Can't tell you," Victoria smiled, casting her eyes downward.

Just then, a man swung away from the bar, holding his drink, and almost bumped into Victoria. "Hey, Vic, so this is where you hang out when you're not with me!" he said with an Australian lilt. Were it not for his accent, he could easily have been mistaken for a Sicilian, with his olive skin, dusky eyes and thick, almost jet-black hair. She had never really noticed a resemblance before, but it suddenly struck Victoria that he looked a lot like Josh.

"Simon! Great to see you! So this is where you scope out new women to conquer, huh?" They exchanged a kiss on the lips that lasted just long enough to imply they were more than friends.

"Who is this knockout, and why have you been hiding her from me?" Simon's gaze moved from Maribeth's face and lingered at the area where her pendant hung.

"This is Maribeth, and I'm keeping her away from you for her own good." Victoria winked at Maribeth.

"She looks like she's old enough to take care of herself," Simon grinned. "Say, Vic, you're still coming tomorrow night, right?"

"Wouldn't miss it!" she turned to Maribeth. "Simon's new art gallery in the city is having a gala grand-opening tomorrow night."

"And I would be most honored if you would come, too." Simon reached for Maribeth's free hand and, with an exaggerated gesture, brought it to his lips and gave it a light kiss.

"Oh, that's very nice of you, but ..."

"You can bring your husband or boyfriend. It's all right, I don't mind the competition," Simon assured her.

"I don't have—"

"Ahhh! Then you absolutely must join us!" Simon raised his glass in a toast to Maribeth.

She looked over at Victoria.

Victoria nodded. "Yes. You should definitely come. We can go together. It will be great fun. There will be lots of interesting people there."

"Okay, sure. I'd love to go." Maribeth grinned shyly at Simon.

Victoria's cell phone rang again. She looked at the screen, then hurried outside to take the call. When she returned, Simon was describing the art that would be on display at the opening. "Very cutting edge," he was telling Maribeth.

"Sorry, I've got to run," Victoria told them. "One of my clients wants to put in an offer on a house first thing tomorrow, so I have to put the paperwork together and get their signatures. Simon, can I trust you with Maribeth?"

"I have to go, too," said Maribeth, looking at her watch.

"Why? Come on and have another drink. I promise I'll be a perfect gentleman." Simon bowed slightly.

"No, really, it's been a long day. But I look forward to seeing you tomorrow at your opening." Maribeth put her empty glass down and started to shake Simon's hand. Once again, he raised her hand to his lips and planted a kiss.

"Until then," he said.

Maribeth followed Victoria to her car. The wind had picked up and the fog was flowing over the mountains in multiple gray rivers that would soon pour into the city. The temperature had dropped at least ten degrees since they had arrived at the bar. Maribeth hugged her cardigan. Her cheeks were flushed, and her eyes still had that new brightness.

"That was a great day!" Maribeth said. "I mean, once we got to the spa. Thanks so much, Victoria, for arranging everything and for suggesting this place for drinks. I had a lot of fun."

"My pleasure! And you certainly did wow them there at the Fogscape."

Maribeth giggled. "Those two guys were very sweet. I mean, I know it was all in fun, but seriously, that's the most attention I've gotten from a man in the last couple of years."

Victoria threw her head back with a throaty laugh. "I don't know about that red-haired Kevin guy, but 'sweet' is not the word I'd use to describe Simon, for sure. He did definitely like you. And Kevin was obviously hitting on you when I got back from my call."

"He wasn't hitting on me; we were just chatting."

"Maribeth, you've been out of the game too long. Take my word for it; he was flat-out flirting with you. And by the way, there were other guys checking you out, too. Whenever you're ready to start dating, you'll have them stacked up on your doorstep."

Maribeth shook her head in protest, but her eyes beamed. "Dating! That's not in the cards for a long, long time. Maybe never. But it was so nice of Simon to invite me tomorrow. What should I wear? Is it formal?"

"Not exactly formal. More kind of artsy."

"I don't think I have anything like that."

"Yes, I know." Victoria caught herself. "At least from what I've seen you wear so far. Hang on a second; let me look at my appointments for tomorrow." Victoria scrolled on her cell phone. "If you like, I can take you shopping in the late afternoon, say around four?"

"Okay. That would be great."

"I'll meet you in front of the Starbucks on Bridgeway in Sausalito."

"We're not going to the mall?"

"No, the mall doesn't have what you're looking for. See you then!" Victoria got into her car, then had another thought and lowered her window. "Don't forget to wear your new makeup. Come to think of it, bring it with you, in case you need a touch-up." She waved as she pulled out of the lot.

Punching numbers into her cell phone with her right hand while she steered with her left, Victoria pulled onto the freeway toward her client's house. "Just calling to say thanks," she said. "Though I must say, I think you laid it on a bit too thick."

Simon stood at the bar laughing into his cell phone. "No, I don't think so. She ate it up. Speaking of which, are you going to take her to a gym, now that you've made her over? She's a little chunky."

"Be nice. But I just might," said Victoria. "You did such a convincing job of drooling all over her; I thought maybe you wanted to invite her *instead* of me tomorrow."

"Don't be ridiculous. Pink zinfandel isn't my style. And

by the way, is this a little sideline business you've got going?"

Victoria tightened her grip on her cell-phone and held her breath. Forcing a breeziness into her voice, she faked a southern accent. "Whatever do you mean, Mister Chile-dress," intentionally drawing out the first syllable of his last name and mispronouncing it in a way she knew he hated. She bit her top lip, waiting for him to answer.

"You know, your makeover clinic for dumpy divorcées. I mean, I'm happy to be of service, but I hope you're getting something out of this. If not, you should be! You really have a knack for turning the dumplings into sexy little pastries."

Victoria exhaled, turning it into a giggle. "Why thank you, honey chile. I just may give it some thought. You could be my partner. You know, I transform the outside and you get the inside job, so to speak!" She didn't mention that the latter role was already cast.

Even though she had put him off this time, she began to worry. Simon had gotten too close to the truth. She had used him four times now. That was at least once too many. She should have known better.

She would have to diversify more in the future. *Wake up! Pay attention! If you're not careful, you're going to crash and take Theo down with you.*

When this one was over, she would take a nice, long break. Maybe even a permanent break. The thought took her by surprise. But she didn't have time for that now. Couldn't take her eye off the ball. Concentrate. Focus. Make it happen. And since she had brought Simon in to work on Maribeth, that piece had to play out its course. There wasn't much more she needed from him for this one anyway. Just another pass or two at her current dumpling, as he would say.

"I'm looking forward to my next inside job," he was saying with a huskiness in his voice. "Tomorrow night? After the opening?"

"Let's play it by ear," Victoria said, turning on her southern accent again. "Who knows? You might get smitten by the lovely Miz Maribeth."

"Squashed would be more like it. A little hefty for my taste. Besides, I told you, I won't actually sleep with them, just get their juices flowing. You know, so they're primed for the next lucky guy who comes along."

"We'll see. Anyway, thanks so much for tonight. I think the juices are stirred. See you tomorrow."

"Can't wait."

She pulled into the Safeway parking lot and found an end spot at the outer edge of the lot, facing a row of trees. The two slots to her left were empty. She found the $100 bill in her wallet and pulled out the rejuvenator jar. She inhaled quickly from her compact mirror, her gaze darting alternately from left, to rearview mirror, to right. Feeling the familiar shot of courage, she took a final snort, and threw her accessories back into her purse.

Then she dialed again. "Kevin, thanks so much for tonight. You did great!"

"No problem, glad to help out," he said. "She wasn't half-bad, actually, for a midwestern Catholic girl."

"She's Catholic?" Catholic. That was likely to make it harder. All that guilt. "Well, hopefully next time you see her, she'll be a little more relaxed."

"Next time? What do you mean?"

"Well, I thought maybe you could run into her just one more time at the Fogscape? I'm not asking you to date her or anything. Just one more brief encounter to give her a little confidence."

"Vicky, look, I'm a nice guy. Maybe too nice, as you've pointed out for many years. But in case you forgot, I'm gay. Remember?"

"You don't have to kiss her, just flatter her!"

"Yeah, but if people see me chatting up women in bars, they're going to assume I'm *into* chicks. What's that going to do to my reputation?"

"Okay, maybe not at the Fogscape. Maybe at Whole Foods or something, where your reputation isn't as likely to be tarnished?"

"Yeah, well, maybe. We'll see. I know I owe you, after all the favors you've done for me. It's just, you know, I'd really like to meet someone." He paused for a moment. "Hey, how come you don't have me help you out with *male* clients who've been dumped and need an ego boost? Maybe I could get them to switch sides?"

"When was the last time you met a man who needed an ego boost? The terms are mutually exclusive."

"Just sayin'!" Kevin chuckled. "Okay, okay. Maybe Whole Foods, just one more time, but that's it."

"You're the best! Love you! Gotta run!" She clicked the phone shut and parked outside her client's house. Tomorrow, she would send the spa staff a fruit basket for playing their parts so well.

TEN

THEO SPRINTED BY THE CHILDREN'S PLAYGROUND and rounded the bend, choosing the path that led to the forest-like area of the park. This was the part that was farthest from the main street and therefore usually the least crowded. Branches formed a natural awning over the path, allowing only glimpses of the bright sky. He could feel the air become cooler as he ran farther into the thick woods.

This was one of his favorite jogging routes. He could always count on relative solitude. The screen of trees and foliage made him feel secure and protected. Johann, producer of fake IDs, had introduced Theo to this section of the park. It was the location of the first drop the two had used about three years ago.

He remembered how nervous he had been that first time, his heart racing with fear that he would be caught. He had circled the spot numerous times, his eyes darting from side to side to ensure no one was around. Then he had fumbled with the large rock at the base of the tree, his hands shaking with such force that he had trouble sliding it to the side to access the nook where the documents had been hidden. He chuckled out loud, thinking back to the moment when he had removed the large envelope from its hiding place, only to realize he had forgotten to bring something to put it in. Quickly replacing the rock, he'd had no alternative other than to jog out of the park holding it against his chest in plain view.

The story was still good for a laugh when he retold it for the hundredth time to his aunt and sister, but when it had actually happened, he'd thought it was catastrophic. He had bolted back to his apartment at top speed. Not even waiting for the elevator, he had leapt up the fourteen flights to his penthouse, finally collapsing on his couch. He sat in the same spot, virtually without moving, reliving the escapade, trying to will his heart rate back to normal, but expecting someone to come knocking at his door at any moment.

Until now, the drop locations had always been different, but this time he was going back to the original one. He thought about how much he had changed since that time. When they'd first started, he put a lot of effort into playing characters who were confident and smooth, exactly the opposite of his own persona at the time. With every project, though, he had gained strength, until now that part didn't require any acting, really. He felt like he was almost back to the old Theo, the Theo who had not just existed, but thrived, the Theo before Isabella had left him.

He hadn't made a complete comeback, of course, but at least he no longer felt like he was walking on a precipice that might crumble at any time. No, he was doing a lot better than just keeping it together. He felt pretty strong. Like he could live a normal life. Better than a normal life, thanks to his earnings.

His role in Victoria's schemes now came easily to him. In fact, he relished it and couldn't wait for the next project. He felt self-assured, though hopefully not overly so. You can't get too cocky. It was so easy to make a simple mistake that would sink the entire project or worse yet, land him in prison. But that wasn't going to happen. His every cell was totally focused, on alert. Every aspect of the execution would be flawless.

With that thought, he made a sharp right into the woods, glancing back to make sure no one had seen him. His legs moved easily. He mounted the gentle upward slope and disappeared farther into the forest. For about a quarter of a mile, he continued on, coming to a stop just below the crest of the hill. Once there, he snapped his head briskly from side to side, checking to make sure that he was alone. Then he bent over quickly and moved a large rock that was resting against the broad tree trunk in front of him. He reached into the compact cavern and pulled out the packet.

Again, he rotated his gaze like a human searchlight, then stashed the documents in the slim pouch at his waist and replaced the rock. As arranged, he placed a small rock on top of the large one, signifying that he had emptied the drop. He turned, ran back to the base of the hill and rejoined the path, as if on a smooth entry ramp. To celebrate his successful retrieval, he took another lap around the park, looping once again past the drop-off exit, but bypassing it with an extra spurt of energy.

When Theo returned home, he popped open a bottle of Dom Perignon and checked his watch—five o'clock in the afternoon, eight o'clock in the morning in California. Not too early, he thought. He picked up the phone and hit the autodial for his sister.

ELEVEN

THEO HEARD HER VOICE AND SMILED. "Hey, Vic, it's me. I'd like you to join me in a glass of champagne to celebrate the birth of yet another dashing, dastardly devil."

"I'd love to, but I've got a meeting to go to," Victoria told him. "Tell me quickly, though, whom exactly are we celebrating?"

"We are welcoming into this world, or should I say back into this world, the devastating, the charming, the knock-your-pants off ..." He looked at the driver's license on top of the stack again. "Rufus McCain. Do you believe it? Rufus! That's a fucking dog's name. What were his parents thinking? Must have been a real loser. How do you even get through first grade with that name? I was thinking I should go by 'Ruff-Ruff.' What do you say?"

He heard Victoria laughing on the other end of the line. She tried to talk, but couldn't compose herself. Finally, she got some words out. "It's cute. I'm picturing a rumpled-haired, professorial type. Every Rufus I've known has been gorgeous, incredible in bed and clever as a … Clifford." She paused for a moment. "The sound you don't hear is of me raising a virtual flute in honor of the mighty Rufus and drinking it all down in one big gulp."

"Okay, me too, but mine's deliciously un-virtual. Say, what are we calling this one, anyway?"

"Steeplechase."

He tipped his glass and emptied it. "To Steeplechase!"

"To Steeplechase!" she answered.

"Hey, by the way, what's her name and what is she like?"

"Her name is Maribeth Simmons, and—"

"Mary Beth? Are you kidding? No one is named Mary Beth anymore. Is she a sixty-year-old former nun or something?"

"No, she's in her thirties, and if it makes you feel better, it's M-A-R-I-B-E-T-H—all one word."

"Oh, thank God! Yeah, the 'I' and all one word make it totally different. Now I'm thinking a real fox, huge boobs, red hair, legs up to there, can do it all night. That's Maribeth with an 'I' and all one word. Mary Beth with a 'Y'—the totally opposite, two-word variety—never had sex before she got married, and even then, only once a month, when the Pope said it was okay. She's a size fourteen and her hobbies are crocheting and reading the Bible. Now, on the other hand, Marybeth with a "Y," but all one word …"

He could hear Victoria laughing again on the other end of the line. When she caught her breath, she tried to reassure him. "She's not that bad, I promise you. And I'm working on her. Don't worry. Besides, it's a job, you know. It isn't supposed to be fun, just lucrative."

"All right, if you say so. Do the best you can, though."

"You have my word."

"So, what is she worth?"

"I don't know yet. I had a spot of bad luck when I went

through her house. I'll have to go back. But don't worry, I know she has a lot. Her husband worked for a pre-IPO dot-com that went public. He got lots of stock. Plus, their house should go for at least five mil."

"Good. As long as it's worth my while, I can keep my eyes closed and pretend she's someone else. Anyway, I'll be arriving the day after tomorrow. The flight from Zurich lands there at six o'clock in the evening. Can we meet at Caesar's?"

"Sure. Let's say eight o'clock at Caesar's. I can't wait to see you. It's been too long!"

"Me, too. Say, have you worked out where I'll meet Betty Sue?"

"You should talk, Rover! Yes, well, I haven't told Maribeth yet, but it will be the Mill Valley Wine Festival the fourth Sunday in June. It's an outdoor event, in the town square."

"Brilliant. Can't wait to see you, Vic. I'll call you the instant I get in. One more toast … to Steeplechase!"

"To Steeplechase!" Victoria repeated. If Theo had been with her to celebrate, he would have seen her drizzling the line of white powder down neatly on her cocktail table and inhaling first through one nostril, then the other.

TWELVE

VICTORIA CROSSED THE STREET TO STARBUCKS. She spotted Maribeth at the cashier, large cookie in hand.

"Hey there, sorry I'm late," Victoria said, trying to mask her disapproval with a quick hug. "Let's go; we don't have much time!"

"Wow, you look gorgeous!" Maribeth stared at Victoria's lace-up, ankle-high black boots with copper heels. Victoria had paired them with a calf-length, rust-suede skirt and a cream silk blouse. Her hair was pulled back in a chignon, exposing large, gold-rimmed topaz crystals on each earlobe. As usual, the effect was one of understated elegance.

Victoria grabbed Maribeth's arm and started to move through the afternoon crowd of shorts-clad tourists and chic locals. But Maribeth was rooted to the spot.

"Aren't you coming?" Victoria shot a glance back at her. For a moment, she thought the woman was going to start crying.

"Don't you like my dress? I wore the snazziest thing I have just for you. I mean, I know it's not appropriate for tonight, but I thought just for shopping ..."

Snazziest? Victoria looked at the multicolored, flowered shirtdress that covered Maribeth's knees and wondered how to reply without damaging the woman's already precarious self-confidence. "It's a lovely dress—really. I'd definitely wear it myself" ... *in a nightmare, maybe,* she thought. "I'm sorry I didn't notice. I was just in such a hurry. But hey, you did a great job with your makeup!"

Maribeth grinned. "Yeah, I tried really hard to do what they told me at the spa. It took forever, but I guess it was worth it. You know, I've got to admit, I've really enjoyed going out with you these last few weeks, Victoria. I haven't had this much fun in ages!"

The fun's only starting, honey! Victoria pushed open the steel-rimmed glass door emblazoned with ebony block letters that spelled "Fuzio." The boutique had an air of ultra-modern sophistication. Clothes were arrayed by color on padded, black-satin hangers suspended from Lucite rods, as though they were floating in space. The pieces were simple and unfettered—of the finest fabrics and superbly cut. Muted electronic music played in the background and the air was infused with a spicy orange scent. Victoria and Maribeth were the only patrons in the shop.

Kenji, the owner, greeted them. He was unusually tall for a Japanese man and carried himself with perfect posture. A large amethyst ring flashed from his forefinger. He gave Victoria a gracious bow. "How wonderful to see you again, Ms. Clifford. And I see you've brought a friend?"

Victoria explained that they were there to pick out something for Maribeth to wear to a gallery opening that evening. Kenji studied Maribeth expertly, then nodded and led them to a rack of black skirts. He turned to the two of them, but seemed to be addressing Victoria mainly. "I'm thinking a simple black skirt, maybe calf length or ankle length, and one of these semi-sheer net tops with a muted design. What do you think?"

"Absolutely!" Victoria said.

Kenji selected a few pieces and escorted a dubious-looking Maribeth to the fitting room. "Please come out and show us how you look," he said as he closed the mirrored door behind her.

Victoria chatted with Kenji for several minutes before she realized that Maribeth had not yet emerged from the fitting room. "Maribeth? Come on out and give us a fashion show!"

There was no answer.

"Maribeth? How are you doing? Come on, don't be shy," she joked.

Still no answer.

Victoria frowned at Kenji and walked over to the fitting room. "Maribeth?" she said, knocking on the door. As she cocked her ear to the door, she could hear the faint sound of crying on the other side. "Maribeth? Are you okay? Can I come in?"

When there was no answer, Victoria gently turned the knob and peeked in. She saw her client crumpled on the rose leather chaise, her hand covering her eyes, weeping quietly. She was wearing one of the sleek skirts Kenji had selected, along with a form fitting, partially transparent top.

"Hon, what's wrong?"

Maribeth shook her head slowly and continued to cry.

"What happened? Do you feel okay?"

Maribeth looked up, her eyes brimming. "Look, Victoria, it just won't work."

Victoria shut the door behind the two of them. "What won't work?" she asked carefully.

"Trying to turn me into something I'm not. It's not going to happen. Look at me. You've got to admit; this outfit is ridiculous on me." She stood up and held out her arms and twirled in front of Victoria. It was true. The fitted top hugged the extra pounds around her midriff too closely, and the tea-length skirt ended exactly at the fullest part of her calves. What had she been thinking when she told Kenji these pieces would work? She should have known better.

Maribeth was well into her litany of self-pity. "I'm dumpy and I've been dumped. Not even for another woman. For a man, of all things. That tells you how hopeless I am."

Victoria resisted a visible sneer. *You deserve to be cheated on, you sniveling cow.* She fought her repulsion and eyed her watch, knowing she didn't have much time to turn things around.

"Come on, hon, sit down for a sec." She patted the seat next to her on the sofa.

Maribeth slumped down next to Victoria and blew her nose.

"Maribeth, you are a beautiful woman. Charlie didn't leave you because you were missing anything, except a penis. You had men crawling all over you at the Fogscape. And you're absolutely right about that outfit. It doesn't suit you at all. And you know what, it would look awful on me, too."

Maribeth looked at her dubiously.

"Just wait a minute." Victoria left the dressing room, went to a nearby rack and selected an item. She brought it back to Maribeth. "Here, try this."

While Maribeth was changing, Victoria went over to Kenji. Whispering, she explained the situation. Seconds later, Maribeth emerged tentatively from the fitting room. She wore a bias-cut, midnight-blue dress that skimmed her figure flatteringly. The diagonal seams were trimmed in pale silver, creating an elongating effect. The silver was picked up in a gray, voile-trimmed neckline that rested on the crest of her breasts.

Victoria and Kenji watched Maribeth scrutinize herself in the three-way mirror as though she were looking at a stranger. Almost imperceptibly, her back straightened and her shoulders lifted. Suddenly, she looked like someone who was sure of herself and knew where she was headed.

Victoria understood exactly what was happening. Ever since she had been a teenager sewing knock-offs of the latest styles in her tiny bedroom above a fabric store, she'd realized that clothes could change her mood in an instant, that they could make her anyone she wanted to be. Now Maribeth was learning the same thing.

"Fabulous!" Kenji said. "And these will complete the picture!" Kenji handed Maribeth a pair of silver hoop earrings. She put them on, looked in the mirror again and smiled.

"Maribeth, you look absolutely stunning," Victoria said. "See, it's just a matter of picking the right thing." She checked her watch and did a double take. "Look, I hate to rush you, but we really have to go now, or we'll miss the opening. Leave your car here. We'll go in mine."

◆◆◆

The gallery affair was everything Victoria had hoped it would be. A lively and obviously affluent crowd filled the high-ceilinged rooms of the former warehouse in an industrial area of San Francisco. The art was largely abstract, huge pieces, each of which would have filled an entire wall of her townhouse. Elegant metal sculptures depicting couples in various forms of embrace were suspended from the rafters in the centers of the rooms. Wait staff in tuxedos served caviar and sushi.

Simon was a gracious host, welcoming them with glasses of champagne as soon as they entered. He put his arm around

Maribeth's shoulder, and with a wink to Victoria, guided Maribeth away on a tour of the gallery, explaining the techniques of the various artists represented and making sure her glass remained filled. About an hour later, Victoria spied the two in a far corner, talking intently. Simon's slim body leaned against the wall, his eyes bright with interest. Maribeth was clasping her hands at her waist, holding her empty glass in front of her, as if to keep him at bay. She was blushing.

Victoria snuck another look at Simon. The first few buttons of his pale-blue shirt were open, exposing his tanned chest. Maybe later. She concentrated on working the event, chatting up the people she knew, being introduced to some she didn't, and scoring listings in Ross and Belvedere, two of the most exclusive neighborhoods in the county. She also managed to get introductions to a few East Coast transplants who were going to be looking for homes in Marin. Not bad for an evening's work, she thought.

It was nine fifteen. The event would be over in less than an hour, time for her getaway. She grabbed a flute of champagne from a passing tray and made her way to Simon and Maribeth, who were now engaged in conversation with a small group. She pulled Maribeth aside, handing her the full glass. "Looks like someone is having a good time!" Then she leaned over and whispered, "Simon can't take his eyes off of you!"

Maribeth took a drink and grinned into her champagne. "He is kind of cute."

"Kind of cute? He's a hunk! I'd jump him myself if I didn't have someone waiting for me right now. Look, I have to leave. I got a call from the guy I'm seeing, the one I told you about. He had a really bad day and I told him I'd cheer him up. You'll be okay here, right? You can take a cab home, or …" Victoria switched to a mock-sultry tone. "Maybe someone will give you a ride."

"Oh, no, I'll just go with you. You can drop me off at my

car." Maribeth looked for somewhere to put her glass, setting it on the top of a display case.

"Sorry, hon, I'm going in the other direction. And you're having fun, so you should stay. Want to do brunch on Sunday? I'll give you a call!" Not waiting for an answer, Victoria gave her a quick wave and disappeared into the crowd, leaving Maribeth to fend for herself.

She walked to her car, charged with energy. *This* was why she did it. This feeling that was like no other—things going exactly according to plan, falling into place, all under her orchestration. Pure euphoria.

She remembered the first time she had felt it. She was fourteen and in the ninth grade, the year after her father had left. Since he had taken all their savings, there was no money for class trips, books or clothes. Her mother barely made enough to feed them and keep the heat on. It was Girl Scout cookie selling season. She wasn't a Girl Scout, but her friend Amy was. Victoria knew Amy's locker combination, and one day after school used it to get Amy's Girl Scout uniform and cookie-selling kit. She made copies of the sales forms and, dressed in the uniform, went door to door in an area a few miles from her house. She told her customers that the Girl Scouts no longer accepted checks, just cash, and that they could use the receipts she gave them for tax deductions. In the first afternoon, she made $50. She returned the uniform to Amy's locker, and borrowed it whenever it was available during the next three weeks.

That first escapade netted her $600 and a lifetime addiction. Not only to the money, but more to the rush of pulling it off without a hitch and not getting caught. The highs just got better and better with each caper after that. And now, here was yet another one on the horizon. She gave a little skip as she got to her car.

Two hours later, back at home, Victoria answered her

doorbell. Simon grinned at her. "What I won't do to spend the night with you!" His Australian lilt was heavily tinged with champagne.

She stepped outside. "How did it go?"

"Just fine, I think. She wouldn't let me go to her house, so I drove her to her car and we made out for a while. I felt like I was back in high school. I thought she was going to let me get to second base, but it didn't happen. Guess I didn't get her drunk enough. I think it's safe to say, though, that she's convinced I want her."

He put his finger under Victoria's chin and lifted it until their eyes met. "I must say, it is incredibly noble of you to go to such lengths to build up your dumped clients' self-esteem," he said with mock sincerity.

She rolled her eyes. "I've told you; altruism has nothing to do with it. It's a good business practice. They're eternally grateful and that translates to great referrals and more business."

"So, I'm just a business asset, is that it?" He feigned a pout.

"You, my friend, are a very special *personal* asset." She stepped forward until their bodies touched.

"Happy to be of service, my dear. I've fulfilled my part of the bargain, so now I'm claiming my reward!" Simon stepped into the house and pulled Victoria to him, closing the door behind him. But not before the camera in the shrubbery clicked twice.

THIRTEEN

SUKI WAS STAGING THE HOUSE, for real this time. So, Victoria had arranged a full schedule for herself and Maribeth. They started with a morning aerobics class, a regime Victoria was trying to instill in her client with mixed results. It was all she could do to stop from laughing as she watched Maribeth struggle through the routines, always several steps behind everyone else, waving her arms up when the others were down, lunging left instead of right, thighs and arms jiggling all the while. By the end of each class, Maribeth was sweating heavily, her hair stuck to her head, her sopping tank top clinging to her ripples.

After brunch, they went to San Francisco for shopping and manicures, followed by drinks. Maribeth went straight to dinner with her attorney. Victoria went straight to Maribeth's house to see the results of the staging.

Even though she knew from experience that Suki's ability was nothing short of magical, she was astonished by what she saw. She walked from one room to another in awe.

The place looked completely different.

The designer had actually retained most of the Simmons' furniture, but only a practiced eye would be able to tell. It was hard to believe that such an extraordinary metamorphosis had been created largely by moving existing furniture around, adding a few key pieces and accessorizing.

The living room had been transformed. The dreary taupe sofa and love seat had been pulled from their refuge along the walls to form the centerpiece of the room. They were placed at a 90-degree angle to each other and diagonally faced the large wall of windows that looked out to the bay. Silk cushions in shades of yellow and orange almost totally hid the drab upholstery.

Victoria studied the coffee table. The surface was a multicolored design with a glass top and steel border. It took her a few seconds to realize that Suki had taken a framed poster with a geometric pattern and placed it on top of the Simmons' tired maple coffee table. Genius.

The two somberly flowered armchairs were hidden by yards of copper-colored silk that had been artfully draped over them, tucked into seams, pulled taut over armrests and fastened underneath. Victoria was reminded of her mother's far less successful attempt to mask an old couch with velvet remnants in the small apartment they'd shared after her father left. The artificial floral arrangements and potpourri were gone, of course. Instead, a few real palm trees in attractive lacquer pots encircled the living-room conversation area.

Every single part of the house was reconceived with creative brilliance. Suki had really outdone herself this time. Victoria couldn't wait to hear what Maribeth's reaction would be.

She was rewarded the next morning when she clicked on her voicemail.

"Oh, my goodness! I can't believe my eyes!" Maribeth

gushed. "The house looks so great! If it didn't hold such bad memories for me, I would seriously consider staying here. It's amazing what that woman can do with a little reshuffling. She actually kept most of our furniture. But it looks so fabulous, I almost didn't recognize it. That was a terrific idea—to have her come. I'm sorry I gave you such a hard time about it. Thanks so much. You're incredible!"

FOURTEEN

TWO FULLY PACKED SUITCASES LAY OPEN on Theo's bed. He added a black cashmere sweater to one, then zipped them both shut. The taxi driver called from the lobby. Theo buzzed him in, taking a last quick look around to make sure he hadn't forgotten anything. He thumbed through the packet of documents in the brown leather folder, then closed it and placed it in his carry-on. The elevator door opened; the taxi driver stepped out and went over to pick up the luggage. Theo turned to the window and stared out at the mountain for a moment. He bowed slightly as if in homage before joining the driver in the elevator.

The next time he saw his apartment, he thought, he would be even richer than he was now.

◆◆◆

"Mr. Schurer, would you like a drink before take-off?" the flight attendant asked. Theo had made the short hop from Geneva to Zurich and was settling in for the transatlantic flight. For a split second, he blinked, caught off-guard by his traveling name. "Yes. Campari on the rocks, please," he said.

"And Ms. ..." the flight attendant glanced down at her list, then addressed Theo's seatmate. "Ms. Chapman, what would you like?"

"Champagne, please," the woman sitting next to him answered. Then she turned to him. "What exactly is Campari? I've always wondered."

"It's an aperitif, made from various herbs. But the actual ingredients are a closely guarded secret."

"What does it taste like?"

"Uhh, hard to describe, really. Bitter, I guess."

"How long were you in Zurich?" Her lips were unnaturally glossy and spread in a smile that ended at her mouth, with no other evidence of it anywhere else on her face.

"I live here," he lied.

"Oh, really?" She leaned toward him a couple of inches. "That's exciting. What do you do, if you don't mind me asking?"

"I'm a business consultant," Theo answered. He looked at her left hand—no ring. He glanced up to study her.

Ah, he knew the type immediately: forty-something with major resurfacing. Her short brown hair had streaks of red and was sprayed into place, no doubt able to withstand winds of up to 50 mph without a single displaced strand. Her face had a tan, which ended abruptly at her chin. He could see tiny flakes of what looked like Kleenex on her right cheek, the side he had to face. Her blouse dipped below her artificially sculpted cleavage. The cloying scent of vanilla-tinged roses assaulted him every time she moved.

In short, a nightmare seatmate. He knew what was coming. If he wasn't careful, he would be held captive by her for the entire flight.

"I'm Tess, by the way. I live in the Bay Area." She extended her hand to him. He shook it politely, noticing the garish dark-orange polish. "I was in Zurich on business. My first time here. It's such a cool city." She gestured with her hand, her bangles clanging in accompaniment.

"Yes, it's quite a pleasant place."

The flight attendant brought over their drinks. Theo reached into his briefcase for a sleeping pill. His seatmate leaned over to him and raised her glass. "Here's to a good flight!" she said, her eyes too bright.

He touched his glass to hers, then popped the Ambien into his mouth while she was looking at him.

"Headache?"

He resisted giving her one of the many wiseass retorts that came immediately to mind.

"No. Sleeping pill. I have to go to a meeting right after we land."

She did a poor job of hiding her disappointment. "Are you staying in the Bay Area for long?"

"Only about a week, I'm afraid."

"How long have you lived in Zurich?"

"About four years now." Theo was hoping that his curt answers would send the desired message, but she was undaunted.

"Do you have family in Zurich?"

Holy fuck! There it was, the bald question, without artifice or grace. He had given her credit for a little more imagination.

Theo smiled politely through his disdain. "No immediate family. Many friends, I'm grateful to say." He could feel the warm cloud of sleepiness creeping through his body. "I think my pill is kicking in. Please excuse me." He positioned his Bose earphones on his head, reclined his seat, covered himself with a blanket and turned his head the other way.

A couple of hours before landing he awoke and was relieved to see that she was asleep. He noted that the rest hadn't improved her appearance in the least. If anything, she looked even worse in repose.

Turning from the distasteful sight, he took the opportunity to study his notes on Rufus McCain. Like memorizing lines, he thought. Little had he known when he graduated from drama school that his talents would be put to use in this way. Ironically, the income from his current gigs far surpassed what he could have ever earned doing occasional commercials, industrial films or supporting roles in local theaters. Maybe he should volunteer to attend his alma mater's career day to mentor undergraduates on how they could use their thespian training for maximum financial advantage. He grinned at the idea.

Tess awoke just before the plane began its initial descent into San Francisco. Obviously realizing that he had seen her at less than her best, she darted into the lavatory clutching a large cosmetics bag. A quarter of an hour later she returned, freshly primped, sprayed and painted. The garish orange lipstick stood out like a beacon in the dim cabin. "Did you sleep well?' she asked with that overly wide smile.

"Very well, thank you. And you?"

"Oh, yeah. I passed out after my fourth or fifth glass of champagne," she gushed. "Good thing I don't have plans for tonight. Where are you staying, anyway?"

"My company is putting me in one of those executive apartments in the city." He was appalled by her obviousness. Thankfully, the wheels hit the tarmac and they were braking to a halt. He began to collect his things, which seemed to give her an increased sense of urgency.

She reached into her bag and jabbed a business card in front of him. "I'm Tess Chaplin, by the way. I don't think we ever formally introduced ourselves. Here's my card. If you have a free evening or something, give me a call. I live in the South Bay; it's not far from the city."

"Thanks, Tess. It was nice to meet you. I'm Anthony

Schurer." He didn't offer a business card. Instead, he flashed one of his charming smiles and shook her hand brusquely. Passengers were filing out of their section. "Bye, now," he said as he turned and quickly made his way down the aisle.

Once out of the jetway, he practically sprinted to the nearest men's room. He entered a stall, locked the door and pulled out his red cell phone. "Hey, I'm here!" he announced when Victoria answered. "Well, if you must know, I'm in the loo," he said, in answer to her next question. "I'm hiding out from this hideous creature who sat next to me on the plane. If I reek of vanilla beans when I see you, you'll know why. I figure I'll give her at least twenty minutes to collect her luggage, and then I'll be off to meet you. Are you on your way?"

Victoria told him she would be at Caesar's in about an hour.

"Okay. See you as soon as I can. I'm flushing at the thought of you!" he said, pushing the toilet lever as he clicked off the line. Theo left the men's room and spent the next twenty minutes browsing through magazines in the gift shop before cautiously making his way to the luggage carousel. Thankfully, she was gone. He collected his suitcases and headed for the taxi stand.

He sank into the back seat. Soon the gentle jarring of the car lulled him into a light sleep. Suddenly, the cab lurched as it switched from one freeway lane to another, jolting him awake. The San Francisco skyline sparkled in the distance. It was so great to be back. There was no city like it—the world's most beautiful, he was convinced. What a shame he and Vic couldn't retire here.

The evening was unusually clear and warm for June. Normally at this time of year, the fog would have already sunk in and people would have been bundled up against the chilly winds. Tourists would be wearing their just-purchased, heavy sweatshirts stamped with "San Francisco." But not tonight.

The temperature was a balmy 72 degrees, according to the cab radio. As they drove into the city, he saw the outdoor restaurants and cafés jammed with customers. Bicyclists were out in force, threading fast and fearlessly through the traffic.

He got out of the taxi at his hotel, noting with pleasure the four-piece orchestra playing on the sidewalk. A fit woman who looked to be in her 70s, wearing black exercise tights and a tie-dyed T-shirt, zoomed by on a skateboard. A group of young men in oversized, low-slung jeans strolled by, their steps in perfect sync—no doubt to a rap song piped into their earbuds. Well-dressed theatergoers scurried to make their curtain times. Residents of nearby Chinatown shuffled home, scents of bok choy, ginger and fresh fish wafting from their plastic bags. God, he loved this city.

Theo checked in quickly and had his bags sent to his room, then returned to the cab. On the way to the restaurant, he thought about other exceptional cities they could retire in: Rio, Paris, Sydney, or maybe a remote island. But none of them were San Francisco.

The driver's voice jolted him to reality. "Sir, we're here!"

Theo quickly paid and entered the small cantina. The décor looked like a page from "The Guide to Decorating Small Mexican Restaurants." Standard-issue plastic red-and-white-checkered cloths covered the plain wooden tables. On top of each, a salsa bottle featuring a devil on the label stood like a religious statue. The pungent smell of Dos Equis, mixed with various varieties of chiles, filled the air. Boisterous Latin music gave the place an upbeat, party vibe.

He caught sight of her at a table in the back. She had pulled her chameleon act, fitting right in to the environment. In a plain black T-shirt and blue jeans, her hair pulled back in a ponytail, she looked like she lived in the neighborhood. The only jewelry she wore was a pair of earrings, plain gold loops that could have come from Target, but didn't, he knew. The single detail that possibly could have set her apart, and only to the most discerning eye, was the way she held herself. Even in her casual garb, in this common place, her presence stood out. She seemed regal, from another sphere, at least to Theo.

Victoria looked up and saw him, lighting up instantly. She jumped out of her chair and hugged him. He kissed her on the lips and wrapped his arms around her. They held each other for a full minute, swaying back and forth, not saying a word. Then he stepped back and looked her over. "My, you are more marvelous than ever!"

"And you!" she said, "Every woman in Geneva must be after you."

"Exactly right. Why do you think I'm out of breath from running each time I speak to you?"

"We'd better sit down. Everyone's looking at us." Many in the restaurant were smiling at the two, assuming they were reuniting lovers. And indeed, settled across the table from each other, leaning forward with eyes locked, they certainly could have been.

Theo looked around a bit nervously. "Are you sure it's okay to be seen here together?"

Victoria took his hand and patted it. "Don't worry. It's still early in the game for Steeplechase. We'll spend enough time meeting in stuffy hotel rooms. I figured we could risk just one night out. Who's going to look for Victoria Clifford and Rufus McCain in a little hole in the wall under a freeway overpass, anyway?"

"Well, hopefully, nobody's going to be looking for us period, right? Okay, let's enjoy it."

They had a leisurely dinner, catching each other up on the last few months. From time to time, they reached across the table to hold hands. Hours went by, until finally they were the only two customers left in the restaurant.

Their waiter approached sheepishly. "I'm so sorry, but we have to close now. The staff is going home."

"Oh my God, it's almost midnight!" Victoria said. They apologized, quickly paid their bill and left. The plan had been to drop Theo off at his hotel, but they decided that just for this first night, he would stay at Victoria's townhouse. It was a small risk to take, they thought. And there was still so much to talk about.

On the drive to Sausalito the topic turned to Steeplechase. "So, when do I meet Peggy Sue?" Theo asked.

"Down, Fido. In about three weeks at the Mill Valley Wine Festival. That gives you enough time to set yourself up."

"Okay, but now that I'm here, you can tell me what she really looks like. She's a troll, right?"

"Not at all. She's cute, in a midwestern kind of way. And I've already made a lot of progress. She looks much better than she did a few weeks ago. And after you work your magic on her, she'll be totally hot. You know, I've been thinking about it. This is really a service we're providing these women. We get something from them, of course, but they get a lot out of it, too."

"Yeah, the world's most expensive makeover!" Theo chuckled. "I love your twisted mind. Only you could rationalize a major swindle as an act of charity."

"Chalk it up to my good Catholic upbringing." Victoria grinned as she pulled into her driveway.

Theo jumped out of the car and gave Victoria another long bear hug before they tramped happily up the walk. Again, a casual observer would assume a handsome boyfriend was coming to spend the night. At least that's what the man in the gray Lexus parked half a block away figured. He leaned out of the car and snapped a few photos of the couple before they closed the door behind them.

FIFTEEN

VERA MADE HER WAY to the neatly dressed young woman sitting at the far corner table. She had that same air of self-assurance as she'd had the first time she came to Vera's office for advice on whether to leave her job at Coro Biosciences. Carolina Crespi stood to greet her with a hearty handshake and a warm smile.

"I'm so glad you could make it," Carolina said.

"Thank you for inviting me. Though I'm not quite sure what this is all about."

They ordered lunch quickly. Then Carolina leaned forward. "Ms. Peterlin, I wanted to thank you so much for what you did for me."

"Please call me Vera."

Carolina nodded. "You helped me a lot. Thanks to you, I got a great package from Coro. Actually, it was so good that I could have taken a couple of years off and just vegged. But that wouldn't be me."

Vera smiled in agreement. The woman was ambitious and a go-getter. The type who wouldn't know what to do with a week off, let alone a couple of years. "I'm glad I was able to help. But there was really no need for you to take me to lunch."

"Well, it's not entirely altruistic. There's another reason I wanted to talk with you." Carolina stopped while the waiter served them their orders.

When he left, she continued. "See, right after I left Coro, I got a job offer from Kinney Pharmaceuticals. An incredible offer for a position a lot higher than I had at Coro. And of course, I took it. But wait a minute. You probably already know all this, right?"

Vera laughed. "No, I don't already know it. Maybe, if I set my mind to it and we had a session together, I would come to know it, but I don't walk around automatically aware of everything that is going on in everyone's life. Thank God. That would be exhausting!"

"Oh, okay, I get it. Anyway, now I'm the VP of Corporate Development at Kinney. I have my own department, my own team, and I report directly to the CEO. It's a dream job!"

"Well, that's wonderful, dear." Vera wondered what else Carolina could possibly need from her.

"Yes, it's terrific. Except there's this one problem. This guy who reports to me really wanted my job. He has a lot less experience than I do, but he thinks he's more qualified somehow. Ever since I got there, he's shifted into slow motion on his projects and does everything he can to undermine me. He's basically sabotaging our work."

"Surely you can fire him for nonperformance, can't you?"

"Yes, eventually, I could get rid of him. But I'd have to write him up a few times, document everything to the nth degree. All that would take months. In the meantime, I can't get any real work done. I got to thinking, if I could somehow get him to come to you, indirectly, of course. Could you get him to see that leaving would be a positive career move for him? Kind of like you did with me, except in his case, I really want him to leave. Maybe you could get him to think it was his idea."

Vera had a hard time suppressing a grin, but managed to form a surprised expression.

Carolina continued. "It's out of the ordinary, I know, and not what you usually do, but I thought I'd ask you if you'd be willing to do it. I have a hefty budget at Kinney and I could pay you well."

Vera sized up her lunch mate. A solid professional of good character, obviously very smart and on an upward trajectory career-wise. Probably safe, but of course she would have to check her out, just to be sure. "As you say, Carolina, this is quite out of the ordinary. I will have to give it some thought. Give me a few days and I'll call you."

Carolina looked disappointed, but recovered quickly. "Yes, of course, I understand. It's an unusual request. But please do let me know when you've had a chance to think about it."

Two weeks later, after a thorough investigation, Vera called Carolina. "I am willing to do what you asked. However, I have to tell you that under no circumstances will I lie to any client. If we go forward with this, then we will decide on a dignified, fair departure for the man. You will tell him that you are restructuring your department and that his position is being eliminated. That being the case, you will give him a generous severance package and you will ensure that at your end, everything actually plays out as we agreed. So that when I describe it to him as being in his future, I am telling the truth. Do you understand?"

"Yes, of course!"

Vera grinned to herself as she hung up from the conversation. Even she could not have predicted this turn of events. But as she thought about her client, the strange foreboding she'd felt the first time she met Carolina edged into her consciousness. What was that about? Should she not take her on as a client? Would it get her into trouble? No, that wasn't it, she was fairly sure. It wasn't directly related to the work she would be doing for Carolina. It was something else. But what else could there be? There was no other connection. She would just have to be on guard.

SIXTEEN

VERA DROVE INTO THE CITY and handed her key to the valet at the St. Francis Hotel on Union Square. She entered through the large, gilded front door, walked through the lobby and made a stop at the ladies' room. If anyone had been standing outside of the restroom area for the next half-hour, they would have wondered what happened to the elegantly dressed woman who went in, but never emerged. Had they been watching closely, however, they would have noticed another woman leaving who had never entered.

The second woman wore blue polyester pants and sneakers and carried a backpack. All that could be seen of her head were black-framed sunglasses under a wide-brimmed canvas hat.

With a manly gait, the woman with the canvas hat walked out the side entrance of the hotel. Glancing behind her slightly, she continued two blocks east and entered the Hyatt. In less than a minute, she was knocking at the door of room 1021. Both Theo and Victoria were waiting for her.

Theo hugged her heartily. "Teta Vera, it's so good to see you!"

Vera took off her sunglasses and looked him up and down with a broad smile. "Theodore, you are more and more handsome every time I see you." Her eyes misted a bit.

"Must be the Peterlin genes! You look pretty sexy yourself!" he said.

Vera rolled her eyes, removing her hat and backpack. "What I go through for the two of you."

Victoria hugged her, then the three settled in the sitting-room area of the suite. It was so rare for all of them to be together. Victoria and Vera occasionally met up in a small town a couple hours up the coast or had dinner together in a hotel room such as this one. But since Theo lived in Geneva, he saw his aunt and sister for only a week or so each summer, when they got together for a holiday in the Slovenian countryside. Unless, of course, they were working together on a project, like they were now. And then there was little time for socializing.

They popped open a bottle of champagne. For the first couple of hours, they just enjoyed each other's company, catching up on all that had happened since they were last together.

Too soon for Vera's liking, the discussion turned to the task that lay before them—Steeplechase. Victoria started by explaining the details and timeline of the project. She spent over an hour relaying everything she had learned about Maribeth: her personality, financial standing, the status of her divorce settlement, her strengths, weaknesses and anything else she could think of that might be important in carrying out their plan.

"I didn't spend as much time as I wanted in the house, but I think I got enough for you, Teta Vera," she said. Vera took notes on her iPad as Victoria gave details about aspects of Maribeth's past and her relationship with her husband, Charlie.

Until late in the evening, they revisited the plan from every angle, went over each step, brainstormed what could possibly go wrong and how they would deal with it if it did. Finally, they were satisfied that once again, they had planned a perfect crime.

Vera could see that Theo and Victoria were ebullient, in their element. As for herself, she was just tired. Not only from the evening's work, but also, more fundamentally, from having to participate in the scheme yet again.

As they started to say their goodbyes, she made a point of asking. "Do we really have to keep doing this? Don't you already have as much money as you could possibly ever need?"

Vera could see that Victoria was annoyed with her, but she needed to be reassured once again, this time in front of Theo, that Steeplechase really would be the last time. Victoria was stealing a look at Theo. Her niece was clearly uncomfortable talking about this in front of him. *She probably hasn't told him about her promise to me*, Vera guessed. *Well, no time like the present.*

"Teta Vera, I've already assured you this would be the last time you'll have to help us," Victoria said.

Theo's brows arched.

Vera pressed on. Might as well go for broke. "Yes, I know, but I'm also concerned about you and Theo stopping this."

Victoria appeared to regain her confidence. "Since you mention it, I've been thinking about that, too. Maybe we don't have to do this at all anymore."

Theo shot her a surprised look. Vera grinned to herself. This was obviously the first he had heard about it. Good. At least all the cards were out there.

"I'm so glad to hear that, *mičkena*," Vera said, genuinely pleased. "I've got to go now. "*Lahko noč!*" She hugged them goodnight.

The door had barely shut behind Vera when Theo blurted out, "You told her she didn't have to help us anymore and you've been thinking of calling it quits?" He was staring at her like she had turned into someone else.

Victoria hadn't planned to discuss this with him yet. But thanks to Vera, she had no choice.

"Look, hon," she said, "it's clear Teta Vera's heart hasn't been in this for a long time. In the beginning, she went along with it to help us out. I guess she thought it was part of her obligation to Mother.

"Anyway, you know during the last couple of gigs, she complained the whole time that she didn't want to do it, saying that it was wrong, we should stop, and so on. When I told her about Steeplechase, she was really upset that we were going to do it again. So I told her it would be the last time. The last time for her, or the last time for all of us, she wanted to know. I told her I'd been thinking about calling it quits, too, mainly to shut her up.

"The most important thing now is that all three of us are totally focused on Steeplechase. I figured if I told her it was the last time, she'd lay off the complaining and concentrate on doing her part. That's all I care about now.

"Look, the last thing we need on our little team is someone who doesn't want to be on it. I was afraid that consciously or unconsciously, she'd throw the game."

Theo shook his head. "No, she wouldn't do that to us, Vic. She's always played her part perfectly, not one single mistake. She's a pro!"

"You're right. Until now, she's played everything exactly by the script. But at some point, I'm afraid, her feelings are going to get in the way and she may slip up. Not on purpose, but because her heart's not in it. We're lucky it hasn't happened yet. And it better not happen this time, either. But after this, I'm just not willing to take the risk again. So, I think it's best all-around if we don't use her anymore. And if we decide to keep going without her after Steeplechase, we sure as hell aren't going to tell her."

"*If* we decide to keep going without her? You mean you really are thinking of quitting after this one?"

Victoria poured herself the last of the champagne and sank into the sofa. What she couldn't tell him was that she really wished she could manage it entirely on her own—without him, even. He was fragile. She'd seen him on the brink of insanity. Granted, that was a while ago, and he seemed to be pretty much back to his old self. He, too, she had to admit, had played his part flawlessly time after time. But you never knew with someone like that. If they lost it once, it could happen again.

She had never been able to hide her feelings from Theo for very long. She might as well level with him. Not tell him she had doubts about *him,* of course, but ...

"To tell you the truth, hon, I have to admit that lately I've been thinking that we may need a change, too. Obviously, after we let Vera loose, we'll have to figure out a new con. That will take some time and a lot of brilliance."

"A lot of brilliance is exactly what you have. I have complete faith in you. You'll figure out something stunning!"

"Theo, I know you don't want to hear this, but maybe we should also *consider* ... I'm just saying *consider* ... hanging it all up after Steeplechase. Teta Vera's right. We certainly don't need the money."

Theo faltered, stumbling over his words. "Vic, I can't believe you're actually thinking of stopping!"

"Look, I just said I was *thinking* about it, *considering, thinking,* okay? But right now, you're right. I absolutely shouldn't be thinking or considering anything except Steeplechase. I—*we*—can't afford to spend our energy on anything else. Every single one of our brain cells has to be focused on making it spectacularly successful. Then, when we're done, we can take our time and figure out what to do next.

"I promise, before we decide anything, we'll talk through all the alternatives, see what other schemes we might be able to come up with, give it a lot of thought. There are *tons* of possibilities. Okay? Deal?"

This seemed to calm him down. "Okay. As long as all our options are still open. As long as we consider all possibilities."

SEVENTEEN

VICTORIA GOT HOME AND WAS LOOKING through her mail when she heard her stomach rumble. With a thrill, she realized that she hadn't eaten since the morning, just a couple of glasses of champagne. Normally, she knew to the minute how long it had been since she'd had any food, how many calories she'd had so far that day and how soon it would be before she could eat again. But today, she had been on a Steeplechase high and hadn't even thought about food. It was better than any diet pill.

But now that the adrenaline had subsided, she was disgustingly hungry. She should capitalize on it. Turn it to her advantage.

She took the packet of frozen asparagus out of the freezer and popped it into the microwave. Moments later, she withdrew it and cut an opening in the pouch, spilling its contents into a bowl. Her stomach lurched at the smell of the slimy green chunks. "Safeway Asparagus in Water," the package read. She kept a stock of it, the cheapest brand of asparagus she could find—butterless, sauceless, nothing to disguise its natural, vile essence.

Steeling herself, she delivered several forkfuls to her mouth, chewing rapidly and then swallowing. She forced herself to continue breathing through her nose, allowing the full impact of the disgusting smell and taste to be absorbed. As expected, waves of nausea soon began churning in her stomach. She scooped up more and swallowed it down. Finally, she felt the bile rising in her throat, accompanied by strands of the objectionable, sinuous stuff. She bolted to the bathroom.

EIGHTEEN

IT HAD BEEN SLIGHTLY MORE THAN THREE WEEKS since Theo had arrived in San Francisco. In that time, he had established a local identity, formed a corporation and found a place to live. Having gone through the drill several times, he now had the timing and sequence down to a science. The first time had been a bit rough, since he found out the hard way that he needed at least one local employment reference and a local bank account in order to get a short-term lease. And he needed a p.o. box and phone number to create an employer, and so on.

That time, thanks to his learning curve, the process had taken almost two months. He'd been Steven Cooper then and the company was Wavelength Systems. The woman was Jenny Russert, their first mark. They had made their first three million off of her, split two ways, fifty-fifty. They had tried to persuade Vera to take at least twenty percent, but she wouldn't hear of it.

For the Wavelength caper, he had rented a fairly modest,

furnished flat in Pacific Heights. With each con, his living accommodations had gone up a notch. Now for Steeplechase, he had specified an executive suite of at least 2,000 square feet, preferably a penthouse, with a view of the bay and within walking distance of the city's financial district.

The first property the leasing agent showed him was perfect. Theo paid the deposit and signed a three-month lease immediately. He had a new address: Mandarin Towers, 514 Sacramento Street, Suite 2002.

It wasn't a penthouse, but an expansive loft, with a sweeping view of the Golden Gate Bridge, Alcatraz and the Marin Headlands. He'd had it furnished entirely from Roche Bobois. A brown-leather sectional sofa and Brazilian-marble coffee table defined the living room area. A sprawling, pale-ash laminate desk, placed against one expanse of windows, served as the office. The bedroom featured a king-size, platform bed frame in the darkest shade of brown. A switch on either side of the bed ejected the flat-screen TV from the base of the bed frame.

The layout and décor were right up his alley. At $12,000 per month, it was an expensive alley, but he deserved it. He had an image to project for Ms. Maribeth Simmons, whom he was about to meet for the first time.

Victoria had used the intervening time since Theo's arrival to solidify her friendship with Maribeth and to continue working on Maribeth's image. While Maribeth certainly looked more stylish and put together than when she'd first met Victoria, there was still evidence of a few too many cupcakes under her belt. Nonetheless, it was a respectable transformation so far. Along with Maribeth's cosmetic changes came the expected boost in self-confidence and bonding with Victoria. The two now met for lunch, dinner or some other social event at least twice a week.

While Victoria's efforts with Maribeth had been quite

successful on the social front, she had not made any progress at all on selling Maribeth's property in the time since Maribeth had signed the listing papers. This would seem surprising, given the current seller's market. But on deeper investigation, it was not the least bit unexpected, since Victoria was doing everything she could to ensure the home wasn't marketed. After all, it wouldn't do to have the property sold before everything was in place. If Victoria did her part—and she always more than delivered—the house would close at exactly the moment it was supposed to. And the profit from the sale would end up exactly where it was supposed to.

Maribeth had insisted that the house be listed on MLS. But Victoria was able to convince her to dispense with a "For Sale" sign. And indeed, in spite of the lack of a sign, Maribeth said she was thrilled with all the attention the house was getting from real estate agents and potential buyers. Nearly every day, there were at least a couple of realty agent business cards on the foyer table when she returned from appointments or errands.

What Maribeth didn't know was that not a single prospective buyer or real estate agent had seen the house yet. Nor was it listed on MLS. Nor was there a confidential listing. In fact, the listing papers hadn't even been filed yet. They were neatly ensconced in Victoria's desk, conveniently undated, just waiting for Victoria to decide when they should see the light of day.

NINETEEN

"HERE YOU GO, LADIES, YOU'RE ALL SET." The balding man with the full gray beard took their money, stamped their hands and gave Victoria and Maribeth each a complimentary wine glass engraved with the "Mill Valley Wine and Food Festival" logo. This was the annual festival sponsored by the Canepa family, whose ownership of the Mill Valley Market went back several generations.

Jim Canepa, the family patriarch, took great pride in bringing in the best wineries, mainly from Napa and Sonoma, for an afternoon of wine tasting in Mill Valley's main plaza. When the festival first started, about fifty wineries participated, but now well over a hundred labels were represented at the annual affair. The event always drew a large local crowd, as well as a sprinkling of out-of-towners.

As usual, Mill Valley's many specialty stores and boutiques had set up sidewalk sales to attract the festival crowd. Attendees wandered easily from the wine stalls on the square to the neighboring streets, wine glasses in hand.

Mill Valley's main plaza covered about two square blocks. Several large oak trees splattered pools of shade here and there. A small but regal grove of redwoods stretched skyward from the far corner. The wineries were set up alphabetically along the perimeter of the square. Interspersed among them, as well as in the center of the plaza, were a variety of food booths offering free samples of everything from tacos to ice cream. The smell of roasting sausages and grilling hamburgers drifted in the air.

By the time Victoria and Maribeth arrived, a good-sized gathering of wine tasters had already formed. They represented a cross-section of the county's residents, which wasn't a cross-section at all, given Marin's demographics. Essentially, it was a gathering of fit, middle-aged, wealthy left-coasters.

Festival patrons chatted with the winemakers, asking all the right questions. Given the proximity of the Napa and Sonoma wine-growing regions, most Marin residents fancied themselves to be wine connoisseurs. At one-thirty in the afternoon, the temperature was an uncharacteristic 92 degrees, which was sweltering for fog-friendly southern Marin.

Victoria looked cool and relaxed in a linen sundress that was the palest shade of lime. The crisp, luminous fabric was the perfect complement to her tanned skin and taut figure. One would have had to look very closely to see the slightest hardening of her jaw and to notice that her left hand gripped her cream-colored leather bag as though it were a life raft.

Both Victoria and Theo had critical parts to play. Which one of them, Victoria wondered, was the better actor? The one who pretended to have feelings he didn't have, or the one who didn't show the feelings she had? All their lives it had been Theo who'd been recognized for his talent to mimic characters of all types, culminating in an actual career as a minor-league actor. In the meantime, Victoria's skill, if it could be called a skill, went unnoticed. Everyone saw her as strong, unemotional—a rock. But only Theo sensed, and only she knew, that she was none of those things.

Almost from the first time she'd felt a negative emotion, Victoria had hidden it, instinctively knowing that was what was expected. She learned quickly that the list of inappropriate emotions, in the Clifford family at least, was a long one: anger, fear, sorrow, need, pain, dissatisfaction, to name only a few. So, she had become adept at pretending not to have them.

Did it take more will to make your hands tremble or to stop them from trembling? Or was it an equal accomplishment? Both talents would be put into play today.

It was a crucial day: the day that would test how successful Victoria had been in building Maribeth's confidence; the day that would set the next few weeks in motion and hopefully culminate in yet another financial coup. It took all of Victoria's strength to squelch the anxiety that threatened to break through at any moment. She concentrated on her hands to keep them from shaking; one clutched her purse while the other gripped her wine glass. She focused on her voice, forcing a normal pitch and not permitting the slightest waver. She needed a drink—or something more. But she would have to settle for the drink.

Victoria and Maribeth surveyed the booths. They decided to start with white wines. Within half an hour, they had made their way from Acorn to Matanzas Creek and were beginning to feel the heady combination of alcohol and heat.

"Wait right here," said Victoria, handing Maribeth her half-full glass. "Al Fresco is serving my favorite mini fish tacos. I'm going to grab us a couple."

Maribeth slipped under the shade of a sprawling oak tree

to wait. She was sipping the last of her chardonnay when her arm was jostled, splashing her drink and Victoria's onto the front of her pink sundress.

"Drat! I'm so sorry." His voice had a European clip. He was already flushed from the heat, but reddened even more when he looked at her. "I'll get some napkins or something. Hang on, I'll be right back!"

A couple of minutes later, from her vantage point near the restaurant stand, Victoria saw her brother awkwardly dabbing the front of Maribeth's dress, his head shaking in obvious apology. Maribeth was laughing and waving him off, apparently telling him not to bother. As Victoria watched, Theo led Maribeth to a nearby booth and got their glasses replenished with a fresh tasting sample. She could see Theo lean in toward Maribeth in his characteristic style, as though sharing a secret for only her to hear. Maribeth was playing with a strand of her hair, twisting it around her fingers. Victoria's grin spread, and she gave her brother an unseen nod of admiration. If only he had made it in legitimate theater or the movies.

She balanced a couple of mini-tacos in her hand and walked over to them. "Sorry it took me so long. I ran into a client who wanted to give me a new listing—business first, you know!" She handed Maribeth her taco and looked quizzically at the man standing next to her.

"Oh, Victoria, this is ..." Maribeth began the introduction, then looked at Theo. "Wait, you haven't told me your name, have you?" She giggled.

"Rufus." He shook Victoria's hand and gave a slight bow. Then he looked at Victoria. "Unfortunately, I relieved you of your drink, thanks to my clumsiness. What can I get you?"

As he hurried to get Victoria another glass, Maribeth leaned over to her and whispered. "Isn't he adorable? He seems foreign or something."

"Definitely hot!" Victoria agreed.

Theo returned with her drink and the three chatted for a while until Victoria waved to someone across the square. "Excuse me, I have to talk to my client over there about a property I just saw that is exactly what he's looking for. I'll catch up with you later." Victoria raised her glass to them and headed toward the other side of the plaza.

More than an hour later, Victoria returned to find Theo and Maribeth on a bench in the small nook of redwoods. Both of their glasses were half-filled with red wine. Victoria could tell that Maribeth was well on her way to being drunk. Her voice was a few notches louder than usual and every sentence ended with a giggle. Her normally bright eyes had a pinkish tinge and a dazed look. Theo was gesturing dramatically and laughing heartily every time he spoke. His arm was draped around Maribeth's shoulders as though they were long-time friends. He whispered something in Maribeth's ear, sending her into a new round of laughter. Victoria knew he was perfectly sober.

"So, this is where you're hiding. I almost gave up looking for you!" She joined them in the natural alcove.

"Oh, damn, she found us," Theo said. "I told you we should have escaped before your chaperone came back. I have a feeling I'm in big trouble now!"

"Not at all," Victoria laughed. "I just wanted to let you know I have to leave now, Maribeth. I can drop you off at your house or ..." She shot a glance at Theo.

Before Maribeth could open her mouth, Theo jumped in. "I would be most honored if you would allow me the pleasure of giving you a lift home. After all, we've only sampled half the wines here. The afternoon is yet young!" His eyes darkened with just a hint of seduction and then it was gone, replaced by a chaste earnestness. "Unless you have other plans, of course," he said, pulling slightly away from her, as if it just occurred to him that she might not be single.

Maribeth looked uncertain, her gaze shifting back and forth between Victoria and Theo. Victoria could almost hear the inner debate. The good girl, the one who had never slept with someone just for fun, the one who only dated one guy at a time, the one who was never the dumper, always the dumpee, the one who had been unfailingly cautious, honest and true and had the scars to prove it. This Maribeth battled the new one: the one Victoria had worked on for the last few weeks, the one who, now in her thirties, was finally starting to look and feel like an adult instead of a girl, the one whose self-assurance was emerging, one halting step at a time.

"Okay. If you don't mind, Victoria, I'd like to stay a little longer." Maribeth turned to Rufus apologetically. "Are you sure it's not too far out of your way to give me a ride, Rufus? I could just take a cab."

Still miles to go on the confidence front, Victoria thought. But she's going for it, that's what's important right now. Victoria shook Theo's hand. "Rufus, I'm entrusting her to you. But as her chaperone, I'm warning you, be careful. She's not as sweet and innocent as she looks!" Victoria winked at Maribeth and took off. When she was out of their sight, she dialed Theo's number on her red cell phone. She waited for him to answer, then hung up.

◆◆◆

Knowing that Theo was successfully absorbing all of Maribeth's attention, Victoria drove to Maribeth's house. She let herself in and headed toward the office. As she moved through the wide corridors, she was once again struck by the unlived-in quality of the place. Yes, the home had been staged, but usually if the owners were still living in the house, they left some traces of themselves in the unfamiliar setting. In fact, Victoria realized that the house had felt staged in its own way before Suki had set to work on it, yet with an entirely different effect.

She entered the office, which still looked like no one had set foot in it for months. She examined several file drawers before she found what she was looking for. Leafing quickly through the folder, she selected five pages and carefully laid them out on the top of the desk. From her tote she pulled out her cell phone and took a shot of each page. Just as she was snapping the final page, she heard voices at the top of the stairs. Fiona's voice.

It took a full three seconds for the thought to register. Someone was in the house! Not only in the house, they were just a few feet away. How could that be? How could she have missed them pulling up the driveway? Fiona had a silent Tesla, true, but … what about the noise they probably made coming in the front door? Stop analyzing. Just move, she told herself. Hands shaking, she jammed the pages back into the file and closed the cabinet drawer. She made it out into the corridor just in time to come face to face with Fiona Chang and her clients.

Like Victoria, Fiona Chang was one of Marin's top real estate agents. She had been a member of Peabody Realty's millionaire club for many years and was always named as one of the top ten agents in Marin. In the last few years, though, Victoria had outranked her on the list. This did not sit well with Fiona. It didn't help that Victoria was also about a decade younger and easily more beautiful. The two often found themselves working together—perhaps sparring would be a more accurate description—on real estate deals.

Fiona had been born to Chinese immigrants. She was an "ABC," American-Born Chinese, as they were called in the Asian community. She had worked very hard to earn her remarkable success in the real estate world, starting out as a secretary in one of the smaller Peabody offices and gaining more and more responsibility as she aced every assignment she was handed. Not knowing Victoria's history, she assumed that her rival's success was due to her good looks instead of plain, hard work. And she resented it.

Fiona looked startled at the sight of Victoria in the office doorway. Her face crinkled, emphasizing the deep lines around her eyes. Her thin lips parted into a surprised "O."

Victoria was relaxed and friendly, greeting Fiona and her clients breezily and asking them their impressions of the house. She released a measuring tape back into its holder while they spoke and threw it into her tote. Out-of-state clients, she explained, needed some measurements before considering whether they would make an offer on the house. She asked Fiona if her clients had any questions about the house. Fiona politely turned to her clients, but it seemed there were no questions.

Excusing herself, Victoria left. Once in her car, she allowed her hands to tremble again. What was happening to her? Why hadn't she kept an eye out for a car driving up? Why wasn't she on high alert for this possibility? And most importantly, most bizarre of all: How in the hell had Fiona heard that the property was for sale, since it wasn't even listed? How in the hell could that even happen? She would have to figure it out later. Right now she had to act fast, formally and immediately listing the house. What was more, word would now get around that the house was for sale and she would have to prepare for potential offers. This would give Theo less time to do what needed to be done. There was no doubt about it, she was losing her edge. It wasn't over-confidence; it was a lack of focus—carelessness. *You lazy piece of shit!* She heard her father's anger as though he were right there.

The jar was jammed in a corner of her purse. It took her a few seconds of shuffling to get it out. A few seconds after that, she had regained her confidence. Whatever was thrown her way could be managed. She would prevail as she always had. Victoria was sure of it.

TWENTY

THEO KNOCKED ON THE HOTEL ROOM DOOR a few minutes after ten that evening. A pregnant woman opened it. She had short, spiky, platinum hair and wore a flowered maternity dress and sensible flats.

"For a minute, I was sure I had the wrong room!" he laughed.

"Do you like my new get-up?" Victoria asked. "Another selection from my Steeplechase line! Hang on, I'll be right back!"

They had agreed to meet at the Hyatt in Walnut Creek, a bedroom community about twenty-five miles east of San Francisco. Victoria was still dressed in the traveling outfit she had worn for her train ride over there. She ran to the bedroom to change and reappeared barefooted and some twenty pounds lighter, dressed in a T-shirt and sweatpants. Theo was looking through the minibar selection.

"So, how did it go? Did she agree to see you again? Did you sleep with her?" She fired the questions at him.

"Whoa! Can I at least sit down for the interrogation? Maybe even pour myself a drink?"

"A drink? Are we celebrating?"

"You never quit, do you? That's why I love you ... a trap like a steel mind. All right, all right, yes. We're celebrating!"

She gave a whoop and jumped into his arms, wrapping her legs around him. "Congratulations, my studly brother. You've done it again!"

"Hang on. Not so fast. I haven't won the lady's heart yet. I haven't even gotten into her big cotton knickers. But I think she's interested and I think I know how to play her."

"Okay. *Now* you deserve that drink!" Victoria went to the minibar and poured a Glenfiddich, straight up, for him and a Courvoisier for herself. She raised her glass to his. "To Steeplechase!" she said with a clink.

"To Steeplechase!" he replied.

"Now, I want a blow-by-blow. What happened?"

"She hasn't blown me yet, Vic, but I'm giving it two, maybe three dates before she will."

"Incorrigible, as ever. Stop stalling."

They sat on the sofa for the next hour, each cross-legged, facing the other, knees to knees, rocking back and forth like they'd done when they were children. Theo told her about his encounter with Maribeth, embellishing each detail, replaying his part, imitating her as though enacting a scene from a play.

He had told Maribeth that she reminded him of his first girlfriend. "That's actually true," he chuckled. "What I didn't say was that I was about ten at the time and that Stella was the biggest girl in the class. She had me beat by at least four inches and twenty pounds. The reason I liked her so much was that she always carried an impressive stash of M&Ms on her and could be relied on to share them with me if I pretended to be her friend. You'll note the uncanny resemblance.

"Speaking of getting her to share her stash with me, I took your call as soon as you left us at the wine festival. Our little pumpkin seemed curious that I'd be getting a call on Sunday afternoon. I told her this was my broker in Tokyo who handled my Asian stocks. I could see her eyebrows go up, along with her opinion of me, hopefully. She started to ask me about my interest in Asia, but I quickly changed the subject."

Theo went on to describe how it had only taken a couple more wine tastings before she started to let her guard drop. The two had discovered they had a lot in common: both recovering from emotional breakups with longtime partners, both favoring old movies, both recovering Catholics, both attended private schools and had strict parents. "She named it, and that was me, too!" Theo bragged. "I had to stop when she said she loved southern cooking and piña coladas. I wouldn't have been able to live with myself."

He had upped the compliments with each wine sampling; the thicker he laid it on, the more she ate it up. "But not as fast as she went for the food samples," he laughed. "Tell me, Vic, why can't you come up with a mark that's a knockout. Just for a change. Are all rich divorcées in Marin County either old, fat, or ugly—or all three? Surely there must be at least a few who would meet my minimum standards."

"Theo, *not* being a knockout is precisely the profile we're looking for. It's easier to sweep them off their feet if they're already wobbly. Not that you would have the least bit of trouble either way," she added hastily, remembering his recently shaky ego. "We want them to fall hard and fast, so we can swoop in before they know what's hit them. And the more precarious they are, the quicker they'll fall." She paused and frowned. "As long as *they're* the ones to fall," she said slowly.

"What?"

"You know, as long as it isn't us."

"Why? You think we'll get caught?"

"God, we'd better not." She took a deep gulp of her drink at the thought. "But I …" she started to chew the little finger on her left hand. A sure sign, he knew, that something was troubling her.

"Vic, this doesn't sound like you. What's up?"

She took another long swig and grasped his hand. "It's just that lately I've begun to feel like I'm … losing my cool."

"You, my dear, will be forever cool," he said, putting down his drink and taking her other hand. "You were born cool."

"No, hon, I achieved cool. And I did it the hard way. I don't want to blow everything we've worked for. I don't know what it is. Sometimes I feel I'm not as sharp as I used to be. My mind keeps wandering and I just can't let it. I've got to stay focused or we'll be screwed.

"Case in point … right now. Here I am babbling about my insecurities instead of concentrating on where we are with Steeplechase and what comes next. So, let's get back to you and Maribeth. Tell me what happened after you got our little cream puff sloshed."

Theo told her he had led Maribeth to a bench in the redwood grove and put his arm around her. That's when Victoria had found them. After Victoria left, he had kissed Maribeth behind her ear when her head was turned. She had swung around with a shocked expression, as though he had slapped her. He had apologized, claiming the wine, coupled with her irresistible neck, had gotten the best of him.

"Her irresistible neck! You really said that?"

"Hey, she bought it," Theo grinned. "But it was at that point I knew I would have to go slow, at least for the time being."

"Shit! You mean this one's going to take a long time to seduce?"

"No. Like I said when I got here tonight, if you'd been *listening* instead of thinking of your next question, I think I know how to play my little strudel." His eyes danced, waiting for her to ask.

She mimed pulling a rope, hand over hand, until he told her. It was obvious that Maribeth was scared of being pursued, so he would make *her* the pursuer. And how was he planning to pull that off? Easy. Play hard-to-get. He planned to develop another woman who would be taking up some of his time and attention. A woman he would clearly be sleeping with. But he would give Maribeth the impression that his affections lay with her, that it was only his libido seeking another outlet, so to speak. He figured it would then be only a matter of days before he had her where he wanted her.

As always, Victoria was impressed with his instincts about women. He had never been wrong, at least in knowing how to seduce them. Keeping them was another matter, but that was irrelevant in this case.

"Look, time might be an issue now." Victoria told him about seeing Fiona at Maribeth's house. "We won't have as much control over the timing as we planned, so you might have to speed things up."

"I'll do my very best," he assured her.

By then, they had polished off several drinks. They each stretched back on their arm of the sofa, legs intertwined. Theo immediately fell into an inebriated sleep. Victoria watched as he started to snore peacefully. What a long way he'd come in the last three years. She would never forget what he looked like when she visited him right after Isabella left. He had scared the shit out of her. For a moment, she hadn't even recognized him. His hair was a matted, muddy brown and he had a full beard, which was totally gray. He wore badly stained sweatpants that hung on him like a skirt. His eyes gleamed, she remembered, like he was on some crazy drug. And he had the weird, dank smell of despair.

Right away she had hugged him hard, like she had when they were kids and there was no one else to comfort him. She had bathed and shaved him and cut his hair. And she had fed him, mouthful by mouthful. Still, he hadn't uttered a word.

For two entire weeks, he said nothing. She kept talking to him. She kept talking *for* him, describing his feelings, the vacant cavern in the pit of his stomach, the enormous energy it took just to walk, the dullness that enveloped his body like a soundproof cocoon, as though they were her own feelings. She plunged with him into the darkest, solitary, most horrendous caverns and joined him in hell.

Eventually, he began repeating her words—starting slowly, as though in a trance. Gradually, he added a word of his own here and there. And then finally, he began to talk.

She had saved him, no doubt about it. Now she had to get them all through this scheme at least one more time. Then he would pretty much be set for life, at least financially. They both would. She would still worry about his sanity, but at least this would be one big piece out of the way. One piece not to worry about anymore. *Just get this done. Just one more time. You can do it.*

TWENTY ONE

THE NEXT MORNING, VICTORIA COULDN'T WAIT to call Maribeth to hear what she thought of Rufus. But she didn't. First, she went to the gym for her early-morning workout, then she drove by a new listing in Belvedere and even forced herself to sit through the entire Monday morning Barnaby Wells staff meeting before going to her desk to make the call. It wouldn't do to seem too eager. But when she finally got to her desk after eleven o'clock, she was excited to see a message from Maribeth. "Please call ASAP," it said.

Without even asking how Victoria was, Maribeth launched immediately into an ecstatic account of her afternoon with Rufus. She gushed about his looks, his perfect manners, how he tried to make a pass at her, how much they had in common and on and on. After the first thirty seconds, Victoria knew what she wanted to know. She spent the next twenty minutes reading her email, interspersing an occasional "uh-huh" or "great!" or "wow" into the conversation, which was really a monologue. When she sensed that

Maribeth was winding down, she turned from her computer and gave her full attention to the conversation.

"Tell you what," Victoria said. "I think this deserves a celebratory lunch—on me—at the Monte Cristo. Are you free?" The Monte Cristo was probably the most exclusive and expensive restaurant in Marin County. It sat at right on the bay, overlooking the city. And it had another important geographic advantage.

Victoria arrived at the restaurant parking lot a few minutes early. She parked at the edge of the lot, away from most of the other cars. A lovely oak grove lay in front of her. There seemed to be a narrow path that wound from there through the trees and up the mountain. Deer, she thought. She scanned her side mirrors and rearview mirror. The lot was quiet.

Quickly, she pulled the jar from her purse, sprinkled some of the contents onto her compact mirror, rolled up the hundred-dollar bill, leaned over the passenger seat and inhaled. Suddenly, there was loud knocking on her window. She jumped in her seat. The mirror dropped onto her lap, spilling a splotch of white powder onto her black slacks. With her head still turned toward the passenger seat, she quickly brought her hand to her nose and rubbed hard, hoping to brush away any remnants of her activity. Then she turned to the driver-side window. It was Maribeth.

"What on earth are you doing?" Maribeth yelled through the window.

Victoria looked down and noticed the spray of white on her pants. She rested her arm over the patch and pushed the window control down with the other hand.

"You startled me. I had something in my eye. I was trying to get it out." She was working her arm slowly over the powder splash as she talked. She put on her sunglasses, grabbed her purse and stepped out of the car, glancing down to make sure the spot was gone. Good enough, she thought. But as she stood up, the mirror fell on the asphalt and broke, the partially rolled bill beside it.

Victoria dove for the mirror and bill and swept them up. Small pieces of glass from the mirror fell to the pavement. She slipped both items into her bag and sighed as though dealing with a minor annoyance. "One of those days!" she said to Maribeth, shaking her head. Inwardly, she railed at herself. *Damn! Broken mirror. Seven years bad luck. How could I be so clumsy? My own stupid fault. Get a grip.*

Victoria's sunglasses allowed her to get a hard look at her companion without being obvious. Maribeth seemed a bit confused by what had just happened, but not overly concerned. Maintaining her composure, Victoria reached for Maribeth's arm and led her toward the restaurant.

As they walked, she gnawed again on the little finger of her left hand. *Another stupid mistake. Could have been fatal. Could have been a cop, for God's sake.* There was no way Maribeth would have known what the mirror and rolled-up bill were for. Thank God she had lucked out there. *But for how long? Maybe not for another seven years! Just an old wives' tale. Superstition. Forget it. Concentrate. Don't blow something else worrying about this screwup. You escaped. You're safe.*

Victoria tried to slow her breath down to a regular rhythm. "I can't wait to hear all about the devastatingly irresistible Mr. McCain."

"Well, I pretty much told you everything this morning."

"Ah, no. I want to hear about it in person and see that big smile of yours."

Through their entire lunch, Maribeth talked about her afternoon with Rufus. Victoria had already heard Theo's version, of course, but it was interesting to hear it from Maribeth's point of view. By both accounts, he was off to a superb start.

They'd had a few glasses of wine by the time they headed back to their cars. Victoria squinted at the office building to her left. "Oh, that's the Cascade," she said, as though noticing it for the first time.

"Yeah?"

"Funny, a client just mentioned it this morning. She goes to a psychic there."

"A psychic? In an office building?"

"Yeah, and it's not the first time I've heard about this psychic. Her name is Vera. I've heard about her several times over the last few years. Everyone raves about her."

"Isn't that a weird place for a psychic? I thought they worked out of Victorian mansions … or circuses."

"Apparently, this is not your grandmother's psychic. She has an MBA and is super chic. But most of all, what I've heard is that she's right on—can tell you things you didn't even know about your past and is incredibly accurate about the future."

"Not my cup of tea, I'm afraid. I just don't believe that kind of stuff."

Victoria was used to that reaction. She was prepared. "Well, I think I'm going to try her out. I'm going to go over and make an appointment."

With that, she gave Maribeth a hug, and walked toward the Cascade.

TWENTY TWO

FOR THE NEXT COUPLE OF DAYS, Victoria didn't contact Maribeth. She didn't want to seem to be pushing things. And what she had to convince Maribeth to do next was pivotal. Finally, three days after their lunch at the Monte Cristo, she got the call she was waiting for.

"Victoria, are you free for lunch or dinner this week? I have so much to tell you!"

Victoria knew about one of the topics. Theo and Maribeth had had a date last night and according to Theo, it had gone very well. Since Victoria was seeing a client in Tiburon at the end of the day, she and Maribeth decided they would meet up for dinner that night. Maribeth was waiting at her front door when Victoria came to pick her up.

She doesn't look half-bad, Victoria thought, appraising Maribeth. Her client was finally getting the hang of her new hairstyle; it no longer looked like a pageboy gone wrong. What's more, she had evidently done some clothes shopping on her own and bought an outfit that Victoria herself would have chosen for her: black jeans, a ruffled white linen blouse with an unbuttoned tan linen vest over it. On her way out the door, Maribeth had picked up a cherry-red Louis Vuitton bag that she had bought on one of her shopping sprees with Victoria. Victoria complimented her, telling her she looked fabulous. Maribeth beamed and confided that she had returned to Fuzio, where Kenji had helped her select some more pieces.

But it wasn't clothes Maribeth wanted to talk about. "I have to tell you; you were absolutely right about Sam Wheeler!"

Victoria searched her brain. *Sam Wheeler?*

"You know," Maribeth said, "the attorney Charlie and I were using."

Victoria noted with pleasure the use of the past tense. "You're not going to believe what Sam and Charlie were trying to pull on me."

Whatever it was, Victoria could believe it. She had seen it happen many times. The very first time was with her own mother.

When they were settled at their table, Maribeth began to explain. "Ever since you told me you thought it wasn't a good idea that Charlie and I have the same attorney, it nagged at me. But to tell you the truth, I kept dismissing it. Charlie's been very good about staying in touch with me and keeping me posted on how the settlement's going. Then, I happened to call a friend of mine from St. Louis. Her husband works for the same company as Charlie and they're now posted in Philadelphia. She told me that the company is going to be bought out. Charlie hasn't mentioned anything about it, even though I've been talking to him at least once a week.

"My friend said that subsidiary heads like her husband and Charlie are going to get big severance packages. But here's the thing. The new company wants the subsidiary managers to stay on for six months. So, Charlie and Ed, her husband, won't be getting their severance packages until early next spring. By that time, our divorce settlement will be finalized and I wouldn't have gotten any part of that severance package. Can you imagine?

"Well, once I heard about that," she continued, "I called Charlie and told him I would be getting my own attorney. Charlie was speechless. There was dead silence on the phone for almost thirty seconds. He asked me why, of course. I told him I just thought it would be better this way. He tried to tell me that Sam was working in both of our best interests, and that he was committed to doing the right thing, splitting everything fifty-fifty. But of course, I stuck to my guns.

"You were so right, Victoria. I owe you big time! By the way, can you recommend an attorney here?"

Hiding her elation, Victoria gave her the names of two divorce attorneys well-known for securing large settlements from cheating husbands.

Maribeth then launched into her next topic. "Oh, and guess what? I called some headhunters. I decided to restart my job hunting."

Victoria blinked in surprise. "Oh? I didn't know you wanted to work. You should be in great shape after the divorce settlement, right?"

"Yes, but I had already started thinking about looking for a job before Charlie left me," Maribeth reminded her. "Obviously, I've been too overwhelmed to think about it until now. But to tell you the truth, I'm starting to get bored again. Don't get me wrong, I really enjoy going to lunches and spas, but I'm not the type to spend all of my time doing that kind of thing. Besides, I don't have a house to work on anymore or a husband to take care of, so I need something meaningful to do. It's a good sign, right? It means I'm starting to get over Charlie and focus on me, right?"

"Absolutely," Victoria said, though she wasn't so sure.

"Besides, I've got to start thinking about finances," Maribeth said. "Sure, I'll make a good chunk when the house sells, plus there's Charlie's settlement, but that's probably not enough so that I don't have to work for the rest of my life. I'll have to buy a new place. And if I don't do anything, I'll run out of money at some point. So, getting a job seems to make sense.

"The thing is, I'm trying to figure out if I should try to get a job here in the Bay Area, or if I should go back to St. Louis—or maybe even Kansas City, where a lot of my family lives. I keep going over it again and again, the pros and cons. At this point, I think I'm leaning toward staying in the Bay Area."

"So, you contacted headhunters here?" Victoria asked.

"Yes, but the ones I've called are big firms. They have offices everywhere. I told them I was mostly interested in the Bay Area at this point, but that I might also consider Missouri. So, I figure I can cover all my bases."

"You should have told me. I have a couple of very good friends in the search business here. One's with Heidrick & Struggles and the other is with Russell Reynolds."

"I called Russell Reynolds, but not the other one. Maybe you can give me the name of the person you know there, and I'll call them."

Victoria made a mental note to tell Vera about this latest development. They definitely didn't want Maribeth hanging around after it was over.

"Oh, and guess who I went out with last night?" Maribeth had a glint in her eyes.

"Well, there have been so many lately; it could be one of several."

"No, there aren't several, just Rufus!" Maribeth practically sang his name. "He is soooo cute and so sweet." She recapped her date with Rufus detail by detail, how handsome he was, what he wore, compliments he gave her, comments he made that led her to believe he was quite rich, his taste in wine, and so on.

Victoria pretended to pay attention, chiming in with the required enthusiasm over every one of Rufus' incredible qualities. She had to hand it to her brother: He was a master, knowing just how to play women. This was confirmed by what Maribeth said next.

"The thing is, he probably won't ask me out again. I mean, he is such a catch, I'm sure he has tons of girlfriends. In fact, he got a call from one at dinner."

"He did?" Victoria asked with too much surprise, jolted out of her stupor.

"Yeah, I'm sure it was a woman. He blushed when he answered his cell and told whomever it was that he couldn't talk, saying he was in the middle of something. His voice was kind of soft … it must have been a girlfriend." Her smile shrunk to a pout.

Brilliant, Victoria thought. "Hey, don't be so sure," she consoled Maribeth. "It was probably his mother, or his sister."

"That was not a mother or sister tone of voice, believe me. Besides, I don't think he has any family. He's never mentioned any, anyway. I'll have to ask him about that."

Victoria returned to the main topic. "So let's get to the good part. Did he spend the night?"

Maribeth blushed. "Oh, gosh no. Just kissed a little, you know. Of course, I didn't invite him in. I hardly know him. I've only seen him twice. Besides, I'm still married. I don't have a clue about how to start dating and it's way too soon." She started twirling the thin gold chain at her neck. "Let's talk about something else. What's new with you?"

Finally, Victoria had the opening she had been waiting for all evening. "Well, I do have some really interesting news, but I'm going to need a drink first." Victoria chose Courvoisier and Maribeth ordered an Amaretto.

Victoria could feel her knees tighten as she prepared to launch into the next phase. She took a sip from the snifter and began. "I went to see Vera. Remember? The psychic I told you about? I know you don't believe in that sort of thing, but wait until I tell you what happened!"

Victoria replayed the fabricated visit, revelation by revelation, starting with Vera's first question, which was about how the real estate market was faring these days, even though Victoria had given her no information about her occupation. In fact, she told Maribeth, she purposely had given no background at all about herself. Even when Vera asked her what aspects of her life she wanted to explore or what questions she had about past or future events, Victoria had said that she wanted the session to be completely open— to let Vera talk about whatever she thought was important, whatever came up, giving her no clues about her background or current situation. Nothing.

Victoria told Maribeth how, after making the real estate comment, Vera had correctly pegged Victoria's age, number of siblings, town where she grew up and the fact that she was poor as a child.

Victoria went on to tell Maribeth about some of the more personal aspects of Victoria's past that Vera had described accurately. First, she'd described a scene where Victoria and an older British gentleman named Alistair were dining at a restaurant overlooking the Eiffel Tower. Vera saw the man place a small box on the table, saw Victoria opening it and then saw tears on the man's face.

Victoria leaned forward and lowered her voice. When she had been in her early twenties, she told Maribeth, she'd lived in London with a British man in his sixties. His name was Alistair Alsop. After they had been together for several months, Alistair took Victoria to Paris for a romantic weekend. During the last evening, he had proposed over dinner. Victoria had been shocked—and had turned him down on the spot. She had been too stunned to even feign regret or other niceties that would have softened her answer. Alistair, normally proper and composed in public, had cried, right there in the restaurant, in front of anyone who cared to watch.

Victoria's voice softened as she related the event. It was, in fact, a true story. And to this day, she wished she had handled the situation better. For her, it had been just a fling, which had started as a means of revenge. She'd been at Oxford University on a Rhodes scholarship. Her English Lit professor was Mrs. Alsop, Alistair's wife. There was almost instant dislike between the two women. And their relationship became increasingly antagonistic as the first semester progressed.

Mrs. Alsop came across as someone who thought of her profession as an unsavory chore, a burden she had been saddled with. Victoria found out that Mrs. Alsop had settled on a career in academia only after her attempts at jobs in publishing and editing didn't pan out. The professor treated her students as frivolous, stupid beings who should consider themselves lucky to have someone of her stature and expertise teaching them the basics of literacy. Her classes were almost entirely in lecture format, delivered in a dull monotone, allowing no time for questions or discussion. Students were there to absorb what she had to tell them. They were to take notes, commit facts to memory and recite them back verbatim on the exams.

Most of Victoria's classmates quickly learned to play along in this compliant role, but not Victoria. She had always lived by her brains and wasn't about to hide them. She challenged Mrs. Alsop frequently and publicly, often showing the professor's statements to be flat-out wrong. And she did it with obvious enjoyment, earning admiration from her classmates and smoldering fury from Mrs. Alsop.

Of course, much of the animosity between the two women was personal. If Victoria reminded Mrs. Alsop of everything she herself had been as a student—attractive, popular and with brilliant prospects for the future—Mrs. Alsop represented everything Victoria did not want to be in thirty years: stodgy, unexciting and in a job that repeated itself day after day, year after year. What clinched Victoria's disdain for the woman was her air of superiority: the way she answered questions in a style designed to make students feel stupid for asking, to the point where they asked no more, which was clearly Mrs. Alsop's objective. It would not have been so bad if the teacher's hubris had been warranted, if the woman had been brilliant in her area of expertise. But her arrogance clearly far exceeded her knowledge.

Even so, Victoria would not have set out to put her in her place, had it not been for the teacher's fatal mistake. Mrs. Alsop consistently gave Victoria marks in the 70th percentile, when her work was obviously exceptional. At first, Victoria couldn't believe that the woman was grading her unfairly based on petty bias. So, after her first few "70 percents," she decided to confirm her theory. She wrote papers for a classmate and close friend who typically scored in the mid-90th percentile, submitting them under the friend's name. The friend submitted her work under Victoria's name. The papers written by Victoria for her friend came back with marks in the mid- to high 90 percents, accompanied by comments of "outstanding," "great insight" and the like. The friend's papers came back to Victoria with scores in the 70th percentile.

Victoria was furious, an emotion she didn't often feel. But when she did, the object of her rage was made to pay, often in a way that far out-measured their crime. Which is what happened to Mrs. Alsop.

Victoria got the idea one day when she saw the professor with her husband at the university dining hall. Observing them at lunch, she sensed that there was no real connection between them. They barely spoke, and when they did, there was no direct eye contact. They both seemed bored, enduring the eating ritual together out of habit. She guessed, correctly, it turned out, that the marriage had long ago lost its passion.

With a little research, she found out that Alistair was a well-known attorney specializing in estate matters with one of the most prestigious law firms in the city. Victoria went to him for help in setting up a trust for her assets, which were as fictional as they were sizable. It only took a couple of meetings before his interest turned to her nonfinancial assets.

Soon they were sleeping together regularly. Victoria led him to believe that she was deeply in love. On the days they were apart, she called him at the office every couple of hours to tell him how much she missed him. She made sure to leave physical evidence of their trysts that Mrs. Alsop would notice: lipstick marks, hickeys and the like. Victoria wasn't sure, though, that the Alsops ever got very close to each other, so she had to take it a step further. She secured stationery from a local hotel and sent Mrs. Alsop a note.

Dear Mrs. Alsop,
After your departure from the Halstead on November 10th,
the cleaning attendant found the enclosed article in your
room. We took the liberty of laundering it before returning
it to you.

*Thank you for choosing the Halstead. We look forward to
seeing you again in the near future.*
Sincerely,
Marissa Clements
Hotel Manager

Victoria placed a pair of black-lace panties in the
envelope and mailed it to her professor, who promptly kicked
her husband out of the house. Alistair took up a cozy luxury
flat, which he and Victoria shared until shortly after the
dinner in Paris.

Naturally, Mrs. Alsop found out whom her husband was
seeing, and visibly seethed each time she saw Victoria.
Luckily, the semester was almost over, so the two didn't have
to interact much. Victoria got a "Pass" for the class, which
she was able to turn into a "95%" on appeal to the Dean of
the English Literature Department. Mrs. Alsop was put on
probation for her unfair grading practice and assigned to
teach introductory classes to an auditorium full of first-year
students.

While Victoria had absolutely no regrets about bringing
down her pompous and mean-spirited teacher, she had felt
remorseful for leaving a crushed man, a rare sentiment for
her. Alistair had fallen for her so completely that when she
pulled the rug out from under him, he went into a tailspin
for several months, taking a leave from his job, immersing
himself in the study of meditation, and coming down with
a host of physical ailments. She heard that he had returned
to his law practice eventually. She hadn't given the matter
much further thought until tonight, when recounting the
story—at least some of the story—to Maribeth. Of course, she
left out the part about Mrs. Alsop.

Maribeth had stopped drinking her second Amaretto
when Victoria got to the part about Alistair's proposal in

Paris. As Victoria recounted each detail that Vera had described accurately, her companion's stare grew wider and wider. *She's biting, thank God!* Victoria thought. But Victoria had more in store.

Before Maribeth could express her awe, Victoria went on to another account, calculated to have a double-barreled effect.

"As you know, I'm seeing someone," Victoria began.

"I had the feeling you were seeing several, at least!" Maribeth laughed.

"Well, yes, but there's someone I've been seeing more than the others, and ..." Victoria swished the liquid in her glass, working the coating in upward spirals until it almost reached the rim. "He's married."

Maribeth inched back almost imperceptibly. "Oh."

"Yes, I knew you would feel that way. I wasn't going to tell you, but I decided I had to tell you. You'll see why when I'm finished." Victoria went on to relate what Vera had said about him. "She said she saw the letters 'J' and 'O.' His name is Josh. She said he had something to do with my work. He's an associate at Barnaby Wells. She described exactly what he looked like and said she thought he was younger than I. He's ten years younger. She said he was married and that his wife suspected he was having an affair. Lately, Josh has told me that he has the feeling that his wife thinks something's up, especially when he comes home late. Vera said we wouldn't be together for much longer, but that it was best that way, because he wasn't right for me."

Victoria could see Maribeth struggling between disapproval and fascination. She decided to stop talking and wait. Long ago, she had learned the power of silence in a conversation. Most people were uncomfortable with it to the point where they would say whatever was foremost in their mind, just to fill the void.

"Gosh, it's amazing that she knew all that," Maribeth said cautiously. "Look, I don't mean to judge you. It's just, you know, I was brought up in a certain way. And I'm trying to get over being on the wrong end of an affair. Whatever you decide to do in your love life is none of my business."

Victoria considered ending the topic on that note. Maribeth was clearly impressed with what she had heard so far. Victoria would be taking a big chance by pushing it further. But Vera had been insistent that she bring up a final subject, guaranteeing that it would hit the mark—spectacularly.

"There's one more thing." Victoria could feel her heartbeat quicken. "When I was getting up to leave Vera's, she told me that I should send a friend of mine to consult with her, that she could see I knew someone who had recently gone through a traumatic split and that she had several messages for this person."

"And that's me, right?" Maribeth said with sarcasm.

Victoria felt a jolt at Maribeth's uncharacteristic response. "Well, she gave me a name ..."

"Mine, right?" Maribeth said, smirking.

"No, but somewhat similar."

"Oh well, so much for her psychic powers," Maribeth sniffed and reached for her bag.

Victoria bent down to get her own purse, so that she wouldn't be looking directly at Maribeth. "She said her name was Bethany Foster. Since there was the 'Beth' part in it, I thought I'd mention it." When she looked up, Maribeth's eyes were locked in shock—or terror. Victoria couldn't quite tell which.

"What's the matter?" Victoria asked.

"What was the name again?" Maribeth said slowly, color deepening in her cheeks.

"Bethany Foster. Does that mean something to you?" Victoria asked, thrilled that it obviously did.

There was a long silence. Maribeth was now scarlet. She propped her elbow on the table, letting her head sink into her hand. "That's me," she said quietly.

"Foster was your maiden name?" Victoria asked.

"No. It was my birth parents' name. I was adopted when I was six months old. They were drug addicts and couldn't take care of me. Their name was Foster. And they named me Bethany, after a beach resort on the East Coast where they met on spring break. When my new parents adopted me, they changed my name to Maribeth. They wanted to leave a little of my original name." She shook her head, as though trying to dislodge what she had just heard. "That's incredible. I can't believe she came up with that name. I haven't even thought about it for years."

As they walked together toward the car, Maribeth stared into the distance, seemingly lost in another world. She settled into the passenger seat and was silent for most of the ride home. Victoria's efforts to restart the conversation were met with half-hearted, short replies. Finally, as they pulled into her driveway, Victoria heard the words she had been hoping for.

"I guess I'm going to have to see her."

Victoria studied Maribeth as she got out of the car. Her passenger certainly looked shocked, but there was something else, too. She couldn't be sure, but she thought it was fear.

TWENTY THREE

VERA'S MESSAGE LIGHT WAS BLINKING. She picked up the receiver and smiled when she heard the voice.

"Hey, Vera, Jake Longworth here. I need your help with a project. Give me a call." Jake was CEO of EQuate, a financial modeling company. She punched in his number, gave her name and was connected right away.

"Vera, thanks for calling back. I need your help again with a deal I'm working on. I'm trying to buy a company called Bottom Line. It's a start-up that's developed technology to analyze business financials for M&A transactions, essentially streamlining the decision-making process. Here's the thing. Bottom Line's CEO and board are very interested in the deal. But the CFO—his name is Nick Slade—is resistant. He keeps coming up with roadblocks to stop the acquisition from happening. I'd like you to convince Slade that going ahead with the deal is the right thing to do. Like the help you gave me with Suzanne Hill and the CloudChord deal. Can you do it?"

"I will certainly do my best, Jake. Who is the intermediary?"

"Stan Harper. Stan had been Slade's boss at Intel; Nick was his golden boy. He promoted him three times in two years. Stan will take care of the hand-off."

The intermediary had to be someone whom Nick Slade trusted completely and who could be relied upon to point him in Vera's direction without seeming to do so. The hand-off role was particularly tricky in this case. Executives in general weren't naturally drawn to consulting psychics, but CFOs in particular rarely had patience for business discussions that weren't grounded in analytics. For them, the idea of going to a psychic to find out whether or not to proceed with an acquisition sounded like the first line of a joke. That was why Stan Harper's part was crucial.

"Stan is a great choice," Vera said. "I'm sure he'll get Nick to call me. Now, give me some details about the EQuate/Bottom Line deal structure."

Jake filled her in on the background, operations and management teams of both companies and outlined the key components of the acquisition agreement on which consensus with Bottom Line management was needed. Finally, he told her exactly how much he wanted to pay for Bottom Line—$110 million. Before hanging up, Vera confirmed her fee arrangement: $150,000 now and the remaining $150,000 upon completion of the project.

"I'll do the best I can. You can count on it," Vera said. Her red cell phone was blinking with a call from Victoria. "I've got to go now, but I'll let you know when I hear from Slade."

Vera could hear the excitement in Victoria's voice. "I have to hand it to you, Teta; you really outdid yourself this time."

"What happened?"

"The name 'Bethany Foster' hit a nerve in a big way. I must admit, I was anxious about bringing it up, but you were so sure. I should know by now to trust you completely. Did you try googling it yet?"

"Yes, I did, but I can't find anything. The name kept repeating itself over and over in my head when I looked at her picture, though. So, I knew it must mean something."

Victoria filled Vera in on Maribeth's explanation of the name. "It makes sense, I guess," Victoria said. "If someone had a name for only the first six months of their life and then was adopted and got an entirely new name, the original name wouldn't show up anywhere except on birth records. And we don't know where she was actually born, just where she was conceived. Anyway, you're incredible, as always. I'm sure she'll be calling you. In fact, judging from her reaction, I'd say you'll hear from her right away."

TWENTY FOUR

VICTORIA HUNG UP AND MADE HER WAY to the conference room where Fiona Chang, her nemesis from Peabody Realty, was waiting with an offer on the Simmons house. It was sooner than Victoria would have liked, but once she was forced to formally list the property, she was deluged with calls from other realtors wanting to see it. There was no way to stall any more. They would just have to speed things up on Steeplechase.

"Well, hello, Fiona," Victoria said testily, as though finding an especially distasteful hair in her soup.

"Victoria, good to see you," Fiona said, her smile too wide.

Victoria sat at her end of the table and arranged her files in front of her. She leafed through them quickly, appearing to prepare herself for the discussion ahead, even though she already knew each detail by heart. Fortified by a sniff from her jar, she could feel the adrenaline coursing through her. She forced herself to wait for her opponent to speak first.

At the other end of the table, Fiona had already buttressed herself with her own stacks of files. She was sitting upright in her chair, almost vibrating with anticipation. "Shall we get started?" Fiona's saccharine voice marked the battle's opening salvo.

Victoria nodded coolly.

Fiona began. "My clients are Mr. and Mrs. Lazenby, the couple I was with when we bumped into you at the Simmons house. Mr. Lazenby is an international banking executive who has been working with his current employer for over ten years. His annual income is about a million. Mrs. Lazenby is a stay-at-home mom, who looks after their three children. The Lazenbys are making an offer of $5.3 million, the asking price, with no contingencies. They have transferred here from London and are currently staying in temporary housing, so they're anxious to move. They're looking for a quick settlement, with closing in thirty days. Given their assets and income level, financing should be no problem." Fiona settled back into her chair with a satisfied smirk.

Victoria forced a blank expression on her face. *Fantastic ... a superb offer*, she gloated to herself. Her voice was perfectly neutral when she responded. "That sounds pretty good," she said, jotting down a few notes in her Day-Timer. "I'll take it to my client and get back to you." She stood up, taking the offer file Fiona had given her, and walked toward the door. "Oh, I should tell you that there is likely to be another offer coming in tonight," she said casually.

Fiona's lip formed the slightest sneer. "Of course," she said, as though she had expected something more creative. "I'm sure you will let me know if it comes through. In any case, our offer is good for twenty-four hours. The Lazenbys have seen another property that also interests them. If this one doesn't work out, they may make an offer on the other one."

"Of course," Victoria countered with a glazed smile.

Victoria went to her desk and called Maribeth. Naturally, Maribeth was thrilled with the offer. Victoria suggested, however, that they could do even better if she went back asking for a higher price.

"A higher price? But they're giving us exactly what we asked for. And a very short closing, so I can get out of there fast."

Victoria explained that in the current market, properties frequently went for over the asking price.

"But how can we go back and ask for more if they've agreed to pay the listed price?"

"Leave that to me, honey," Victoria said. "So, are you okay with turning down their offer?"

"But what if we don't get another offer? Isn't this a big gamble? I mean, it could be a long time before someone else bids on it. In the meantime, I have this mortgage, and we may not get an offer this good the next time around."

"Maribeth, you have to trust me. I am very good at this. Believe me; I can get you more if you let me."

"No, Victoria. I'm sorry, but I really want to sell this. I want to accept the offer."

Victoria frowned at the phone. "Okay, if you're sure," Victoria said, masking her disappointment.

"Yes. I'm positive."

"So, I have your approval to accept the offer?"

"Yes."

"Great. It sounds like we have a deal, then. I'll call the Lazenbys' realtor, get the formal paperwork going and get back to you."

Victoria weighed her next move. It was very risky, but worth it. There was no way in hell she was going to let fucking Fiona win this. She went to the gym for a couple of hours to kill time. At around 6:30 p.m., Victoria dialed Fiona's home number. She caught her in the middle of dinner, she could tell. And Fiona was having wine with dinner, she could tell.

She told Fiona that she had spoken with another realtor who said they would be presenting an offer on the Simmons house in the next couple of hours. This wasn't the second potential offer that she had mentioned to Fiona earlier in the evening; it was a brand new one. She didn't know the details of what would be presented, but she did know that these other prospective buyers were very interested. They had just seen the house earlier in the day and had flown back to their current home in Hawaii. When they got there, they had called their realtor immediately, saying they wanted to sign an offer tonight.

"Did you present the Lazenbys' offer to Ms. Simmons?"

"No. I have a call in to her. I haven't been able to reach her yet. The Lazenbys' offer is a very solid one."

"No kidding," Fiona said with an audible smirk. "So, what do you want?"

Victoria noted the use of "you" rather than "your client." "I don't want anything, Fiona. I'm just advising you that there will very likely be another offer presented in the next couple of hours. Of course, I don't know how much these other clients may offer for the property. Perhaps we priced it a bit too low ..." She let her sentence trail off.

"Okay, I get it," Fiona repeated, not hiding her disdain. "If you ask me, there's something fishy about this house. When Suki told me about it, she said it had been listed weeks ago, but there was no listing anywhere—until the day after I brought the Lazenbys by to see it. When I showed up with the Lazenbys, there was a lock box, which luckily was open since you were inside. Why was there a lock box and no listing?"

"Just a timing thing," Victoria explained. "The listing

was still in process when you came by."

"Right," Fiona said dryly. "I'll get back to you on the Lazenbys' offer." She hung up.

Victoria grinned at the phone.

Early the next morning, Victoria called Maribeth. "I've got great news for you!" she announced. "We got a revised offer from the Lazenbys—$5.5 million."

"What? I accepted their offer of $5.3!"

"Yes, and I put in a call to Fiona right away last night to let her know, but I couldn't reach her. In the meantime, apparently Fiona heard from another realtor at her agency that they were working with clients who were also interested in your house. And they were apparently thinking of offering more than the asking price. So Fiona called the Lazenbys and they upped their offer right away. They didn't want to take the chance of losing the house."

"Well, what about this other offer that was going to be over the asking price? Should we wait for it to come in?"

"That's up to you, Maribeth. We certainly could. But I thought you were interested in a sure thing. We do have to get back to the Lazenbys on their revised offer by late this evening."

"No. Of course! Let's accept the 5.5. It's way more than I had hoped for! That is so incredible that they raised it!"

"Yup! It was meant to be! Okay, now get your pen out and come on over. You've got papers to sign!"

TWENTY FIVE

VERA STARED OUT AT THE DEEP GREEN PEAK of Mount Tamalpais, waiting for the wave of serenity that inevitably followed. She transported herself into the midst of the woods, breathing in the minty eucalyptus, feeling the damp ground under her feet, comforted by the veil of green that enshrouded her. A cool, quiet cocoon. She wished she were there, instead of here in her office, preparing to do something she didn't want to do. One last time, she told herself. This was it. Victoria had promised.

But first she had to actually get through this one. No, not just get through it; she had to absolutely nail it. For Mara, she told herself. Just think about Mara. If she told herself it was for her sister, she could do it this one last time.

Reluctantly, she swung her chair away from the window and faced the iPad in front of her, trying to ignore the knot that had formed in her stomach. For the next hour, she studied diligently. Closing her eyes from time to time, she repeated facts to herself, committing them to memory. The buzzer on her phone jarred her into the present.

"Maribeth Simmons is here," Cynthia said.

Vera removed her reading glasses and smoothed the front of her beige linen skirt, admiring for a moment how perfectly the marbled grain of her pumps matched the shade of her skirt. She stood to greet Maribeth.

Vera had seen pictures of Maribeth, but most had been taken around the time when Victoria had first met her. Vera could see that in the last few weeks, her niece had made significant headway in influencing Maribeth's outward appearance. At first glimpse, she seemed hip and stylish, with rakish hair and a well-cut, flirty leather jacket. But once Maribeth started talking, her cover was blown.

Maribeth thrust her hand out to Vera and introduced herself, her face flushed, gaze darting from side to side. Gripping her hands together at her waist, she stared at the floor and asked, "Where should I sit?"

Vera touched her client's shoulder lightly, trying to put her at ease, and steered her to the sitting area. She could feel Maribeth's muscles harden under her hand. The two sat across from each other, Vera leaning forward, all senses tuned to the woman who faced her—or more accurately, who wouldn't face her. Maribeth sat like a child who was being punished, hands clenched on her lap, eyes cast downward. Vera offered her coffee or water. Maribeth politely refused.

"You seem nervous." Vera couldn't help stating the obvious.

"I am. I don't even know if I should be here. In fact, I'm pretty sure I shouldn't be."

"Why do you say that?"

"I don't believe in this kind of thing. I mean, nothing personal. I don't want to offend you. It's just that I'm Catholic; my religion doesn't condone psychics. It's kind of a sin to go to one. No, not kind of. It is."

"Yet you came anyway." Vera knew how to draw people out—to get them to tell her things they didn't want to tell her.

"Yes, I came because you knew my name when I was born—something almost no one else knows. I couldn't explain to myself how you knew it. And I thought that if you knew *that,* then maybe you knew other things. I could do with some help right now. I'm going through a lot." Maribeth spoke haltingly, her eyes continuing to scan the floor, as though the words were written there. "By the way, what else do you know about me?"

Vera's eyes drifted past her client's head, looking back at her history. What she saw were a series of walls, offset from each other, with only a narrow space in between, like a corridor winding through a labyrinth. Normally, she could discern people's past through their eyes, but Maribeth wasn't allowing eye contact, so Vera was left to fly blind.

Here and there from behind the walls, certain scenes or figures emerged briefly, only to dart back into obscurity. Vera told her what she was able to see: a brown house with a welcoming, wrap-around porch; a family of five sitting at a dining table; Washington D.C.; what looked like a college class with Maribeth as one of the students; Maribeth kissing a young, dark-haired man with a beard, who appeared to be a classmate; Maribeth shooting a gun. Then the walls slid firmly shut, blocking off any further images.

Maribeth's head dropped even farther down toward her chest. She rubbed one thumb against the other rhythmically. "Wow. That's pretty good. My house in Kansas City, my family growing up, my college in D.C., and my first real boyfriend, who took me target shooting. What else?"

Vera tried to return to the walled city, but the narrow passageway had disappeared. "That's all I can see right now."

Maribeth nodded, as though in agreement. "What I

really want to know is about the future. What's going to happen to me next?"

Vera reached for the tarot cards, but noted that Maribeth's eyes followed her, her eyebrows arching. "I'll tell you what, let's not use the cards. I don't need them anyway." Her client's clenched hands relaxed slightly.

Vera closed her eyes and inhaled deeply. She moved her eyes back and forth under her lids, as if viewing her own private movie. After almost a minute, she spoke. "You are alone now. Your husband is gone, and you are by yourself in a very large house. I have an image of you that is suspended in mid-air—as though you are not really participating in life, but have withdrawn and are watching it from a distance. You are unsure of where you want to land. You are unsure of where you fit in. You clearly shouldn't be in that house anymore. It belonged to you when you were someone else."

Vera went on to relate what she saw of the early years of Maribeth's marriage, then of the events leading up to its recent conclusion. She included as many details as she could from Victoria's notes. When she was finished, she shifted slightly in her chair. "I see that you are planning to move out, but you don't know what to do next."

"Yes, that's why I'm here." Maribeth's fingers pulsed on her clenched hands.

"You have met a man recently, a man who will play a significant role in your life. He is blond, tall. I see the two of you drinking wine in an outdoor setting—other people are milling around. You will have a romantic relationship with him, and it will be good for you. It has been quite a while since you have been connected intimately with a man."

Vera tried once again to see into Maribeth's prior relationships, but again ran up against a wall. It was as though a thick screen had been erected, hiding the woman's past. Vera rarely encountered a block like this, and when she did, it was usually limited to one or two incidents, or a year or two of a client's past. But with Maribeth, it was the opposite. Only a few pieces of her past allowed themselves to be seen.

While she rarely ran into psychic blocks in her own practice, Vera knew that the phenomenon was not unusual in her line of work. Generally, it happened when clients had particularly painful histories and had done everything in their power to bury the past, so that even the best in her profession couldn't penetrate it. At other times, clients who didn't believe in psychics or who feared that they might be told something frightening about their future sealed themselves off from being "read." Perhaps one or more of these reasons came into play in Maribeth's case, Vera guessed.

The future, though, was easy to see in this case. "This man will pursue you quite rigorously and the two of you will become close." Vera cocked her head to one side, as though hearing an unexpected noise. "And there's a financial aspect to this relationship, as well."

Maribeth sat forward.

"It seems that your divorce will leave you fairly well provided for, but some proceeds that you are expecting from it may not materialize."

"What do you mean?"

"It looks like you are counting on getting certain sums from your husband in the next several months. It appears that some of what you are expecting may not pan out. This gentleman that you have met appears to be quite an astute investor. He may even make his living that way. In any case, through him you will learn about an investment opportunity that looks very lucrative." Vera's eyebrows lifted. "Yes, very lucrative."

"So, he is going to advise me on my finances?"

Vera shook her head, her eyes still closed, "Not exactly. What I see is that through him, you will come to know about an income-generating opportunity. It will require some research on your part, evidently."

"So, I won't hear about it from him?"

"Well, it's not totally clear. What I see is that you will hear about something through him, but you will then pursue it yourself."

"What's the name of the investment?"

The lines between Vera's eyebrows deepened and she was silent for several seconds. "I can't see the name."

Maribeth slumped back in her chair.

"But it has something to do with horses, I think."

"Horses! I don't know anything about horses. And I'll make a lot of money on it?" Maribeth leaned forward again.

"It looks like a superb investment."

"What about romantically? Will he and I end up together?"

Vera closed her eyes and took a couple of deep breaths. "Hmmm ... I cannot see an end point to your relationship right now. That doesn't mean there isn't one—just that if there is one, it isn't in the near future. You haven't known him for very long. Maybe when you have a little more history with him, your future together will become clearer. In the meantime, remember that everything that is sent our way is on purpose, to teach us something we need to learn. Think about how you feel when you are with him and what it is you can take for yourself from the experience. No matter how long it lasts, it's clear that this will be an important, positive event in your life."

Abruptly, Maribeth reached for her purse. "Okay, thanks. You have been very helpful." She locked her gaze on Vera's hand and shook it brusquely, then walked out the door.

Vera was surprised to have the session end so abruptly. Usually, clients used every minute of the allotted time and pumped her with questions until the very end. However, in this case, she was glad to have Maribeth go—to have the session over with. An almost audible dissonance hung in the air, like a badly played chord that wouldn't fade into silence. First, her inability to read the woman's past was highly unusual and quite perplexing. And secondly, Maribeth's behavior during the session was odd. Vera was used to clients who were afraid to discuss intimate details of their life or who were nervous that they would hear of some awful news about what awaited them in the future. But in all her years of practice, she had never encountered anyone like Maribeth. The woman had professed to not believe in psychics and said her religion forbade using them, but Vera was convinced there was more to the strange demeanor and to her own inability to connect with Maribeth than that. She just couldn't figure out what, exactly, was going on. All in all, though, it had gone reasonably well, she told herself. She was pretty sure that she had scored points with her knowledge of Maribeth's past. And she felt confident that Maribeth would be back.

The message light was flashing on her phone. "Vera Peterlin, this is Nick Slade. I'm the CFO at Bottom Line. I have an appointment to see you next week. Stan Harper gave me your name. Listen, I don't want to meet at your place— or at my office, either. Call my cell." He left his number.

Vera remembered her conversation with Jake Long- worth. Stan Harper had obviously been successful in getting Nick Slade, CFO of Bottom Line—the company Jake wanted to buy—to her doorstep. From the tone of the message, though, it sounded like the last thing Mr. Slade wanted to do was to actually cross her doorstep. The confident staccato of his voice, along with the command at the end, suggested someone who was accustomed to giving orders and being in charge. Vera was used to dealing with no-nonsense exec- utives, but it was the underlying tone that gave her pause.

She let the voice float in her mind, dissecting it into the components that made up its basic essence: arrogance, derision, anger and ... most disturbingly ... a tinge of what she could only label as evil.

She called him back.

"Nick Slade."

There was that brusque tone. She identified herself.

"Look," he said. "I don't want to meet at your ..." She could tell he was searching for the right word.

"Office?" she offered.

"Yeah, whatever. That's all I need for my reputation is to be seen going into a fortune tellers'. How about grabbing a cup of coffee or something?"

Vera assured him that would not be necessary. She told him that her office was set up to accommodate people who didn't wish to be observed availing themselves of her services. She explained that her official address in the Cascade Building was suite 112. That was the office number listed by her name in the foyer index. However, he should go to suite 214 on the second floor, where he would see a nameplate that said "Dental Imaging." If he pressed the bell, her assistant, Cynthia, would buzz him in. She advised him that suite 214 was actually one of her private waiting rooms. An internal staircase led directly from that waiting room to a door to her personal office. "We use 214 for clients like you who prefer to keep their visits confidential."

"All right. That'll do. Got to go." He hung up.

She took a deep breath. This man was going to be trouble. Cynthia buzzed her, interrupting her thoughts.

"Carolina Crespi is on the line for you. She said she just needed a couple of minutes. Shall I tell her you're busy?'

"No, that's okay, I'll take it." Vera punched the blinking light. "Carolina, how are you?" she asked pleasantly.

"I am absolutely terrific, thanks to you! Oh my God, I

can't believe how well it went with Jason, the guy I sent to see you. You're a miracle worker! He's off my team for good. And don't worry; I gave him a great severance package. So good, in fact, that he's taking a few months off to travel before looking for another job."

"I'm glad I was able to help, Carolina."

"Thanks so much, Vera. I feel like this huge obstacle is out of my way and now I can really move forward and make my mark here. The future's looking great, thanks to you!"

Vera settled the phone into its cradle. A dull pain drifted through her head, then disappeared. No. The future would not be bright for Carolina, she feared. At least not in the short run.

TWENTY SIX

THE ELEVATOR DOORS PARTED and Maribeth stepped in. Vic had outdone herself with her powers of transformation this time, Theo thought. Every time he saw Maribeth, she looked better and better. The neckline of her black silk blouse was frankly seductive. She wore close-fitting, black-satin jeans that showed the progress, albeit minor, that had been made with her personal trainer over the last few weeks. Not bad.

They had been on several dates since they met three weeks ago at the wine festival: movies, dinners and a concert. As it turned out, Maribeth was more attractive, in a wholesome sort of way, than most of the other women Victoria had selected for their projects. He wasn't getting very far sexually, though. Until now, with the women Victoria had assigned him, three dates were the most it had taken to get them into bed. He was at almost twice that with Maribeth and the furthest he had gotten was passionate smooching. She kept referring to her religion, the fact that she was still technically married, that it was very soon after her breakup, that she wasn't used to dating yet, and so on. Tonight, though, she wouldn't be able to resist. He was sure of it.

He reached for the bottle of Dom Perignon cooling in the bucket and poured them each a glass, then offered her a prosciutto-encrusted fig. They sat on the deck overlooking the city, watching the sunset framed by the Golden Gate Bridge.

Maribeth followed him to the kitchen and watched while he broiled the filets and prepared tarragon vinaigrette dressing for the fresh haricots verts salad. When dinner was ready, he took her over to the dining table that was lit by a pair of candles in the palest platinum. A single white orchid with a deep amethyst center floated in an oval Baccarat bowl between them. The meal was long and leisurely, accompanied by several glasses of wine.

For the first time, Maribeth plied him with questions about his past and his family. Victoria had warned him that this was coming, so of course he was prepared. His parents, now deceased, were working-class people, he told Maribeth. He was an only child who had lived in London until his early twenties, when he decided America was the place to make his career. He'd spent some time in New York with a boutique investment firm, then moved to San Francisco, where he branched out, forming his own business.

How had he been drawn to the world of international finance, Maribeth asked—given his middle-class background and the fact that he hadn't left the U.K. until after college?

His uncle, he explained, had been a director of capital markets for a multinational bank. His uncle loved talking about his work and told Rufus all about his travels and the types of deals he was working on. On a few occasions, he even took Rufus to his office and showed him the trading-room floor. He remembered sitting in the leather swivel chair with three computers in front of him and watching the rolling ticker tapes and automatic portfolio updates flashing on the screens. The excitement and possibility of making millions in a heartbeat were infectious. Rufus was hooked.

After clearing the main course, he drained the last of the cabernet into her glass and went into the kitchen. "Damn, I can't believe this!"

"What's the matter?" Maribeth looked over at him.

Theo opened and slammed cabinet doors, one after another. "Bloody hell! I ran out of the Dom Perignon. I could have sworn I had another bottle." He finally stopped searching and threw up his hands. "I'm very sorry, but can you please excuse me—just for a few minutes? I'll dash to the restaurant next door; they're always stocked up."

"Oh, don't bother; we can just drink something else."

"Absolutely not. The dessert I have in store can only be accompanied by Dom. Not to worry, I'll be back in less than ten minutes." He rang for the elevator and was on his way.

Exactly nine minutes later, when he burst back into the apartment with the champagne, Maribeth was standing by the bookcase staring at the phone.

"Did you miss me?" He grinned and kissed her.

"Of course!" She was glancing back at the phone, looking puzzled. "Someone called and left you a message."

"Oh? Who? Did you catch a name?" He began uncorking the champagne.

"Jonathan, I think—British accent."

Theo's grin faded, and he went to the answering machine, pushed a button and listened.

"Rufus? Jonathan here. Look, Steeplechase is really starting to take off. It was up seven percent when the market opened this morning. I thought you might want to increase your position. I know you said five million was as high as you wanted to go, but I have information that says they'll be acquired by the end of the month. As you know, I don't normally do this, but I think you should go for at least another two million. Give me a ring when you get in."

"Goddammit!" He jabbed the "erase" button.

"Can't you just call him back?"

"Yes, of course. That's not the problem. I'm sorry you had to hear it."

"Why?"

"Because I like to keep my business dealings private. I'm sorry you heard what you heard." He went into the kitchen, popped open the champagne and filled two flutes. "Let's forget it and focus on the far more pleasant things in store for tonight," he said. He brought the champagne over to Maribeth and kissed her slowly on the lips. "Ready for dessert?" he teased.

"Sure." She smiled.

"Madam, for this next course, I am going to ask that we move to the living room. Allow me to escort you," he bowed and settled her on the sofa. Then he returned to the kitchen and assembled the ingredients for his pièce de résistance. He heard her voice from across the room.

"So, you've never told me exactly what kind of work you do," she said.

The corners of his mouth tipped upward imperceptibly. "I told you, I'm an investor."

"Yes, but do you invest for other people or just for yourself?"

"Mainly for myself."

"How do you decide what to invest in?"

"Research, contacts in various industries, networking with others in my line of business."

"Do you concentrate on any special industries?"

He allowed annoyance to enter his voice. "Look, I told you, I don't like mixing business and pleasure." He picked up a tray with a large bowl of fresh strawberries and two smaller bowls filled with brown sugar and sour cream. "Now close your eyes and don't open them until I tell you to."

Maribeth lay back into the cozy, mahogany-colored leather cushions, smiling broadly. Theo set the tray down and chose a plump berry from the top of the pile. "No peeking now!" He covered the fruit in the thick cream and dipped it into the brown sugar. "Okay, you can open your mouth, but not your eyes."

She parted her lips slightly, as if expecting a spoon to be offered.

"Wider! You won't regret it!" He eased the fruit gently through her lips. "Take a big bite and tell me what you think."

Maribeth chewed, her eyes still closed. "Wow!"

"Pure decadence, right?" Theo fed her the remaining bite.

"What is it, anyway? I know it's a strawberry, but what's that incredible sauce?"

"Very simple, actually—brown sugar and sour cream, believe it or not!"

"Wow! Can I open my eyes now?"

He was already preparing her a second. He held it over her mouth, stroking her tongue until she took another big bite.

"Okay, now it's my turn." Maribeth picked a strawberry and coated it. She darted the fruit in and out of his mouth until the sweet frosting was gone. "I think I'm getting the hang of this," she said.

They continued feeding each other until the bowls were almost empty.

"Hey, you've got some sugar on your chin," Theo pointed out.

Maribeth reached for a napkin, but Theo leaned forward, stopping her. "I've got a better idea." He licked her chin, and then worked his way up to her mouth, licking her tongue.

He kissed her, reaching for the buttons of her blouse.

She pulled back, "I don't know; I don't think I'm ready."

"I think you are," he said. He slid his fingers over her top button and released it, then worked his way down to the next two, his tongue playing with hers. "Now that's what I call dessert," he said huskily. "Much better than strawberries," he whispered.

Maribeth groaned with pleasure. He started to unzip her jeans, but she pushed him away. "I'm really not ready."

"Oh, come on. Mother Superior isn't looking."

"No, it's not that. It's just too soon."

"Okay, okay, I guess I'll have to content myself with the appetizer for now," he said.

Maribeth pulled her blouse closed, resting her head on his chest and drawing her legs under her.

They listened to the music, barely talking, until Maribeth drifted into sleep. Theo woke her gently and walked her into the bedroom, covering her with his comforter. He glanced at the empty side of the bed, shrugged and got in.

◆◆◆

The next morning, a sliver of light wedged its way between the thick maroon drapes and flickered onto Theo's eyelids, eventually coaxing them open. Careful not to disturb his partner, he turned and peered at the bedside clock. It was already nine-fifteen. He lifted himself slowly from the bed and tiptoed out of the room. A few minutes later, the smell of fresh coffee drifted through the apartment. With the phone in one hand and the stereo remote in the other, he soundlessly made his way back to the bedroom. Maribeth was still asleep. He tapped the stereo remote and Edith Piaf's voice softly filled the quiet. He raised the volume just a notch at a time, until he saw Maribeth stir.

Moving back several steps from the door, he lowered the

volume back down and began to talk into the phone, making sure his voice carried into the bedroom. "How did you hear about the acquisition?" He paused. "What do they think the offering price will be?" He waited a beat, then whistled. "Really? That's astounding. You're right, it's a no-brainer. Double my position. I'll transfer the funds today. Thanks for the heads-up. I owe you a dinner next time I'm in London." He put the phone down and turned to see Maribeth standing at the end of the hallway, wrapped in his cashmere blanket.

"You're up!" He went over and drew her to him, kissing the top of her head. "Sleep well?"

"Yes, great, but I really shouldn't have stayed. I should have gone home. I guess I fell asleep ..." She blushed.

"Oh, so you have regrets?" he said, pushing the blanket off her shoulder and placing his lips there instead.

"No. Well, I mean yes. ... I'm not divorced yet ... and I've only known you for a few weeks." She pulled the blanket back to cover herself.

"Maribeth, nothing happened," he reminded her.

"Nothing? Maybe not for you. But for me it wasn't nothing."

"I meant—"

"I know what you meant. But look, I'm still married. And I'm a lot more conservative than you. You're probably used to a faster crowd."

"But you had fun, right?"

"Oh, yes, I certainly did." She grinned.

"How about some more fun?" He tried to gently pry the blanket loose from her grip.

"No. I think it's time for a shower. And then I'd love some of that coffee I smell," she said, shuffling off to the bathroom.

They sat on his deck again, looking out over the bay. It was one of those twenty-twenty crisp days when the horizon seemed to be hundreds of miles away. The Golden Gate

Bridge hemmed the view to the west, with the Marin Headlands as a stunning, rugged backdrop. Over to the east, a tourist boat was docking at Alcatraz.

Theo sipped his cappuccino and concentrated on looking as relaxed as possible. He slid down further into his lounge chair and rested his head on the pillow. His free hand lay open, palm up. He closed his eyes and slowed his breath.

Even before his professional acting career, he'd had years of practice faking emotions. He had learned from the best— watching his sister as she distracted him gaily with games while their parents argued, studying her as she took insults unflinchingly and seeing with his own eyes how she stopped hers from tearing when things were at their worst.

"So, tell me about Steeplechase." Maribeth's voice jerked him back to the present.

He stared at her and struggled to hold on to his cup. He spoke slowly, without inflection. "I told you, I don't discuss business."

"Look, Rufus, I'm about to be a divorcee. Right now, I have no job; I don't know what the future holds. It looks like you make a very good living on your investments. Can't you just tell me a little about them? I might be interested in putting my money in them, too."

Theo stood up and looked down at her in the lounge chair. "I could not be more serious, Maribeth. I absolutely will not discuss my business with you. If you insist on bringing it up, quite honestly, this relationship will be over, because that's an area that is simply off limits." He turned briskly to go inside. "I'm taking a shower," he said flatly. He went down the hall, through his bedroom to the bathroom, closed the door, turned on the shower and switched on the TV that was embedded in the wall-wide mirror over the vanity.

He watched her on the closed-circuit video. She remained on the deck, swirling the coffee in her cup. After a couple of minutes, she looked over her shoulder and went back inside.

Theo could see Maribeth wrap her sweater more closely around her as she made her way to his desk. "Can I have some more coffee?" she called out in the direction of the bedroom.

When there was no reply, she shot another look at the hallway. Seeing that the coast was clear, she started leafing through the few pages in his inbox. He couldn't see her face, but he could see that she was studying each page carefully. When she was finished, she returned them to their original position and walked back over to the sliding doors that led to the deck.

A few moments later, fresh from a very quick shower, he slipped behind her, his hair still damp. "How about another offering from Chef McCain?" he asked.

She jumped, but recovered. "That would be terrific!" she said.

They lingered over a hearty brunch: fresh fruit salad, omelets bubbling with cheese, baguettes, perfect chocolate truffles for dessert and expertly made mimosas as the accompaniment. Theo asked Maribeth about her childhood and her family, then eased into the sensitive topic of her marriage.

When she had told him the whole story, she leaned forward. "Okay, now it's your turn. I want to hear more about little Rufus growing up."

Theo looked embarrassed and slid a look at his watch. "I have a business meeting in an hour. Sorry, but I have to get going."

Maribeth jumped up. "Oh, I've overstayed my welcome. I should have gone home a long time ago."

He grabbed her and hugged her to him. "You have absolutely not overstayed. How soon can you come back?"

"I don't know. I'll have to see. I'm just not sure about all this. It's moving kind of fast for me."

"Okay. You have twenty-four hours to think about how soon I can see you next." He gave her a long kiss.

After she left, he poured himself another mimosa and walked over to his inbox, smiling to himself as he leafed through the pages. The solitary sparrow perched on the balcony was startled into flight by Theo's whoop of victory when he noted that the business card next to the copier was gone.

He called Victoria.

"So, did you sleep with her?" she asked.

"My dear better half, have you totally lost all of your finesse? You're supposed to ask me how the evening went: how she looked, what she wore, what I wore, what I prepared for dinner, what champagne I chose, whether she heard Jonathan's message, how I seduced her and so on—allowing me to elaborate at length on each salacious detail, drawing it out, keeping you on the edge of your seat, describing each titillating little move until you couldn't take it anymore and began to scream for mercy—for the final climax, so to speak. But no, you crassly ask whether I slept with her. How very American of you."

"Just tell me if you slept with her, then you can fill me in on the excruciating details," Victoria begged.

Theo responded in a maddening lilt. "I guarantee you; the answer will not be enough for you."

"Just tell me, goddammit!" she squealed into the phone.

"Okay. Yes, we slept together."

"I knew it! My irresistible hunk, you've done it again!" she cheered.

"Not exactly. We *slept* together."

"Right—exactly as planned and only slightly behind schedule."

"No, we *slept*."

Victoria's voice dropped. "Oh."

"Well, there was the usual prelude. I got through the first wicket." Theo went on to describe the entire visit, ending with an apology to Victoria.

Victoria reassured him that it was only a matter of time. The important thing was, Maribeth had seen the pages on the printer and taken the business card. Things were proceeding nicely.

"Maybe if I had handled it differently ..." Theo began.

Victoria broke in, telling him to stop second-guessing himself. He should be very pleased that things had progressed so well. Once the words were out of her mouth, though, she wondered. Maybe for him, it wasn't just about getting to the endgame. Maybe for him the sexual conquest was just as important as pulling off the whole con. She made herself focus on the bigger picture. Though she hadn't let Theo know, she was actually worried. Very worried. Time was short. The damned house already had an accepted offer. They only had about three more weeks until closing. She knew she couldn't pressure him, but he *had* to come through and he had to do it fast. Otherwise ...

TWENTY SEVEN

THERE WAS A KNOCK AT THE DOOR. Cynthia brought in Nick Slade, CFO of Bottom Line. Vera crumpled the unlit cigarette in her palm and tossed it into the wastebasket under her desk before standing up to greet him. "Mr. Slade, nice to meet you."

Slade stepped into the office and Cynthia closed the door behind him. Vera could tell he was somewhat surprised by what he saw. She always dressed professionally, of course, but that morning, she had taken extra care to portray the right image. She had selected a classic aubergine Armani pantsuit with a faint pinstripe. Simple diamond studs were the only jewelry she wore. Black Gucci pumps completed the picture.

"Where do you want me to sit?" he asked, glancing around the room.

Vera gestured to one of the chairs at the lacquer table. As he moved across the room, she sized him up, all of her senses tuned. "The picture of arrogance" were the first words that came to mind. He was well over six feet tall and looked to be in his early forties. As he walked, his angular chin jutted out, leading the way. His steel-black hair was brushed back and gelled into place. His metal, rectangular-shaped glasses were the same icy gray color as his eyes. Eyes that, as she looked into them more deeply, seemed permanently narrowed—perhaps as a result of his detail-oriented occupation, or perhaps because of his constitution. She would soon find out which. His scant lips were drawn into a perpetual derisive grin.

The minute he sat down across from her, Vera knew that something was wrong. The session would not go well. She had certainly prepared—over-prepared—for it, studying her notes on the EQuate/Bottom Line deal and calling Jake Longworth for clarification on a couple of points. But what she sensed had nothing to do with a failing on her part. There was something else. She tried to put the feeling aside and began as she often did. "How did you hear about me?"

Slade's smirk widened, and he gave a short laugh. "Well, I was essentially given no other choice but to come here."

"Really?" Vera was genuinely surprised. Stan Harper, the intermediary, had said everything went well and according to plan. He hadn't mentioned having to force Slade to see her—and she trusted Stan completely.

"Yeah," Slade maintained his insolent grin. "Stan Harper, my mentor, I guess you'd call him—an old guy I worked for a while ago—invited me to lunch, supposedly to discuss this acquisition offer my company's looking at. I think the deal stinks and we'd lose big time if we went through with it. Everybody but me wants to do it, though—the CEO, the whole senior management team of the company and the board. Basically, they all see the huge windfall this would mean for them personally. They couldn't give a shit about growing the company independently and doing an IPO in another couple of years. They don't want to wait that long or work that hard."

Slade slouched further back in his chair and continued. "Anyway, turns out old Harper must have some skin in the game, too. He tried to convince me—none too subtly, I might add—that I should rethink my opposition to selling the company. When that didn't work, he started telling me this long story about his own mentor, the guy who founded Chip Systems way back when Silicon Valley was still just a big orchard. I was having trouble figuring out where he was going with all this until finally, he brought you up. He didn't say who you were at first. He just gave you credit for some of this guy's major scores with Chip Systems. Then he bragged about how he'd pulled off some knockout deals himself, thanks to your advice.

"He went out of his way not to mention your name and pretended not to want to give any details about you, so I figured I was supposed to beg him for the information, which I did. That's why I'm here. So I can say I went, and you can try to talk me into selling out to EQuate. I'm warning you, though; I'm not changing my mind. So, if you want, we can both save ourselves a lot of time. We can just call it a day right now and I'll take off. We can both tell Harper, Longworth and anyone else who put you up to this that we gave it a fair shot, but I was an asshole and wouldn't give in."

Vera's tone was calm and steady, even though she felt exactly the opposite. "I'm curious. Why didn't you just tell Stan that you felt strongly about not selling your company, give him your reasons and leave it at that? If you really thought he was setting you up to come to see me, why didn't you just tell him that you weren't interested? Why play along?" She chewed the inside of her cheek.

Slade rolled his eyes. "Well, of course I did try to tell him why I'm against the acquisition, but it was clear right away that he didn't want to hear it. Why did I play along? As I said, he's my mentor," Slade snickered. "Well, he sees himself as my mentor. As far as I'm concerned, he passed his sell-by date eons ago. But I'm not stupid. If I'm going to continue to have a good future in this industry, I need him. I need his connections and network. I need him to recommend me to his cronies and so on. It's worth humoring him and spending an hour or two with you for that kind of insurance, don't you think?" He gave Vera another fake smile.

By this time Vera, was absolutely certain that there was no way she was going to convince this man to sell Bottom Line, regardless of the price. But there was more to the situation than met the eye, she was sure of it. She needed to keep him there for a while longer to see if she could figure out what it was.

"Can you tell me exactly why you're against the acquisition?" she asked. "How do you see the next couple of years ahead for Bottom Line if you stay independent? Maybe I can at least reiterate your point of view to Stan."

Slade threw his head back with a guttural laugh, his chin pointing straight to the ceiling. "You're the psychic. Don't you know what will happen if we don't sell?" He didn't wait for an answer. He took her through his rationale, condescendingly explaining basic financial concepts in the process. For the remaining part of the session, he told her that Bottom Line's mergers-and-acquisitions valuation product was going to be released in the next six months, and outlined the projected market share and revenue over the next three years. He also described a couple of other new products that were currently in early stages of development, which appeared to be highly promising and likely to be released in eighteen to twenty-four months, again with impressive financial projections.

The upshot of his position was that Bottom Line would be profitable within two years at most. If they waited eighteen months to two years to take it public, the company would be worth far more to its founders, employees and board than it would be if they allowed EQuate to buy it now. If they were acquired right now, the founders and board would be set for life, without having to expend any more effort. Employees, on the other hand, would be left in the lurch; they might be able to work for the acquiring company, but not necessarily.

Satisfied, Vera thanked him for taking the time to share his perspective with her and assured him that she would restate his view to Stan.

"Yeah, right. I'm sure you'll be convincing," he smirked. Then he stood up and headed for the door.

Vera addressed his back in a quiet voice. "Nick, one more thing before you go. I see you have a son. His name is Wyatt, I believe."

Slade stopped and turned to her, his face drained of its former fire.

Vera continued. "It seems that Wyatt has some sort of learning disability. I know you've researched many possible treatments, but there's something I'd like to recommend."

Slade's eyes were dull with shock. His first inclination, she knew, was to dismiss everything she had told him, figuring Stan must have told her. Then she could see it dawning on him. There was an almost imperceptible change in his expression as he realized that Stan didn't know. None of his business associates knew. So how could she have known? Somehow, she must have found out, he was rationalizing to himself.

"You blame yourself for his condition. I can see that," she said. "You think there's something in your genetic makeup, or the way you and your wife raised Wyatt during his first year, that caused him to have this flaw. There isn't a minute that goes by that you don't hate yourself for what you think you did to make him this way. Isn't that right?"

For just a moment, his face softened, and Vera saw a father whose son's condition caused him untold pain and embarrassment. The man was a master of controlling his emotions, though. In an instant, his eyes blazed even more intently than before, if that was possible, but not with anger or despair or sadness; just with a sheer force designed to overcome any real feeling.

"Almost no one knows about his condition, do they?" she said gently. "You're afraid they'll see it as a weakness in you, somehow. Everyone thinks he goes to a special school for the musically gifted. And, in fact, he does have a real talent for music, doesn't he?" She smiled at him.

"Nick, it isn't your fault—or your wife's. It has nothing to do with your genes or the way you cared for him during that first year. There's no reason for you to torture yourself the way you do."

Slade was shaken badly by now, though no one else looking at him, besides Vera, would have been able to tell. She went over to her desk, wrote something on the top sheet of a pad, tore it off and handed it to him. "Dr. Drobnick is investigating a new drug targeted precisely at the type of disability your son has, which I think will turn out to be a form of ADD, Attention Deficit Disorder, even though the symptoms are very different from classic ADD. I have a very strong feeling that this drug will help Wyatt."

He snapped the paper from her. "Yeah, thanks," he mumbled, rearranging his expression back to its usual brashness. "I'll see myself out," he said. She extended her hand in front of him. He quickly brushed his cool palm against hers and strode out.

Vera closed the door of her office and leaned back against it. This was going to be difficult. She went over to the drawer with the cigarettes, took one from the pack and lit it, feeling relief and disappointment at herself at the same time.

She opened the window and dangled the cigarette outside, then brought it to her lips for another drag. Obviously, she would have to let Jake know what had happened, and he wouldn't like it. Inhaling the last of the stub, she ground it into the outside windowsill, wrapped it in a tissue and threw it into her wastebasket. Hopefully, Cynthia wouldn't notice.

Might as well get it over with, she thought, picking up the phone and punching in the numbers. She was put right through to Jake. No doubt he had been waiting for her call, knowing she was meeting with Slade this afternoon.

"Hey, Vera, how did it go? Is he on his way over to sign the papers?" Jake was jovial.

She felt a clutching in her stomach. "No, Jake, I'm afraid he isn't."

"Yeah, he's a tough one. It'll probably take another visit, huh?"

"No. Look, Jake, I hate to tell you this, but I wasn't able to convince him to sell and I'm not going to be able to convince him, no matter how many times I see him."

There was silence on the other end of the phone. Vera bit the inside of her lip and wished she still had that cigarette. She thought about lighting another. "Jake? Listen, I'm really sorry. Sometimes—rarely, I think you'll agree—it doesn't work out the way we'd like."

Jake spoke slowly and in a lower decibel than before. "Vera, you've never let me down. This will be the first time."

"Yes, I know. Listen, I'd need to see you about this. Can we talk about it over lunch, dinner, something like that?"

"Look, I'm really busy these days. I can't spare the time. You told me you weren't able to do it. There's really no point in rehashing it."

"I don't want to rehash it. I need to talk with you about what I picked up from him."

"I'm sure you did your best, Vera. I'm just disappointed.

And I really don't have time for the details of what happened. To be honest, I was counting on you. I already told the board that I was working on a solution to the problem. I basically guaranteed them that Slade would come around. Now I have to go back to them with my tail between my legs and tell them I failed. I don't know how much direct interaction you've had with boards, Vera. But let me tell you, giving them news like that isn't fun."

"I know. But please, don't report back to them until you and I have had a chance to talk about it. I really have to see you."

"Vera, look, I understand that you're upset because you failed. I'd feel the same way if I were you. But things are very busy over here. I have five projects I'm working on that have to be tied up in the next few days. I don't mean to be rude, but I don't have time for social lunches."

"Jake, it's not a social lunch." The tension tightened her voice. "There's something I have to tell you about Slade and I don't want to do it on the phone. The truth is that the outcome you wanted with Bottom Line is not the outcome that would be in your best interest, or in the best interest of EQuate."

Longworth gave a curt laugh. "With all due respect, Vera, I think I know a bit more about the business dynamics of the deal than you, MBA degree and all." There was a pause. "I'm sorry, I didn't mean that, it's just that I'm really overwhelmed right now, and I tend to be a bit too direct."

She took an aggressive tone that was rare for her. "Let me be direct, too, Jake. If you go to the board before you listen to what I have to say, you'll be making a big mistake. I know what I'm talking about. Please give me the benefit of the doubt just this once. Meet me for fifteen minutes and you can decide whether or not it's worth more of your time."

"Okay. You win," he said curtly.

Vera realized he had probably agreed just to get her off the phone. Even though he didn't get what he wanted, she thought, he would get something far more valuable.

TWENTY EIGHT

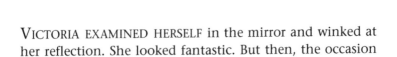

VICTORIA EXAMINED HERSELF in the mirror and winked at her reflection. She looked fantastic. But then, the occasion called for it.

She heard Josh's car pulling into the driveway and went out to meet him. Their kiss was slow and deep. She stole a look over his shoulder and was sure she could make out a crunched figure in the bushes beyond. Her hand glided down his muscular back and rested under his belt. She rocked slightly to the left, to afford a better photo angle. "Ready to come in?" she teased.

"Am I ever!" He stood back and looked at her. She had chosen a very short, strapless black-silk dress, with cutouts at each side of her waist. Around her neck was a slim, diamond-studded choker. And she had worn his favorite shoes—red stilettos.

He slid his hand into one of the slits at her waist and worked his way to her back. The final shots of the two showed them walking side by side toward Victoria's front door, each with a hand tucked snugly under the other's clothing.

Too bad the pictures had to end at the front door, Victoria thought. Otherwise, his sweet little wife would have had some truly impressive visuals that would have stayed with her for decades. As it was, things would never be the same between Josh and his well-educated, accomplished wife. After she saw the pictures, she would always have doubts, would always look into his eyes in a different way, and would always be searching for evidence. And everywhere she looked, she would always see Victoria. The knowledge that Victoria had been with him for so long would eat away at any self-confidence his wife had left.

As for Josh, no pictures would be necessary. No matter how hard he tried to squelch his memory of Victoria, she knew she would always remain with him, too. Because once a man was with her, no one else ever measured up. She made sure of it. Of course, she had never spent more than a handful of months with any of them, so she didn't have to worry about keeping things exciting for a lifetime, like those she had replaced, or those who tried to follow her.

Victoria would never be the one who was left. She would make damn sure of that. She would never put herself in a position where she had to depend on a man or be dominated by one. She would never be her mother. Her mother was a loving, caring woman, but she had no backbone, no character. She let her husband treat her like a child. She let him bully Victoria and Theo. And worse.

Victoria had never told her mother about the visits. After all, there had been only a couple. They had only lasted a few minutes. The next morning, he had been as aloof as ever. And nothing had really happened.

No, she sure as hell wasn't going to be her mother. She poured herself and Josh a glass of wine and they began their favorite tickling game. She had him on his back, pleading for mercy. Suddenly, she felt the playfulness give way to a strange, somber feeling. It pulled at her like a dead weight in the center of her stomach. She tried to brush it off, and launched into another round of tickling, nuzzling her face into his neck and breathing into its crannies, causing him to squeal for mercy. But she didn't feel an ounce of pleasure. The heaviness just rose to her chest. What was going on? She always had a fun time with Josh, and she always relished the "closing night" of her affairs, as she thought of them. Why was this different?

The nameless presence enveloped her now. She saw its unwieldy, bulbous shape and soggy gray color. Regret. The word hit her with shock. It was regret. She hadn't felt it for so long ... since Alistair, actually ... that she barely recognized it. It hung there, draped over her like a somber blanket, dampening the pleasure of this final scene.

She would miss Josh. She *liked* Josh. That wasn't the case with most of her conquests. Usually, she couldn't wait for their wives or girlfriends to find out about her, so she could move on to the next one.

But Josh was different—well, a little different. She certainly wouldn't lose any sleep over the end of their affair, but he had been fun while he lasted. Yes, she would definitely miss him. Most of the others bored her after a couple of weeks. She had to fake it. But no acting was required with Josh. Plus, he was also just a good guy. Most of the men she had conquered were full of themselves and saw her as a prize they deserved. Why should they stay with their wives or girlfriends when they could have *her*? But she had the feeling that Josh actually cared about what she thought and felt. Maybe this time ...

No way you're going to let him get to you! Just get on with it! She pushed the unfamiliar feelings aside and forged ahead. *Get on with it! Just do this. It's time to move on. The very fact that you're having the slightest of second thoughts means you've waited too long as it is. You stupid idiot. Next thing you know, you'll think you're in love.*

What if she ever did actually fall in love, she wondered. She doubted it was even possible. For that to happen, she would have to totally let go and just be herself. She couldn't even imagine doing that. And if, in fact, she did, no man would be attracted to her. *If you can manage to attract one—*her father's voice again. No, it would never happen. There was only one man who really knew her and loved her nonetheless. And it wasn't Josh.

It was definitely time to end it. Josh was getting much too attached, even a little possessive. Besides, it was time for a new challenge.

A few hours later, moonlight peeked through the shutter slats of her bedroom. It fell first on her head, then nestled on his shoulder and flickered onto the muscular arm he had draped around her waist. Finally, it traveled down to his hand where his wedding band glinted back.

Suddenly, a cell phone jangled. Josh rolled over groggily, then jumped from the bed as he recognized the ringtone. "Shit! Where's my phone?" He scrambled around on the floor, looking for it, then realized the sound was coming from the hallway. He ran out there, to where his pants lay in a heap, and grabbed the phone from the pocket—just as the ringing stopped. "Fuck! It was her," he said, looking at the phone. "Oh my God, it's almost one o'clock in the morning. I've got to get out of here."

Victoria helped him gather his clothes. He gave her a hasty kiss and when she tried to draw him in for another, he pulled away. "No, really, I've got to go. I'm in deep shit. I don't know how I'm going to talk my way out of this one."

You're not, she thought. "Bye, hon," she said.

TWENTY NINE

S UNDANCE P ALACE WAS ON ONE OF THE E MBARCADERO piers in San Francisco. On summer weekend nights, the place was buzzing with live music and dancing. Victoria saw Maribeth waiting for her at a booth by the window, already sipping her frozen margarita. She was actually radiant, Victoria was pleased to see, in a strapless sapphire dress that seemed to shimmer in the half-light of the club.

Maribeth caught sight of Victoria, waved and gave her an excited smile. The flush, the radiant eyes ... if Victoria hadn't heard from Theo personally that he had struck out on their first overnight, she would have sworn to the contrary. But maybe for someone like Maribeth, any romantic attention was all it took. Clearly, Victoria thought, her transformation had gone far beyond the surface. Now it wasn't just the clothes and the hair. Maribeth seemed to have changed from the inside out. She finally had a reasonable dose of confidence. Remembering a couple of recent situations, almost too much. Victoria frowned, remembering them.

Confidence was the one quality that made an ordinary woman irresistible; Victoria knew from experience. And in Maribeth's case, it was all due to Theo.

As soon as Victoria got to the table, Maribeth started spilling her news.

"I went to see Vera," she said breathlessly. "I was such a basket case during the session. I mean, seeing a psychic is about the most sacrilegious thing I could do. The whole time, I couldn't even look at her. I was so nervous, I had to hold my hands to keep them from shaking. Goodness knows what Vera must have thought of me!"

But just as with Victoria, Maribeth went on to say, Vera had correctly described her past. It was uncanny. Vera had detailed her childhood home, her college boyfriend and other parts of her past she herself rarely thought about. Vera also knew about her breakup with Charlie and what a difficult time she was going through now.

Maribeth leaned forward. "Here's the best part!" she said. "She knew all about me and Rufus and it seems like we're actually going to have a future together!"

"You guys are going to end up together?"

"Well, at least for a while, maybe even forever. She told me it's too soon to predict very far out into the future at this point. But it looks like we are definitely going to have a relationship—and maybe it will be permanent!"

Maribeth continued with more good news. A headhunter from Russell Reynolds' Midwest office had called. They had seen her resumé and forwarded it to one of their clients, who had a preliminary interest in her. It was a startup magazine that would launch in the fall. They said they should be hearing back from the client shortly.

"That's great!" Victoria said. "But do you really want to leave the Bay Area? I thought Vera said you had a future with Rufus? Why would you want to leave now?"

"She didn't necessarily say we'd be together *here*."

"Vera said Rufus would move with you to Kansas City?" Victoria said, trying to mask her disbelief.

"No, of course not, not in so many words, but I did get the feeling from her that it would be more than a passing fling, so I figure if I move, then ..." She stopped. "I guess I'm over-interpreting what Vera actually said. But no matter what happens, I think it wouldn't hurt to check this job out. I may not get it. I'm just so thrilled that a magazine is interested in hiring me. I owe it to myself to follow up. I also took your advice and put my resumé on a couple of job boards. So maybe something will come up in the Bay Area through one of those. Vera told me things turn out the way they're supposed to. So, if Rufus and I are meant to end up in Kansas City together, great. If I'm destined to stay here, I'll get a terrific job offer here. That's the way I look at it."

"I thought you didn't believe in psychics." Victoria couldn't help grinning.

"I know. I feel so guilty. But at the same time, she was so right-on about so many things about me that literally no one else knows. I'm really torn. But if she's right about what's going to happen ..." A huge smile spread over her face.

This was the happiest and most optimistic Victoria had ever seen her. "I'm really glad for you. And let's hope she's right," she said, and meant it. But Theo living in Kansas City with Maribeth? She had to fight hard to keep from laughing.

"Oh, and you'll never guess who I ran into at Whole Foods, of all places!" Maribeth gushed.

"Who?"

"Kevin! You know that cute redhead from the Fogscape bar—that night after our spa day?"

"Oh, yeah!"

"He was such a sweetie—even asked me out, if you can believe it! But I told him I was going with somebody now."

Going with somebody? Jesus, did the bauble-head think this was high school? She'd have to thank Kevin, though. He always came through for her.

They ordered their second round of drinks. The music drowned out any attempts at serious conversation, so they focused on watching the growing crowd on the dance floor. Like the city itself, it was an eclectic mix: Gen Y'ers dressed in the requisite Internet start-up all-black; the corporate crowd—men, khakied and tie-less and women in pencil skirts and high-heeled boots; those in from the 'burbs for a night out—soccer moms in their nice blouses and dress slacks and hubbies in their polo shirts and belts that sat too high on their waists; and of course, a smattering of tourists, standouts in their pastels and too-bright colors.

A distinguished looking, gray-haired man approached their table and held his hand out to Victoria, pulling her to the dance floor. She looked over her shoulder and mouthed to Maribeth that she would be right back. Maribeth waved her off, shouting after her to have a good time.

He was quite a good dancer. They worked their way up to the front of the floor near the band and stayed for three songs in a row. He was launching into the fourth when Victoria protested that she needed a break and headed back to sit down.

At first, she thought Maribeth must have gotten up to dance, too. She couldn't see her at the table. But as Victoria got to her side of the booth, Maribeth's head popped up from under the other side of the table. An empty margarita glass lay on its side in front of her, the slushy liquid still moving across the table, disappearing over the edge.

Maribeth threw her wet napkin on the table and grabbed Victoria's dry one to mop up what she could of the remaining puddle.

"Oh, I'm so sorry, Victoria. My drink spilled and some

of it got into your bag, I think." She pulled up her other hand. She was holding the rejuvenating cream jar, dripping with slush. Maribeth wiped the jar clean and then bent back down. Victoria lunged under her side of the table. She could see that Maribeth had pulled the tote all the way over to her. She was withdrawing Victoria's Day-Timer, opening the cover and blotting several pages ... the exact pages with the notes she had taken at Maribeth's house. Jutting out from under the back cover were printouts of photos she had taken with her cell phone in Maribeth's office, folded in half, picture side up. By now, Victoria's heart had taken over all of her chest. She was sure Maribeth could hear it thumping wildly through her blouse. Very casually, Victoria sat up and reached across the table. "Don't worry about it. Here, give it to me, I'll take care of it." What she wanted more than anything was to punch Maribeth in the face and yank her bag and Day-Timer out of the fat cow's hands.

"No, no, it's my fault. I'll clean it up," Maribeth said apologetically as she sat up to finish the job.

Victoria could see Maribeth sliding the napkin between the pages of her Day-Timer. She could see the folded photo printouts starting to slip out further from the cover. Maribeth was moving the cloth between the printout pages now, without looking at them. The photographs of *her* personal documents. "I'm so sorry. Are these important?" Maribeth asked. She actually took one out, fanning it in the air.

"No, just printouts of photos for a listing. No big deal." Victoria grabbed the picture out of Maribeth's hand and blew at it, as if trying to dry it off. "Look, really, don't worry, I'll clean it up." She seized the Day-Timer from Maribeth's hand and set it down next to her. Then she reached under the table and pulled the tote over to her side of the booth, propping it up on the cushioned bench next to her. She stole a quick glimpse inside. It looked like the contents had gotten wet, but not drenched. The jar of rejuvenating cream stared back at her; a couple of remaining beads of moisture glinted under the low lights.

How was this fucking possible? She thought about the compact mirror she had broken in the restaurant parking lot. Her turn of bad luck had started, seven years of it. Everything she had to lose was in this bag: details from documents she had found in Maribeth's house; comments Maribeth had made about her life, family and friends that Victoria, in turn, had relayed to Vera; jottings from Maribeth's resumé to which she had referred when impersonating the headhunter; photos of Maribeth's financial statements; and God knows what else that she couldn't remember right now, because she was too terrified to think. And the jar—*the fucking jar was in there.*

While Maribeth blotted away at the tabletop, Victoria studied her carefully, trying to figure out how much she had seen. She was pretty sure the glass had tipped over just before she had returned to the table, so there hadn't been much time for Maribeth to rummage around in the bag. And Maribeth seemed more focused on salvaging the contents than on examining them. She was preoccupied with her dress now, dabbing at a large, soaking spot on her left thigh. A waiter came over with more napkins. Excusing herself, Maribeth slid out of the booth and went to the ladies' room.

Victoria shot a look over her shoulder to make sure Maribeth was gone. Then she extracted the contents of the bag one by one, setting them on the table. The Day-Timer had gotten the brunt of the damage, but the pages were still legible, as were the photos of financial statements lodged between them. Victoria took the jar out and held it under the table, slowly unscrewing the lid. She peered at it. A small amount of powder was left—the same amount as after the last time she had used it.

"How about another dance?" Her dance partner was standing over her.

Victoria jumped in her seat and dropped the opened jar. It rolled and stopped in front of his shoe, the cap twirling the other way. He bent, picked up the jar and squinted at the label, laughing when he saw what it said. She leaned forward over the table, hiding her powder-covered lap, and took the jar from him with an embarrassed grin.

"No, sorry, I'm waiting for my friend. She's having a bit of a crisis and needs someone to talk to. But thanks!" He tried a couple of times to convince her to change her mind before finally leaving. Out of the corner of her eye, she could see Maribeth crossing the dance floor on her way back. She brushed her lap furiously, trying to disperse the powder, but succeeded only in widening the splotch. Seeing a napkin on the table, she grabbed it and rubbed, realizing too late that it was damp and only embedded the powder even more indelibly into her skirt. She flung the Day-Timer and opened jar back into her tote and threw the napkin on her lap as Maribeth came up alongside her.

"I'm going to go. There's nothing I can do about my dress," Maribeth said, looking at the large dark stain on the front. Victoria made a gesture of trying to talk her into staying for another drink, but Maribeth refused.

Alone at the table again, Victoria let out a long breath. She reached for her glass, her hand trembling, and drained the last drop of gin. She noticed that her knees were shaking. *Oh my God. I could have blown the whole thing. I'm not sure I can do this anymore. But there's no way in hell I can quit now. Only about a month left until it's completely over, then a long vacation with Theo. And figure out what to do next.*

THIRTY

Vera had barely put down her bag and removed her sunglasses when she heard voices out in the reception area. She looked at her watch—only nine forty-five in the morning. Carolina was early. She must be anxious to meet with her. Vera felt an unusual tension in her throat, not a common sensation, but one she had learned to heed. In the past, it meant bad news or an unpleasant turn of events. She never knew exactly what was coming, but she knew it wasn't good. It was a warning to be on guard, to be prepared.

She thought back to Carolina's thank-you call a couple of weeks ago. She certainly had been jubilant then, thrilled to be rid of her troublesome subordinate so she could focus on making a mark for herself. The future was rosy. Then Vera remembered her disquieting feeling as she and Carolina had parted—that the woman's future, at least in the short term, was anything but.

Vera straightened her shoulders and went to greet Carolina. Her client was sitting on the edge of one of the plush, deep-purple leather armchairs in the waiting room, her classic Chanel purse clutched in her lap. Carolina's olive skin had a pallid tinge today, an effect she had tried to hide with a little too much blush, Vera noted. She was wearing simple black slacks and a black-and-white-striped pullover, as always conveying confidence, strength and beauty without relying on clothing or makeup to do so.

Vera remembered that she'd had the same impression of Carolina the first time they met. But that time, the young woman exuded energy and vibrance. Today, she was subdued.

As she settled into the armchair across from Vera, Carolina's composure crumbled. Her hands shook, and Vera could see that there was a crumpled tissue in one of them.

"I didn't know who else to go to," Carolina's voice wavered. "But you've helped me so much with my work problems, I thought maybe you could help me with a very personal situation."

"I'm glad you came, my dear. What has happened?"

Though she didn't know her client well, Vera understood that the Carolina who sat across from her was a woman very few people ever met. Her usual poise and control had been knocked out of her by a situation she could not rationalize—one that was at total odds with her framework for making sense out of life.

"I think my husband has been seeing another woman. I think he's been ... having an affair."

The story came spurting out, not neatly and in order, as it would have had Carolina been her usual self, or had she been discussing a problem at work. Instead, it stumbled out erratically, awkwardly, as though she had never uttered the words before in this sequence—as though they were finding their way into the light of day, appalled to be out of hiding.

"I've been suspicious for some time now. All of a sudden, right after he joined this new company, he started having these 'business dinners.' He never had business dinners before, so at first, I thought it was strange, but I told myself that he was moving up in his career, and this probably went with the territory.

"A few months ago, he started to pay more attention to his clothes, which was actually a pleasant change. But lately, he's coming home later and later after these dinners. I can't be sure, but I think he *smells* different. I just want to know if I'm right—if he's having an affair."

Vera saw that Carolina already knew she was right. She just wasn't able to acknowledge it yet. She was silently begging to be told she was wrong—to be reassured that it was going to be all right, that it was a misunderstanding—so she could send those unspeakable words back to where they came from, never to emerge again.

Unfortunately, Vera knew this was not to be. Carolina's husband was, indeed, having an affair. Carolina had come to hear that it wasn't true, that somehow, she had horribly misread the signals. Or failing that, that there was still hope. That she could win him back. Vera was unable to oblige on any of these counts.

"I'm so sorry, Carolina, really I am. This is one of those times I wish I didn't have the gift I have." Vera took a deep breath, then sighed. "I'm going to give it to you straight, because I think you deserve to know. It's true. He's having an affair. And I'm afraid there's no going back. He has made up his mind. The only thing that is uncertain at this point is the timing."

For a full minute, Carolina sat straight up, staring at some indeterminate spot in the distance. Finally, she spoke. "Who is she?" Her eyes brimmed, and she reached into her bag for a fresh tissue.

Vera hated these moments. "What difference does it make?" she wanted to say. She couldn't understand why people—particularly women—were so fascinated by those who had seduced their spouses or partners. Wouldn't it be better not to know? To just form a picture in one's mind's eye of a cheap tart and leave it at that? Apparently not. There had to be a real face on which to pin the rage. A face to put in the fantasy of the plummeting plane, the crashing car, the oncologist's office. So when that particular face was obliterated—either by a real-life fatal event or, more likely, a slow dissipation from the mind over time—everything that face represented was gone and with it the anguish it brought.

She had to give Carolina the face for her agony. As Vera focused on the face, she felt a lurch in her chest. She shook her head, trying to dislodge what surely must be an outrageous mistake, a simple crossing of mental wires. But no, there it was, as clear as a photograph. And unfortunately for Carolina, the face was a stunning one.

Calming herself, Vera reached across the table for her client's hand and held it as she described the other woman, trying to downplay her beauty. "It has been going on for a few months now, as you suspected." As many times as she'd had to deliver a message like this, it always hurt her to do it—literally. She could feel a deep throb in her stomach, aching for the sorrow she was imparting. And in this case, there was something else, too: a stinging anger, an anger that threatened to make its way into her voice. She looked kindly at Carolina as she gave her the final blow. "He wants to leave you. He just can't figure out how to do it."

Vera could see Carolina's wide eyes go from shock, to disbelief, to dismay and back to shock. The young woman let out a wail that seemed to come from the bottom of her soul and began to sob.

Vera went over to Carolina and softly stroked her shoulder. When Carolina finally paused for a breath, Vera tried to comfort her with a slight embellishment of the truth. "He loves you, Carolina. He cares deeply for you … but more as a very good friend. He doesn't want to hurt you and he's trying to figure out how to tell you."

"I want to know more about her," Carolina demanded, her back straightening.

Damn. The need for details. They always wanted the details. Believe me, the more you know, the worse it will be, Vera wanted to tell her. But she knew it would do no good. So instead, she avoided talking about the rival's looks, wealth and lifestyle, and instead tried to think of less enviable attributes. "She's in her forties," Vera exaggerated. "She's had a hard life, never settled down, hasn't had any close relationships," she said, trying to paint a picture of an unhappy, lonely soul—which, in fact, held considerable truth.

"How did he meet her?" Carolina's arms were folded in front of her, each hand bolted to the opposite elbow as though readied for attack.

"They met at work."

"What's her name?" she leaned forward.

Vera closed her eyes and pretended to concentrate. "I'm not getting a name right now."

"So what should I do? I don't really have proof. I can't tell him a psychic told me he was having an affair. Should I just leave?"

Vera's uneasiness grew as she reflected on what would happen next. She considered how to tell Carolina. "Very soon, you will have proof. Once you have it, come to see me and we will work out the best way to use it."

"But in the meantime, how can I stay with him?" Carolina was saying. "It makes me sick to think of him with someone else."

Vera thought hard. "A relative of yours is quite sick, isn't she? A heart problem, I think?"

Carolina blinked, her eyes opening wider. "Yes, my aunt in Florida."

"Unfortunately, she will take a turn for the worse in the

next couple of days. When you hear about it, tell your husband that you're going to visit her for a while. By the time you come back, you'll have the proof. And then we'll decide what to do."

Carolina raised her chin, eyes leveled on Vera. The tears were starting again and her lips trembled, but it was her voice that touched Vera the most. Gone was the assurance, the pride. Instead, in a shaky, uncertain whimper she said, "I just can't believe this. We've been together since college."

◆ ◆ ◆

Vera couldn't believe it either. She felt the anger bulging in her forehead as she opened her bottom drawer and picked up her red cell phone. She clenched it fiercely in her hand and listened to the ringing on the other end. There was no answer. When she heard the beep, she left a message that was short and frigid.

"Victoria, Carolina Crespi came to see me today and I am thoroughly disgusted by what you're doing. I know my opinion on the subject is of no interest to you, but there's something else that you might actually care about. I have the sense that somehow this situation is going to negatively affect your—our—operation." Her hand trembling, she clicked the phone shut. *That should do it*, she thought. *The only thing her niece really gave a damn about.*

Besides Victoria's outrageously inappropriate relationship with Carolina's husband, there was something else that was even more disturbing. She focused every ounce of her powers on trying to figure out what, exactly, that was, but the picture was cloudy. What she did know was that somehow there could be negative consequences for herself and her family.

◆◆◆

A few minutes later, Victoria listened to Vera's message. How the fuck had Josh's wife found her way to Vera, of all people? Having a psychic as an aunt was a real liability at times like these. Vera could often see her secrets. "Get with it," Victoria wanted to tell Teta Vera. Sometimes her aunt's old-style, eastern European morality was just too much to bear. She went to her purse, extracted the jar and tapped out a neat a line. She waited a few seconds, then picked up her red cell phone.

◆◆◆

"Teta Vera, how are you?" Victoria's words rushed into each other, her voice exuberant. Vera had heard this voice from her niece before and hoped it didn't mean what she suspected.

"Not well, Victoria," Vera said curtly.

Victoria went on as though she hadn't heard her, or more likely, didn't care. "Look, I'm sorry you heard about Josh and me. I know you don't approve, but I don't feel like I have to apologize for anything. The truth is, you and I see things very differently when it comes to relationships. It's not as simple as it might look to you. I know you think I'm breaking them up, but if someone has an affair, it means the marriage was already shaky. It's not the fault of the person they fall for. Anyway, don't worry; you'll be happy to know it's over between Josh and me. I've pretty much ended it. Carolina can have him back. It was just a fling."

"Carolina is not going to take him back, Victoria," Vera said tersely.

"Maybe not, but if that's the case, it would have happened anyway, even if I hadn't come along."

"Victoria, you broke up their marriage. Why do you do this? Didn't you see what this did to your mother? You are an exquisite woman who can have the pick of any single man you want. Why do you insist on pursuing the married ones—and ruining lives in your wake?"

Of course, Vera knew very well why. She realized she was wasting her words, but couldn't help herself. Her niece was so selfish and thoughtless; it infuriated her. She was ashamed of her. If it wasn't for her promise to Mara, she would keep her distance. But she couldn't. Not yet, anyway. She realized for the first time that there might actually be a breaking point, even for her loyalty to her sister. There might come a day, she thought, when her niece's ruthless and outright criminal behavior would be more than she could take. And that day might not be that far in the future.

"What was that you said in your message about all this affecting our operation? What do Carolina and Josh have to do with it?" As usual, Victoria was focused on herself and her scam.

Vera steadied her voice, trying to keep her emotions out of it. "I'm not exactly sure, Victoria, but I have the distinct feeling that there may be some connection. In any case, what's done is done." She signed off. "You've said it's over, so we will hope that the story ends here." But she knew it wouldn't.

THIRTY ONE

VERA SAT IN THE CAFÉ, WAITING FOR JAKE Longworth and wishing she had a cigarette. She was still seething from her exchange with Victoria and nervous about telling Jake why his deal to acquire Bottom Line wasn't going to work out as planned. Then she saw him. He came bounding into the café with his usual authority, as though it was a conference room full of people waiting for him. He spotted Vera immediately and went to join her.

In spite of her mood and the awkward subject they were about to discuss, she couldn't help but smile as he came over. They had known each other for nearly ten years now, she reflected, and he still had the same boyishly handsome air as when they'd first met. He was probably in his late fifties now at least, maybe sixty, she thought. But his light brown hair still held its own among the streaks of silver. His face was lined from years of sports in the sun. She knew he had his own sailboat, a ski condo in Tahoe and that he had only recently taken up boogie boarding. Even though he worked fourteen-hour days, he exuded an aura of brimming energy wherever he went, somehow giving the impression that he had just finished a tennis match or a brisk run. When he entered the room, he seemed to bring fresh air in with him.

"Hi. Sorry I'm late. Like I said, it's hectic at work these days."

"No problem. I understand." She bit the inside of her cheek, wondering exactly how to begin.

They placed their order with the waitress: double espresso for Jake and a macchiato for Vera.

"I know you're pressed for time. Let me get right to the point," Vera said, reaching into her briefcase.

"Wait." He stopped her. "First I want to apologize. I was rude to you on the phone the other day. I thought back to our conversation and couldn't believe I actually said some of those things. I'm sorry. I really didn't mean it. I was under a time crunch and was surprised and disappointed that you hadn't been able to get through to Slade. But that's no excuse. Apology accepted?"

"Of course. Just don't do it again, or I'll put a hex on you," she joked.

"You already have, and you know it." He grinned.

That was another trait that set Jake apart from most males in the business world, Vera observed. How many men apologized to colleagues or subordinates for mistreating them? How many actually paused to reflect back on their own actions to begin with? And even if they did, how many would have recognized their own words as being hurtful and unfair? It was rare to find a man with this level of thoughtfulness and compassion, let alone one who was a well-known industry leader.

"Jake, I promised to make it quick, so I will. The bottom line, pardon the pun, is that Nick Slade is a crook. He's bilking Bottom Line out of about a million a year. The real reason he doesn't want to sell is that he has a nice little extra income stream going and he doesn't want to give it up. Okay, I'm finished. You can go back to work now."

The coffees arrived, and Jake waited for the server to leave before reacting. "Are you sure? How do you know?"

"I am sure. And I know the same way I know most things that aren't told to me directly. Remember, I'm not just a brainy MBA; I'm a psychic, too," she couldn't resist lobbing his earlier jab back at him.

"Ouch! I deserved that." He feigned recovering from a blow. "But do you have any specifics? Any hard evidence?"

"I can tell you where to find it." Vera pulled out her laptop and opened up the file with the spreadsheet she had put together. It was a mock-up of Bottom Line's P&L. She pointed to a line near the end of the page. "Here, under 'Contract Services.' It will show a total amount of $20 million for last year. If you look at the detail for that line, I think you'll find an entry for 'Systems Support.' And if you dig deeper into that account, I believe you'll see a contract service by the name of 'Interactive Associates.' You'll discover that's a shell company, with no other actual clients. It's headed up by a Shelby Cockrain, Slade's wife—that's her maiden name. I doubt she actually knows anything about it, by the way. He probably handles all the paperwork, questions from the bean-counters at Bottom Line, that kind of thing."

Jake was uncharacteristically speechless for a few moments. He stared at the spreadsheet, the furrow between his eyes deepening as the meaning of what she had told him sunk in. "How do you know this?"

"You're unusually slow today, Jake. I am actually psychic, remember?"

"Yes, I know, but this level of detail …"

"I'm a very good—detailed—psychic," she grinned.

"Vera, I don't know what to say." He looked at his watch,

annoyed at what he saw. "Unfortunately, I only set aside a few minutes for meeting with you. Obviously, I want to discuss this further. In the meantime, I'll have our auditors look into it. I'll let you know what they find. If it turns out you're right, I owe you ..." He faltered for the right words. "I would really owe you my job."

"I'm glad you're not angry anymore. I know how badly you wanted to do this deal."

"Certainly not under these circumstances. I really am sorry I have to leave. I'll call you when the auditors have checked it out. Thanks, Vera." For a moment he looked like a boy who had been reprimanded for getting an answer wrong in class. Then he was up, striding out of the café as forcefully as he had entered it. On to his next crisis, Vera assumed.

THIRTY TWO

MARIBETH ANSWERED THE DOOR. Theo stepped in and pulled her to him, giving her a slow, lingering kiss. He waited while she got her purse, then took her arm and led her to his Porsche.

In thirty minutes, they got off the elevator at the top floor of the Ritz Carlton Hotel and entered Victor Hugo, one of the top restaurants in San Francisco. The host led them to a private booth by the window and seated them on lush, velvet benches. Richly brocaded drapes, pulled back by oversized cords, separated their table from other, similarly secluded ones. They had a full view of the city's financial district, with the bay and Oakland in the far distance.

"Madam? Sir? Would you like a cocktail?"

Theo and Maribeth had no sooner settled into the booth than a tuxedoed waiter unfurled their napkins and placed them on their laps. Flawless service, as always, Theo noted. He took in the dark wood walls, featuring rows of square insets—each housing a thick, white candle on a silver stand. And a perfect setting. Just as it should be, he thought.

Maribeth broke the mood by ordering a frozen margarita. "Rufus" asked for a Campari. When their drinks arrived, he toasted to their first night together and told her how much he had enjoyed it. Maribeth looked a little embarrassed and said she was still worried that the relationship was moving too fast. She was afraid she was doing the wrong thing, getting involved so quickly after her split.

Too fast? Theo had to keep from smirking. If it had been any of the women he knew in Geneva, he would have been sleeping with them for weeks by now. He covered his derision with a smile and reassured her that things were moving along exactly as they should. As long as they were both enjoying each other and not hurting anyone else, it was right, he told her. Besides, he couldn't help pointing out: They were taking it very slowly.

As though reading his mind, she said, "I'm sure you are used to dating women who are … a lot different from me."

Theo reached for her hands across the table, cupping them in his own. "Darling, that is what I find most intriguing about you. You are not like the others. You are honest, unpretentious and true to yourself. You are not pretending to be someone else just to please me. You know exactly who you are, and you aren't about to do anything that makes you uncomfortable. That's why I find you so interesting … and irresistible."

They clinked their glasses. This was the moment to do it, he thought. He reached into his breast pocket and pulled out a small red box, placing it in front of Maribeth. Suddenly, a shriek pierced the quiet ambience of the room.

"Anthony Schurer, right?"

A woman was standing at Maribeth's side, gawking at Theo. A woman who looked very familiar. He just couldn't quite place her, but he knew he didn't like her.

"I'm Tess Chaplin. Remember me? From the Zurich flight?"

The too-bright eyes, the stretched, lacquered mouth … *Shit!* Theo felt a cold wave pass through his body. For a moment, his mind went numb. "Tess?" He stalled for time.

"You know, we sat together on the plane here from Zurich—must have been a couple of months ago." Her hand was batting the air, her bracelets jingling.

Theo blushed. "Yes, of course, Tess. So sorry. I remember now."

"Still drinking those Camparis, I see." She gave him a pronounced wink. He hoped somehow it wasn't coming, but it was. "I thought you said you were only going to be in town for a week."

"Yes, it was a quick trip, but I'm back again." He smiled broadly.

Tess looked at Maribeth, seeming to size her up.

"Oh, forgive me, how rude of me," Theo said. "Tess, this is Maribeth Simmons. Maribeth, this is Tess." They nodded politely to each other.

"It's so nice to see you again. When are you going back to Zurich?" Tess asked.

"Probably in a few days, depending on how the meetings here go," he improvised.

"Well, with any luck, maybe we'll end up on another flight together again soon." Her heavily coated eyelids blinked. It was clear she was hoping to draw the conversation out.

"Quite," he said, trying to end it as quickly as possible, his mind in overdrive—calculating how he was going to do damage control.

"It was great to meet you," Tess said to Maribeth, then turned and headed to the cocktail lounge.

"Anthony Schurer? Zurich?" Maribeth was gaping at Theo.

Theo shook his head and smiled confidently, his warm eyes doing their magic. "I'll explain." Just then the waiter arrived with second drinks for them both. We're going to need them, Theo thought.

He told Maribeth that he had gone to Zurich for business several weeks ago and met Tess on the flight back. He hadn't been interested in her at all, but she kept trying to engage him in conversation. He had told Tess that he lived in Zurich, hoping she would consider him geographically unavailable. But that didn't put her off. When she asked for his name, he gave her the name of his high school history teacher. He was actually very surprised that she still remembered it. That was it, he told her. That's all there was to it.

Meanwhile, his brain was reeling. *How the hell could this have happened? He probably knew less than ten people in this city. What were the odds of running into one of them? And the only one who knew his traveling name at that? The very one who knew he had flown in from Switzerland? How could this appalling creature intrude into his life again? And she had remembered his name!* He railed inwardly at himself. *Victoria would kill him for giving Tess his traveling name. But how could he have avoided it? The flight staff had called him by his surname, so there was no getting around it. He was sure Vic would somehow blame him for allowing Tess and Maribeth to meet. But again, it was an incredible coincidence—something he could not have foreseen or headed off. Maybe he should just not mention this whole thing to Vic. Yes, it would be better that way. It had nothing to do with Steeplechase anyway.*

The main thing now was to distract Maribeth, draw her mind away from this inconvenient little disruption of the evening. "What I think is that we should forget that bothersome woman and get back to our lovely dinner. We are about to be served the most incredible tuna tartare you've ever tasted. I guarantee it." He raised his glass to hers and noticed her frown recede.

"And there's this small matter of a little red box that you

were about to open before we were so rudely interrupted," he said, sliding it toward her.

Maribeth grinned and blushed, protesting that it was too soon for him to give her a gift. He had the feeling that she wasn't used to impromptu presents—or even romantic gestures in general.

Opening the box, she stared at the delicate, star-shaped gold earrings.

"Oh my gosh, Rufus, this is too much!" She looked at him reproachfully.

He assured her it wasn't extravagant—just his way of letting her know how much he liked her. "Go on, put them on," he encouraged.

Maribeth removed her simple pearl studs and replaced them with her new earrings. Eyes shining, she brushed her hair back and straightened her shoulders. "How do they look?" she asked, posing for him.

"*You* look brilliant!" And he did have to admit that her wholesomeness and unabashed delight were attractive, in a way. A far cry from the jaded sophistication of the few women with whom he'd had casual relationships after Isabella.

They clinked their glasses again. He could feel his shoulder muscles relax. Tess appeared to have been forgotten. *Damn, he was good.*

Almost an hour later they were polishing off an impeccable zabaglione when Maribeth abruptly asked, "What kind of business do you do in Zurich?"

The sweet froth lolling around in his mouth went instantly flat and he swallowed quickly. "I told you— investments." It was condescending enough to provoke more probing.

"Can't you just do that over the phone and by Internet?" she reasoned.

He explained that for investments of a substantial size, he considered it imperative to check out the companies himself and meet with the management to be assured that the business was sound.

"What, specifically, are you researching in Zurich?"

Theo placed his spoon deliberately on his plate. Color rose to his cheeks and he glared at her like a father warning his child for the last time. His own father came to mind. He took a long, audible breath and spoke slowly, as though trying to control himself. "I told you. I don't like to discuss my business."

"Rufus, I need your help," she pleaded. She told him the details of the financial arrangements of her divorce. While it looked like she would be left with a comfortable nest egg, she pointed out that she couldn't be absolutely sure of exactly how much she would get, especially since some of it was in the form of stock options. In any case, whatever the amount was, it wasn't enough to support her for the rest of her life, at least not at the level of her current lifestyle.

So lately, she'd been thinking, she explained, that she should start considering how to invest the money to get the best return. There was a good chance that she would go back to work, but her income as an editor would be modest.

The problem was, she said, that she didn't know anything about investing. Her husband had taken care of all that. But Rufus was clearly an expert. He earned his living at it and as far as she could tell, it was a very good living. She wasn't trying to be nosy about his personal financial affairs; she just wanted advice, as a friend.

"Let's not talk about this here," he said, irritated. He gestured to the waiter for the check.

Once in the car, he was more patient. He explained to Maribeth that if she wanted advice on investments, she should ask an expert, not a friend. It was true that he had done well for his own account, but he didn't want the responsibility of recommending a venture to her, or anyone else, for that matter, then having it go sour. He had carefully structured his holdings so that if one or two of them failed, it would not have a significant effect on his overall financial position. But he wasn't willing to advise anyone else in these matters.

In her case, he told her, it sounded like she would be gambling with a relatively small amount of money. If the investment didn't appreciate very much—or worse yet, lost value—then her entire financial stability would be in jeopardy. He wanted no part in this potential outcome. They arrived at Mandarin Towers and he pulled into his parking space.

"A relatively small amount of money? I said two or three million," she insisted.

He nodded brusquely.

"Okay, forget it," she said sharply, staring out the side window.

He reached over and gently nudged the hem of her dress upward. Slipping his hand underneath, he worked his way up her thigh in an ascending spiral. "Yes, let's forget it and focus on something I really am an expert on." He leaned over, nuzzled her hair and kissed the back of her neck.

He had definitely succeeded in distracting her, he grinned to himself. They played around in the car for a while before going inside. Somehow, he was able to convince her to spend the night again, though it turned out to be just as chaste as their first night together.

Early the next morning, Theo's cell phone began ringing on the nightstand beside him. He pretended to be in a deep sleep, letting it ring several times before answering it. Finally, he picked it up.

"Hello," he mumbled groggily. "Oh, yes. Thank you, Jonathan. Appreciate it. I'll print it out and get back to you. Many thanks!"

"What was that?" Maribeth pulled the covers up to just under her chin.

"Oh, nothing. Business. Just got to print some items off, then a quick shower and an exquisite breakfast for you!" He started to tickle her, but she pushed him away. "Okay, sleeping beauty, you just go back to sleep and I'll wake you when your breakfast is served."

"That sounds so decadent," she said, rolling over.

"Indeed!" Theo headed down the hall to his desk and printed out a couple sheets, leaving them on the printer tray. When he returned to the bedroom, Maribeth appeared to be snoozing again. He wasn't sure if she was faking it or not, so he sneezed loudly just in case.

"Bless you!" she murmured.

He went into the bathroom, turned on the shower and jumped in just long enough to rinse off and get his hair wet. Then, grabbing a towel, he stepped out and turned on the closed-circuit TV. He saw Maribeth approach his desk. She glanced quickly at the two pages on the printer tray, then ran to the hallway entrance, taking a quick look down the corridor. When she saw the coast was still clear, she returned to the printer.

He saw her study the top page, which was a trade confirmation from Smythe and Barnes, showing a purchase of one million shares of Steeplechase Enterprises for a total price of $5 million. She turned over the bottom sheet, which was a summary of account positions for Rufus McCain. The most recent purchase of Steeplechase was shown at the top of the page. Beneath that was an accounting of his other holdings. Twelve equities were listed with a total current market value of $19,242,569. The cost-basis column showed an original total investment of $6,400,876. The unrealized gains reflected that Rufus had roughly tripled his money.

Theo saw her look back at the entrance to the corridor, then lift the flap on the copier portion of the printer. She placed the top page from the printer tray on the glass, closed the flap and pressed the copy button.

She was wearing his silk pajamas. While she waited for the copy of the first sheet, he watched her clutch the thin material tightly around her, simultaneously tapping her foot and moving her eyes from the hallway entrance to the copier, then back to the hallway entrance. Finally, the machine spat out a copy of the trade confirmation.

He gave a malevolent smirk, stepped into the bedroom and began singing loudly. He kept his eye on the TV and saw her open the copier flap, take out the original copy of the trade confirmation, put it on top of the machine and replace it with the account-summary sheet. She jabbed the copy switch.

He darted out to the hallway and began whistling, then raced back to the bathroom to watch. She pulled the copy of the second page from the mouth of the copier, grabbed the copy of the first page and jammed them both down the front of her pajama pants. She placed the account-summary page back in the printer tray and hurried out to the deck.

He turned off the TV, put on his bathrobe and resumed whistling as he went out to join her. He could see that she was shivering, her arms bound around her chest. Standing behind her, he hugged her and drew her to him. He kept his hands dangerously close to the sheets of paper he knew she had slipped into the pajama pants. They watched the morning light as it spilled over the bay. He went to kiss her neck, but she clutched her arms even more tightly across her chest and pulled away.

"Don't get too close. Haven't had my shower or brushed my teeth yet!" she said, her voice a slightly higher pitch than normal. "I'll be back in a jiffy, promise!" She pulled away from him and rushed off toward the hallway.

A jiffy? What was this, the 1950s? Theo shook his head and walked over to his desk. He glanced at the copier. She had forgotten the original copy of the trade-confirmation page on the top of the machine. Smirking to himself, he went into the kitchen and began concocting his homemade banana-pancake batter.

They ate their breakfast on the deck. It was another sparklingly clear day, allowing a view of Sausalito to the north and Berkeley and Oakland to the east. And it was warming up quickly. The temperature had already risen more than ten degrees in the last hour and was now in the high 70s—a rarity for San Francisco mornings, even in August. Theo leaned back in his lounge chair, closed his eyes and let the sun soak into his face. *What a perfect place*, he thought contentedly. *If only he didn't have to work. If only he could live here forever.*

He snuck a peek at Maribeth. She had hitched her capris up over her knees, exposing pale thighs that had maintained their pudginess in spite of Victoria's efforts at a fitness regime. He turned away and slipped a look at his watch.

"Yes, it's late. I've got to go," she said, getting up.

He grabbed her arm in protest. "No, please stay. I was just checking the time, because I have to make a call in a few minutes. I was hoping we could spend the day together."

"No, I've got some business to take care of." She kissed his hand and got up, carrying her coffee cup by the office area on her way to the kitchen. He followed.

Stopping just past the desk, she turned, gesturing out the window and commenting on a huge cargo ship that was making its way across the bay. As she swung her right arm out to point, she knocked the coffee cup from her other hand, sending it tumbling to the floor, where it broke.

"Oh, I'm so sorry!" she said, bending to retrieve the ceramic pieces.

"Not to worry, I'll get a towel," Theo went to the kitchen. He stared at the glass door of the oven, which afforded a reasonably clear reflection of what was going on behind him in the living room. He saw Maribeth's head turned from her crouching position to watch him. Standing on her knees, she reached over to the top of the copy machine where she had left the original of the trade confirmation page and grabbed it. Then, still on her knees in a crouched position, she placed the page on the copier tray in its original position.

Theo turned, holding the towel. "What in heavens name are you doing?" he called over to her.

"Pieces of the cup—they went all over the place," she said. He could see that she was pretending to pick up microscopic bits from the desktop. "I am so sorry, Rufus. I'll replace it. Just tell me where you got it."

"Not a problem, my sweet, I have plenty of others."

◆ ◆ ◆

A couple of hours after she left, one of Theo's cell phones rang. He glanced at the screen and smiled, but didn't answer. Soon, a beep notified him that a message was waiting. He heard her halting voice …

"Uh, this is Maribeth Simmons. I wanted to talk with you about an investment I'd like to make. Please call me back—as soon as possible," she added hastily, then left her number.

Theo waited a half-hour, and then called her back. "Ms. Simmons? This is Jonathan Winslow, returning your call." He used his best Shakespearean voice.

"Yes, Mr. Winslow," she said eagerly on the other end of the line. "I want to talk with you about investing in one of the funds you handle."

"How did you get my number, Ms. Simmons?"

"Oh, through a friend of a friend …"

"What is your friend's name, if I may ask?"

"Oh, it's not important. But I am very interested in Steeplechase," she said.

"Steeplechase?" He feigned surprise. "I'm terribly sorry, madam, but that investment has a limited subscribership."

"What do you mean by *limited*?" she pressed.

"Well, I'm not sure how you heard about this particular fund; it is quite obscure, not well-known at all. In any case, at this point, a minimum investment of $2 million is required."

There was a pause on the other end of the line. "Oh, I see. Well, I'll have to think about it. Thanks." He heard the click as she hung up.

THIRTY THREE

VICTORIA, THEO AND VERA were on their regularly scheduled three-way call to discuss where things stood. Each gave a status update on the project from their perspective.

"She called yesterday and said she needed another appointment with me as soon as possible. I'll be seeing her later today," Vera contributed.

"Yes!" Theo threw his fist in the air and cheered. "She wants advice on Steeplechase, I guarantee it!" Theo recapped Maribeth's numerous attempts to get him to advise her on investments, then related her call to Jonathan to ask about investing in Steeplechase in particular.

Victoria told them that the sale was proceeding nicely, with no hitches. Closing should be in a couple of days, as expected. She read from the pictures she had taken of financial statements related to the purchase of the house on Sunset. "They bought the house for $4 million, with a down payment of a million. At a sale price of $5.5 million, she makes at least $2.5 million.

"Then there's their other assets," Victoria went on. She read from notes in her Day-Timer. "Based on last year's tax return, it looks like they have total investable assets of about $3 million, not counting the house. She'll also be getting a piece of her ex's severance settlement, which is about $750,000 total, but that won't be until next year sometime, and the exact amount is unclear because some of it depends on the valuation of the stock options. So, for the time being, it looks like she'll have $1.5 million to play with, more or less—plus $2.5 million in proceeds from the house."

"How soon is she going to be able to get her share of the assets? How long before they settle?" Theo asked.

"Pretty quickly, now that she's working with her own lawyer. I had a look at her draft settlement. It's in good shape. It's just a matter of whether Charlie and his attorney will fight it or give in and move on. As I said before, though, she won't get her share of his severance—assuming he actually turns out to be eligible for it—until sometime next year."

"So, you think we're pretty safe in going for $2 million?" Theo sounded uncertain. "That's more than half of her net worth right now."

"You tell me, heart-breaker. Is she in love with your brilliant investment strategy or not?"

"That she is!"

"And then there's Teta Vera, warning her that whatever sum she has isn't likely to last a lifetime, which should ramp up the pressure. That will clinch it, right, Teta?"

"Yes, my dear," Vera said tightly.

"Which reminds me," Victoria went on. "She's thinking of going back to work. And that's fine as long as she doesn't stay here. So, Teta, you have to tell her that her next job's in Kansas City. There's already a Kansas City employer interested in her."

Vera was tapping notes on her iPad as Victoria spoke. She considered telling them about another development, but decided against it. After all, it was nothing concrete, just another feeling that things might not go entirely as expected.

They ended their call. Not a minute later, Victoria's red cell phone rang. It was Theo.

"Look, I didn't want to bring this up with Teta Vera on the line, but things aren't going as expected with Miss Piggy."

"Really? What's wrong?"

"I still haven't been able to ..." he stammered, "you know, have sex with her. I was wondering," he said. "Maybe she's gay like her husband."

THIRTY FOUR

"VERA, IT'S JAKE."

Vera was surprised to find her hand grip the phone on hearing his voice. She knew she had been right about Nick Slade's motive for not supporting the acquisition of Bottom Line by EQuate. She was sure Jake would have found the evidence just where she told him to find it—in Bottom Line's accounting records. Why was she nervous?

Sure enough, Jake went on to tell her that she had been absolutely right about Slade. EQuate's accountants and attorneys had confirmed it. Jake had met privately with his board and of course they were relieved that he had uncovered the information before the deal went through. They were most complimentary about his ability to comb through the details and uncover this major problem. Obviously, the EQuate offer was off the table for now. Steps were also being taken to advise Bottom Line's CEO about his CFO's activities and it was likely that a criminal investigation would ensue.

Jake told her that EQuate would use the information about the messy finances to swoop in with a lower bid and get a sweet deal. He couldn't have hoped for a better outcome.

"So, I owe you a lot." Jake's gruff voice was filled with admiration. "To start, I'd like to take you to dinner. Are you free Saturday?"

And then it came to her why she was nervous. Of course! It was obvious. She laughed at herself for missing something so basic. Then again, it had been a decade since she had felt this way about any man. She observed her reaction with detachment and curiosity, as though watching a movie— marveling at the way her heart raced and her voice wavered as she answered him. "Yes, I'm free, but you don't have to take me to dinner to thank me. It's my job."

"Vera, you won't permit me my little pretense, will you? You know as well as I do that I'm not taking you out to thank you. Of course, I'm incredibly grateful that you saved me from a potential financial catastrophe, but that's not the reason I want to get together. I'm taking you out because I'm interested in you. I like you, a lot—and not just as a business advisor." He paused. "There, okay, I've laid it on the table. I don't know what made me think I could beat around the bush with a mind reader. I can't get away with anything!"

Vera's laugh rang through parts of her that had lain dormant for years. "You'd be surprised at what I don't know, Jake. When it comes to clients, I can see complex inter-relationships and sense what will happen in the future. But when it comes to me, I'm usually clueless. So, don't worry, your private thoughts are safe." This wasn't entirely true, but total honesty was rarely a good idea in personal relationships, Vera had found. "And by the way, I'm really glad it won't be a business dinner," she said with a lilt. What delightful surprises life had in store, even at her age!

She put down the phone and allowed herself a moment

of jubilation. Who would have thought? She giggled to herself. Well, she had obviously noticed that he was handsome, and of course she knew he was single. Working with him was certainly great fun, but romantic involvement had never crossed her mind. She had assumed that he had a girlfriend, or maybe several—probably much younger than she. Men with his reputation and financial standing always seemed to have women half their age on their arm. Yet, once again, he didn't fit the mold—and how wonderful for her that he didn't.

She forced herself to push the exciting turn of events aside and steer her mind to a far more distasteful topic. Her second session with Maribeth was coming up in a few minutes. She wished she had never agreed to go through with this caper again, but there was no getting out of it now. She had promised to play her part, so now she just had to see it through. If all went well, she reminded herself, this would be the last time she would have to see the woman. *If all went well* ... The words repeated themselves in her head. She gnawed the inside of her cheek and felt the queasiness that had plagued her for the last several days.

Cynthia knocked on the door, letting Maribeth in. For the second time, Vera and Maribeth settled across from each other at the black lacquer table.

"I must say, my dear, I am a bit surprised to see you. I thought consulting psychics was against your religion. You seemed very reluctant to come the first time."

"Yes, I was," Maribeth said, her jaw taut. "But I had to come back to ask you about some things. You were right about Rufus, the financial stuff—everything, in fact. So, I just had to come back."

Just as it had the last time, Maribeth's gaze zigzagged nervously as she avoided looking at Vera directly. Vera had hoped that the second visit might be more relaxed, but her client seemed equally on edge as she had been the first time.

"Is there something specific you want to know?" Vera asked.

Maribeth shifted in her chair. "A couple of things. First, I'm thinking seriously of making a substantial investment. It happened just like you said it would. I found out about it through Rufus, but he didn't actually tell me about it. I kind of overheard." Her cheeks flushed a bit. "Well, anyway, it looks like a sure thing—very profitable. And I'm just wondering, should I go ahead? I mean, it's a lot of money."

"Two million, is that right?" Vera said.

Vera could see Maribeth catch her breath. "Yes!"

"I do see you going ahead with the investment; it looks like it is a good one."

"Good," Maribeth seemed relieved. "Because I could just keep it in a savings account or money market and live off of it. I might even not have to go back to work."

"Hmmm." Vera shook her head gently. "I can see that you have a comfortable cushion of money, which is about to more than double because of selling your house. However, even though it's a very solid sum—and would be a fortune for most people—it's not really enough to keep you living at this level of lifestyle for the rest of your life.

"While you may expect significant returns from the investment you're considering, I'm not sure even that would be enough to increase your total holdings to such an extent that you would never have to work again. Unless you downscaled quite a bit, that is, which is something you could think about."

As soon as she had said it, Vera chided herself. She shouldn't give her any ideas on that front; that wasn't an alternative they wanted her to consider. She moved along quickly. "Also, I think you would enjoy working. I see you at a job where you're having fun and doing very well, even making a name for yourself in your community. And you will meet a lot of people because of it. In essence, it will form the foundation of your new life. And it will be a rewarding one." Vera felt reasonably good about the advice she was giving now. Except for some tricky wordsmithing on the topic of Steeplechase, the rest of her counsel was pretty solid.

She could see that Maribeth was twisting her hands in her lap. "Was there something else?" Vera asked, knowing there was.

"Yes. Do I have a future with Rufus?" She blurted it out, almost looking Vera in the eye, but averted her gaze at the last minute.

Vera hated lying to her about this topic, almost more than misleading her about Steeplechase. "Let me see if things are any clearer in that respect than they were last time." Vera pretended to revert to her internal film and seemed to watch the frames move behind her lids. "Hmmmm."

"What?" There was unabashed eagerness in Maribeth's voice.

"You are from Kansas City, right?"

"Yes."

"I see you living there again. It's a white-brick, ranch-style house with a large yard—in the suburbs. You've got a job you love. The one I saw earlier, it seems."

"So Rufus dumps me?" There was a catch in Maribeth's voice.

Vera steeled herself. "No, my dear. He's there with you."

THIRTY FIVE

IT HAD BEEN SEVERAL DAYS SINCE Theo and Maribeth had spent their second night together. He could see her name on the screen as his phone buzzed. "What's up?" he answered casually.

Her voice was frantic. "I haven't heard from you for days. I've left voicemails and you haven't called back. Are you okay?"

"Yeah, I'm fine. Sorry, just been busy."

"Busy? I left you so many messages. Couldn't you at least have called me back?"

"I just couldn't get away," he said blandly.

"Get away from what?"

"Darling, you're beginning to sound a bit whiny."

"But we talked about spending the weekend together."

"Yes, I know, but something came up." Theo allowed an undertone of annoyance in his reply.

"But ... we've been together so much these last few weeks, I thought ... I don't know, I guess I thought we had sort of a relationship," Maribeth's voice quavered.

Theo brushed it off. "Of course we have a relationship, my dear, though a bit of an odd one." He inserted a little chuckle. "Not to worry, I haven't flown the coop—just had another commitment and was out of pocket for a while."

"Are you seeing someone else?" The words rushed out, her voice shaky.

"How sumptuously charming of you to be jealous!" he purred. "Listen, I have a surprise for you." But he wouldn't tell her what it was. She had to agree to meet him for dinner to find out.

THIRTY SIX

THE NEXT DAY, VICTORIA AND MARIBETH sat together in a Barnaby Wells conference room, the closing papers of 227 Sunset stacked neatly in front of them. Victoria did her best to go through the details of each before indicating where Maribeth should sign, but Maribeth was clearly too excited to focus on the particulars. She couldn't breeze through the documents fast enough. When they were finished, Maribeth shook Victoria's hand vigorously, then hugged her.

"Victoria, I can't thank you enough. You did a super job with this whole transaction, especially since you had to pull me, kicking and screaming, through parts of it! You got a better price than I could have dreamed of and a fast closing to boot. I'm just so grateful!"

"It was my pleasure. I couldn't be happier that it turned out the way it did," said Victoria—every word of it the truth.

"How soon will the $2.5 million be in my account?" Maribeth wanted to know.

"Twenty-four hours at the latest. What are you going to

do with the money?" Victoria ventured—just to see if Maribeth would tell her.

"Oh, I have plans ..." Maribeth murmured. Then a huge grin spread across her face and she grabbed Victoria's arm. "You'll never guess what! Rufus and I are going on a little vacation together!"

Victoria noticed that Maribeth was wearing her new, star-shaped earrings.

Her words rushed out breathlessly. "We're leaving for Mexico in a couple of days. Rufus is taking me to this small, romantic resort near Zihuatanejo. We're going to have dinners on the beach and massages every day. I can't wait!"

This was news to Victoria, but welcome news. He must have just asked her. It also meant—at least she assumed it meant—that Theo finally got her to sleep with him. Strange that he hadn't mentioned it, though. In any case, the jealousy card obviously did the trick, just as he had calculated.

"So," Victoria gave her a sly grin. "Is he good ... romantically?"

Maribeth looked down at her hands. "Oh, he's very attentive, very sweet."

"No, I mean is he a good lover?" Victoria winked at her.

"Oh, I don't know. I mean, we haven't ..."

"You haven't? You're kidding?" Victoria caught herself. She probably sounded a little too surprised.

"No. I know it must be frustrating for him. I mean, I'm sure he's used to ... you know, a different type of woman. He's been very understanding, a real gentleman."

"But you're going away with him; doesn't that mean ...?"

"Yeah—I don't know—I'll have to play it by ear." Maribeth looked flustered.

They got up to go. Victoria wished her a fabulous time in Mexico and started heading for her office.

"Wait! One more thing," Maribeth stopped her. She

reached into her purse and pulled out a long narrow box, wrapped in silver foil and tied with a smooth black ribbon. Smiling shyly, she handed it to Victoria. "I hope you like it."

"What's this, Maribeth? It isn't my birthday!"

"It's just a small gesture of thanks for helping me so much with the house—and everything else!" Maribeth said with her usual straightforward sincerity. Then a girlish eagerness entered her voice. "Go on, open it. I hope you like it," she repeated.

Victoria opened the box and was genuinely delighted. It was the turquoise and coral necklace with the bronze Buddha pendant that she had admired in Maribeth's craft room the first time she had toured the house.

"I just finished it yesterday."

"Maribeth, it is absolutely stunning. I don't know what to say. Thank you so much!"

"It suits you," Maribeth observed. "And hopefully, you'll remember me when you wear it after I'm gone."

"Gone where? You haven't made your final decision to move yet, have you?"

"I don't know. I'm thinking seriously about it."

THIRTY SEVEN

WHEN THEO GOT BACK HOME, he saw that there was a message from Maribeth on Jonathan Winslow's voicemail. "I'm ready to make the investment in Steeplechase, as we discussed. Please call to let me know what I need to do." She left her number again.

The next morning, Theo called her back using his Jonathan Winslow voice. He switched on the audible, periodic beep, indicating their conversation was being recorded. He started by asking her about her financial status: her investments, her savings, the source of her income, and so forth. He explained that since she was a new client, and since the sum she was about to invest was a sizable one, he needed assurance of her readiness for the size of investment she intended to make.

Based on the information she had given him about her assets and investment experience—or lack thereof—he indicated his concern about the suitability of taking a position as substantial as the one she was considering. Wouldn't she be more comfortable, he suggested, perhaps investing a quarter of that amount in a well-known security?

Maribeth assured him she knew what she was doing and knew what she wanted.

In that case, he told her, as the next step he would send her the Steeplechase prospectus for her to study. She could then call him if she was interested in acquiring shares.

In a clearly impatient tone, Maribeth reiterated that she totally understood what she was buying. She said that she had, in fact, already seen the prospectus, because a friend of hers had it. She just wanted to go ahead with the purchase.

"Very well, madam," he said. Feigning reluctance, he repeated the amount she wanted to invest and stated that on the day her funds cleared, the market value of the stock would be divided into that amount to determine the number of shares she would hold. The beeping in the background continued.

He proceeded to give her directions on how to execute the purchase. He would email her the documents she needed in order to open her account with Smythe and Barnes, along with a confirmation of her intent to buy shares. She was to make out the check for $2 million to the order of Steeplechase Enterprises and send it, along with the completed and signed paperwork, to Jonathan Winslow at Smythe and Barnes, P.O. Box 11860, San Francisco, California 94123. The check should take about a week to clear. Within 48 hours of her check clearing, he would email her the confirmation of purchase.

Did she have any questions about the transaction, he asked. She did not. *Was there anything else he could do for her today,* he asked. There was not.

Theo went to his computer to send her an email. But not

the one they had just discussed. In a few minutes, she would receive a message from an address she didn't recognize. The subject was "Editor Position in KC."

Dear Ms. Simmons—I got your contact information from our local Russell Reynolds search office here. I believe they may have indicated that they sent your resume to us and that we may have an interest in talking with you.

My business partner and I are starting K.C. Focus, a monthly magazine covering people and events in the Kansas City metropolitan area. We are looking for a senior editor—someone with your background and experience. In scouting around for candidates for this position, your name keeps coming up as the ideal person for the job.

If you are at least willing to have a very preliminary discussion about the position, I'd like to arrange for us to talk by phone in the next few days. I can tell you more about the kind of magazine we have in mind, our target readership and how we envision the role of senior editor. Also, you can give me more details about your work history.

Incidentally, we plan for our inaugural issue to come out this January.

Sincerely,
Walter Fox
Editor-in-Chief
K.C. Focus

Then he sent her the message from Jonathan Winslow, with documents attached.

THIRTY EIGHT

THE PLANE TOOK OFF AT TWO IN THE AFTERNOON. Five hours later, they were led to their deluxe suite overlooking the bay. Bright paintings of regional artists warmed the walls and exquisite textiles covered the seating areas. A large deck, as big as the room itself, jutted out over the beach. Solid, stucco walls extended out on either side of the deck, shielding them from the view of neighboring suites. Two lounge chairs were positioned to face the water, a carved wooden table between them. Resting on the table was a sweating Waterford pitcher filled with the hotel's signature, freshly made margaritas. Even Theo succumbed to the drink, which was more like a martini than the usual sugary slush. They finished the pitcher and almost didn't make it to dinner.

When they finally arrived at the open-air restaurant on the Playa del Sol beach, only one other couple was still there, finishing up their meal. The staff was very accommodating, telling Maribeth and Theo to take their time. They were served fresh seafood and more killer margaritas. After the meal, they lingered over coffee. Maribeth leaned back in her chair and perused the sparkling night sky. She swept her hair up into a small, makeshift bun and fastened it with a sturdy twig. "Almost a whole week of this! I'm not sure I can stand this much relaxation!"

Her hair wasn't cooperating with the twig; strands were loosening on all sides. Theo had to admit that he had never seen her look better. She glowed from every pore. He studied her more closely. It wasn't so much her appearance that was different; it was her entire aura. Of course, she was still far from a knockout; her face was plain, and bulges pulled at the fabric of her dress around her waist. She would never be his type—never even catch his attention under normal circumstances. But there was something appealing about her since she had come to Mexico. Her eyes were closed now, head resting on the back of the chair. There was naturalness about her—a letting go that hadn't been there before. For the first time, he thought he was seeing the real Maribeth, the woman behind the cautious, buttoned-up exterior.

Until now, the idea of an entire week with her uptight moods and banal conversation—not to mention her pudgy body—was something he hadn't been looking forward to. But seeing her across the table now, cheeks flushed with the sea breeze, every bone at ease, he thought it might not be so bad.

Of course, it was all due to the fact that he had finally had sex with her. When she had agreed to go away with him, he'd figured it must obviously mean that she would sleep with him. But nothing had progressed normally so far, so he hadn't been entirely sure.

They had been on their third or maybe fourth margarita on the deck. Their bags were still packed in the room inside. Theo had gotten up to use the bathroom. When he returned, he saw that Maribeth was still lying flat on her lounge chair—topless. If she'd had her eyes open, she would have seen him blink several times, as if to clear his vision.

This was the moment he had waited for; he wasn't going to let it pass, even if she was obviously drunk. Ironic, he thought, that after all this time, it was she who was taking the first step. He started to straddle the lounge chair, but was afraid it wouldn't hold the two of them. So he led her to the bedroom.

When it finally did happen, the first thing he had felt was relief; he hadn't lost his touch after all. Maybe it had taken longer than usual, but then again, she was practically a nun compared with what he was used to. The average guy would never have had the patience to wait this long.

His next thought had been to call Victoria immediately. He couldn't wait to tell her—mostly to reassure her—that Theo, the famed irresistible lover, was back in business. Very carefully, while Maribeth dozed beside him, he had reached into his overnight bag on the bedside table, found his red cell phone and texted. "GOOOOOOOOAL!!!!"

But who knew if the new Maribeth would still be around tomorrow? She'd probably come around from those magical margaritas and be back to her remorseful self, second-guessing her decision to come here with him and appalled that she had slept with him. Who knew? Maybe she'd pack up and leave right away.

As the days floated by, though, the reverse was true. She walked with a light-hearted bounce instead of her typical, determined gait. She wore flimsy sundresses and tank tops, revealing a refreshing, free spirit, along with her newly freckled skin.

Most surprisingly for Theo, her inhibitions virtually disappeared. She was unabashedly flirty, dragging him out to the water so she could jump on his shoulders and ride piggyback. Under their beach umbrella, she pounced on him unexpectedly, tickling him until he begged her to stop. In a turn of events that caught him totally off guard, it was now she who often initiated their lovemaking. Her change in personality was a complete puzzle to him. Finally, on the third day, it came to him. She was happy.

He couldn't wait to tell Victoria about his new girlfriend. He texted her several times a day and snuck in brief phone calls whenever he got the chance.

He and Maribeth spent the whole week doing whatever caught their fancy at the moment, not sticking to a schedule or planning in advance. Most days, they lolled on the beach, swimming, snorkeling, napping and taking their meals at the water's edge. They went into the small town of Zihuatanejo a couple of times, wandering through the silver shops, then stopping for outrageously good carnitas and chicken mole.

On their last evening, Theo surprised Maribeth with a private dinner in a secluded cove on the beach. They were greeted by a waiter carrying two flutes of champagne. No doubt he thought the tanned, relaxed couple were newlyweds on their honeymoon. A small spit had been set up on the sand, the aroma of slow-cooked barbecued pork enticing them to the table.

After dessert, they took a final walk on the beach. Like a carefully crafted movie set, their path was lit by a full moon. Cool waves lapped at their bare toes. Theo held her hand. For a long time, they strolled in silence.

"I say, what's this?" Theo bent down, picking up something out of the sand. It glinted as he held it in front of them. It was a thin necklace; in its center a silver mollusk, with a small black pearl at its core. "What a find! You should wear it. It looks like it was made for you!" he said, holding the necklace at her throat.

"We should turn it in at the hotel—see if anyone lost it."

"No, I think you were meant to have it," Theo insisted.

She took the necklace and played with the centerpiece, studying it from all angles. She held it up to the moonlight, examining a particular surface, then gasped, "Rufus! You're crazy!"

Theo laughed. "I told you it was made for you. You should listen more carefully."

She held the mollusk centerpiece up to the moon, letting the light shine on her name, which had been etched on the back.

Theo put his arm around her. "Here's to the real Maribeth, emerging from her shell, so that all can see her beauty," he said, fastening the necklace behind her neck, then giving her a long kiss.

She fingered the mollusk for a while, then let it drop to her chest. He drew her to him as they continued their walk. She kept touching her hand to her throat, cradling the pendant. From the corner of his eye, he thought he could see tears beginning to form. When he turned to get better look, they were gone. But a certain seriousness had settled on her face.

They continued walking for almost an hour without exchanging a word. The Maribeth beside him was not the same woman he had grown to know—and even, he hated to admit, somewhat like—over the last week. Almost with each step, he could see her reverting back to her former self. He watched as her eyes resumed their regular, steady gaze, seeming to steel themselves for whatever lay ahead.

They treaded silently along the beach, arms around each other, her stride labored and reluctant, until they arrived at the hotel grounds. He felt her shiver. The strands in her neck tightened and she raised her chin.

"We have to leave tomorrow." Her voice had an expressionless, resolute tone.

He tried to cheer her up, to bring back the vibrant, carefree woman of the last few days. There would be more trips, he assured her. Now that she had sold her house and her divorce was about to be finalized, there was nothing to stop them from traveling all the time, he told her.

She stopped and traced an outline in the sand with her big toe. "I may be moving to Kansas City," she ventured, not looking at him.

The subject of possibly relocating to Kansas City had come up a few times before, but Theo acted surprised at her revelation. Why would she want to go now, just when their relationship was deepening, he asked, just when she would be free of some of the burdens that had worried her all these months? Why not take some time off and have fun together?

"Well, I've actually been contacted about a potential job out there. It looks like the market for my kind of work is better there than in the Bay Area." She looked away from him, her toe tracing a design into the sand. "I told you before that I'd feel more comfortable financially if I got a job. Besides that, though, more and more I've been thinking that I really want to go back to work, to have a career. And except for having met you—which is a big exception for sure—I really have no ties to the Bay Area. It holds bad memories for me. I don't think I can keep living there, just too many reminders of Charlie."

Theo watched her closely. She was looking out into the bay, seemingly at a point far in the distance. All of a sudden, her mouth gave the merest hint of a smile. "I just know it will work out in Kansas City," she said. "I have it on good authority."

It was, indeed, the old Maribeth who returned to the suite. The one he'd known in San Francisco. She changed into pajamas, which she hadn't worn all week, then slumped into bed. Theo tried to nuzzle her, but she squirmed away. "Sorry, I just don't feel like it tonight," she said.

Maribeth's glum humor continued the next day. She wore a thick sweater on the flight home and with it, her usual, guarded air. He tried to engage her in the easy banter they had enjoyed in Mexico, but it didn't work. It was as if their time in Zihuat had never happened. He pried for clues as to why things had changed so suddenly between them. Had he done something to upset her?

No, she assured him, it was just that the reality of returning to the Bay Area was setting in. Vacation was over and she had to get back to normal life.

But this could be their normal life, Theo insisted. They could leave for another vacation tomorrow, if she wanted to. Hell, they could just hop on another plane once they landed in San Francisco and take off for someplace else.

No, she had things to attend to: interviewing for positions in Kansas City, tying up some loose ends with the divorce, among others. Maribeth faced him with a steady gaze. He saw her grip tighten on the armrest. So what about Kansas City, she asked him. Would he visit her there if she moved? Her eyes searched his in the seconds it took him to answer.

Of course, Theo assured her. But he had hoped that they could spend some more time together in San Francisco before she made the decision to move.

Maribeth looked away, staring out the cabin window as dusk settled among the clouds. Her fingers rolled over the pearl at the center of her necklace.

Theo drove her home from the airport. Victoria had successfully negotiated a one-month, rent-back clause for Maribeth so that she would have the time to decide where to live next. Theo set her bags down in the foyer. Taking her hands in his, he pulled Maribeth to him, wrapped his arms around her and searched for her lips with his. She stiffened under him.

"Hey, what happened to my Mexican girlfriend?" he joked.

"She just has a lot on her mind. She'll be back, don't worry!"

Somehow, he doubted it. "In a jiffy, I hope!" he teased.

"I'll talk to you tomorrow," she kissed him lightly before he walked out the door.

He pulled out of the driveway and sped down the hill, elated that his job was virtually done. A Metallica tuneblasted from the radio and he turned it up even louder, the raw sound echoing his thrill at having pulled it off once again. Just a couple more days and he would be a continent away and a million dollars richer. Not bad for three months of work.

A Mexican flag waved from a roadside restaurant, reminding him of the week that had just passed. He frowned for a moment, thinking about Maribeth's odd change of mood at the end. An unpleasant feeling rippled through him—as though the joy he had felt was oozing out slowly, leaving a sour taste in its place. It was something he hadn't felt for a very long time, and he had difficulty naming it. Finally, he realized what it was. Guilt.

THIRTY NINE

CAROLINA'S HANDS TREMBLED as she took the manila envelope out of her bag. Her eyes seemed to have sunk further into her face since her last visit to Vera. She wore her hair down this time, the thick, dark strands falling around her face like a mourning veil. The top two buttons of her tailored blouse were unfastened, revealing a classic double strand of pearls, a wedding gift from her husband, Vera knew.

Carolina handed the envelope over to Vera, shaking her head. "The proof you told me about. I got it."

The photos were of men coming and going from Victoria's house. For each visitor, there were two photos, time- and date-stamped for arrival and departure. Some had stayed only a couple of hours, some the entire night. The very first photo was of a smiling Josh walking toward Victoria's front door at 8:05 p.m. The next was of him, on his way back to his car, his shirt untucked and partially unbuttoned and his jacket thrown over his shoulder. The time stamp read 1:03 a.m.

Vera glanced through the next few prints, which included evidence of two more visits by Josh. She shuffled through the rest of the images feeling slightly nauseous; photo after photo of different men, one after the other. She flipped through the photos, stopping at one almost at the end of the stack. For a split second, her hand froze. Quickly recovering, she moved on to the rest. "I'm so sorry, Carolina," she said. "I honestly didn't know the proof would take such a shocking form."

She arranged the pictures back into a neat stack. As she was returning them to the envelope, she lost her grip and they scattered to the floor. Both women reached down to retrieve them. When they were back in the envelope, Vera folded her hands, leaned forward toward Carolina and said gently, "So you haven't told Josh about the photos, or discussed any of this with him?"

Carolina shook her head miserably.

"Why do you suppose you were sent all these pictures of this woman with other men, besides Josh?"

"At first, I couldn't figure it out. It seemed weird. I mean, why would I care about the other men? And then I realized. Those pictures weren't just for me to see. They were for Josh, too."

With a sickening lurch in her stomach, Vera knew she was right. "What are you going to do?" she asked.

"Well, I'm going to leave him, of course. Isn't that the only thing I *can* do under the circumstances?"

Vera's tone was kind. "Theoretically, there are a number of options. But for you, you're right. The relationship can never be salvaged and so it should end. But Carolina, he is the one who should leave, not you. Why should you uproot yourself? He is the one who failed the marriage, so he should be the one to move out. You are going to have a difficult enough time getting through this without having to worry about finding another place, packing up and moving."

Carolina agreed that this made sense, but said she couldn't imagine staying in the home they had lived in together, where she would be reminded constantly of him.

Vera nodded, then her lips curled into the tiniest smile. "You won't be alone for long," she said. She explained that, difficult as it may be for Carolina to consider at this point, in the next year she would meet someone who would turn out to be a lifelong partner. And within a couple of years, she would be happily remarried and starting a family. "I know it sounds hard to believe right now, but you'll see."

Carolina shook her head firmly, as though that would be the last thing she could ever imagine. She did concede, though, that it made sense to make Josh move out.

The two discussed how Carolina should approach the topic with Josh. They agreed that the best way was to show him the pictures and ask him to leave immediately. "Yes, I should tell him to leave right away," she said, her voice breaking.

Vera couldn't help feeling particular empathy for this client. Something about what this young woman was going through hit Vera more personally than most cases she encountered. Part of it, of course, was that her own niece was responsible for Carolina's misery. But it was more than that. Oddly, it was almost as though Vera was going through the break-up herself ... or as though she had already gone through it herself. Except that she hadn't. At least not in this life.

It was unfortunate that Carolina wasn't in a frame of mind to believe that things would turn around totally in a year, Vera thought. If only there were some way she could persuade her. This was one of the most frustrating things about her profession. People sought her out to learn about their future. But when she told them something they didn't expect or, worse yet, didn't want, they didn't believe her. Strangely, that phenomenon also applied to predictions they felt were too good to be true. How could she make people believe that what she was saying about the future would really happen when it wasn't what they came to hear? Only by having the future prove her right, she supposed. And that took time.

After ushering Carolina to the door, she returned to her armchair and retrieved the two images she had wedged under the seat cushion of the armchair. "*Ti si čuk!*" she said, the Slovenian slang for "You're a fool." It wasn't enough for her niece to decimate Carolina. She had to make a fool out of Josh, too. Why couldn't she just have broken up with him? Why not just tell him she was seeing other men, or no longer cared for him? Why the pictures?

But she knew why. Words could be reinterpreted, remembered inaccurately. Pictures could not have a different meaning, could not be disputed. They would last forever. That selfish little bitch. Her niece was so intent on carrying out her own brand of retribution on the world that she almost self-destructed, taking Vera and Theo with her. They could have all been ruined, Vera's own career finished.

She stared at the two prints, which showed Victoria and Theo entering Victoria's home, Theo's suitcase in tow, then Theo leaving the next morning. She felt a sharp twinge of anger in her chest. What if these photos had ended up in the wrong hands? Proof positive of a connection—a very strong connection—between Victoria and Theo. Now she understood the premonition she'd had upon first meeting Carolina. Were it not for the coincidence of Carolina's visit … She stopped herself. There are no coincidences, of course. This was meant to happen. But what was she supposed to do with what had been given to her?

Slipping the photos into a plain white envelope, she walked over to her bookcase. She selected *Postojnska Jama*, a photo book depicting one of the most famous of Slovenia's natural wonders—a twelve-mile labyrinth of subterranean passages filled with spectacular stalagmites and stalactites. She lodged the envelope in the centerfold of the book, a panorama of the center of the caves, which served as a concert hall for 10,000 people. The answer would come to her, she was sure.

FORTY

THEY WERE SAILING ON THE BAY. It was a glorious day—sun for miles, the brisk breeze inflating the sail like an enormous pillow. Their cheeks were flush with the sea air and the thrill of new love.

She pulled her chunky sweater closer around herself and reached for another chocolate-chip cookie from the batch they had made last night. Her tongue was savoring the bitter sweetness when he wrapped his arms around her from behind. They stood as a single entity, facing the wind, sea and sky blending together in the horizon ahead. Victoria could not remember feeling more content, more totally at ease. She could be herself, no need for artifice, no need to measure up. She rested her head against his chest and looked up, noting for the first time that he looked remarkably like her father, or maybe it was just the unusual angle that made it seem so. His chin stuck out in much the same way and his thick, dark brows sprouted out like a thatched roof. He had that same ruddy coloring, as if he had spent much of his life outdoors. But that's where the similarities ended.

With her father, she had always been on guard, ready to retreat, ready to protect. She had developed that extra skin, that extra self, to absorb whatever he might sling her way. But now, with this man, it was different. For the first time, she was only herself, exposed to the core, fragile.

Just then, the boat shifted direction slightly, the waves jarring the clamp on the starboard side so that it knocked loudly and rhythmically against the wood. She sank further into his strong frame, reveling in the warmth of his body, feeling so safe. The banging noise became louder and more insistent. She burrowed her face in his arm, nudging the solid muscles, but found only the softness of her pillow. The banging was furious now—not against the boat, but at her front door, interspersed with staccato bursts of the doorbell being punched.

She leapt out of bed and glanced at the clock—twelve twenty-seven in the morning. The illuminated numbers pulsed in the dark. Grabbing her robe, she flew down the stairs to the door. She flattened her eye against the peephole. Josh. His eyes were on fire and he was yelling, "Victoria, goddammit! Open up!" his fist pounding at the door.

Once inside, he grabbed her shoulders. "How could you do it?" His face was scarlet; his cheeks sopped with tears. He was shaking her now. "We were so good together. We talked about the future. I was going to leave her. How could you?"

"Josh, what happened?" She knew Carolina had received the pictures, but he didn't seem upset that they had been caught. It was something else.

His voice choking between sobs, he told her that her house had been watched. Someone—probably a private investigator—had taken photos of his visits and sent them to Carolina.

"I'm so sorry, Josh. Carolina must have been furious."

"I don't give a shit about her; we were over anyway, a long time ago. I'm glad she found out. Now I don't have to tell her. But you ... How could you?"

"What are you talking about?"

He grabbed her under the arms and pulled her to him. "Those other men, goddammit. You were cheating on me!"

Victoria wrestled away from him. "I never talked about it being an exclusive relationship. You were still married. I assumed you were still sleeping with her."

"But I told you I loved you. I told you I was leaving her."

Victoria gazed back at him calmly, detached, taking in his devastation, his desperation. "I never said I loved you and I never asked you to leave her. Yes, we were having a good time. It was fun. But that's all, Josh."

For a moment, she thought he was going to hit her. The fury seemed to pour out of his whole body. He was vibrating with it. His arms went for her. Then, at the last minute, he held himself back. She could tell it took all of his energy not to touch her. His eyes bulged in disbelief as the reality sank in. It had all been just for fun. His anger crumbled into despair.

He bit his lower lip to keep it from trembling and started to reach for her again. This time she thought he was going to embrace her. But again, he held back. He shook his head, then brushed past her to the door. Just before closing it behind him, he looked back at her as though he couldn't believe it was really her, that this had really happened. Then he was gone.

She poured herself a Courvoisier, chose a Coltrane selection from her playlist and stretched out on the moss-colored suede chaise lounge. Outside, the houseboat lights swayed back and forth; beyond them, the hills of Belvedere twinkled. She felt sorry, she admitted to herself. She really did like Josh.

And maybe, if she had let it go on for much longer, it could have turned into something else. All the more reason to nip it now.

Experience had taught her that painful though it was, this was the best way to do it. Or better said, because it was so painful, it was best this way. Otherwise, they didn't get it. They would plead, cajole, and come back again and again, thinking she would change her mind. This way, they would always have the image of those other men, leaving her house just after—or before—she had seen them. They would visualize her with the others and they would be enraged, mortified. They couldn't live with the thought that she had been unfaithful, so they would go away for good. No messy remains to clean up.

There was a reasonable chance Josh would resign from Barnaby Wells. He wouldn't want to see her every day, make small talk and pretend nothing had happened. She took another sip of brandy and felt the smooth liquid wash over a small knot of regret, dissolving it slowly.

Victoria switched her mind to more pleasant prospects. Who would be next?

FORTY ONE

THEO STOOD IN FRONT OF THE FRENCH DOORS leading to his deck. The smoky mist blended into the dark waves, making it look like winter anywhere else. But it was August. That was the thing about this place; the seasons changed daily—sometimes hourly. He would miss it. The city suited him.

He felt especially at home in the fog and the wind. Muffled against the chill, shoulders hunched, he could be anyone. He could be as bleak or as brisk as the elements around him and no one would notice. The almost constant coolness was invigorating, keeping his spirits at a perpetual high.

And here, no one stood out. The streets were filled with the ordinary and the extraordinary. Only the occasional tourist gave anyone a second glance. He could be at home and unknown at the same time. Just the way he liked it. He could blend in without knowing a soul. Yes, he would miss it.

◆ ◆ ◆

The next day, almost to the hour, Maribeth was in the lobby of his building. She headed for the apartment manager's office and explained who she was. She had been trying to reach her boyfriend for twenty-four hours, she said. She had called every hour, leaving messages. She had rung his door from the lobby last night and again this morning, and then again now—with no response. She was worried. Could he please let her into Rufus' apartment, just to make sure nothing had happened to him in there, that he wasn't sick or in need of help.

The manager shifted his gaze away from her and studied his hands. "But madam, he moved out yesterday."

She stared at him for several seconds as though he had spoken in a foreign language, then told him it was not possible. Rufus had left his apartment and met her across the street for coffee yesterday. He was to call her later that afternoon, so they could decide where to go for dinner. They had plans to go away to the wine country today. That's why she was concerned.

The manager twirled his garnet pinkie ring nervously as he reiterated the facts. Mr. McCain had, indeed, vacated the building yesterday afternoon.

She refused to believe it and demanded to see his apartment.

The manager shook his head, his kind eyes unsuccessfully suppressing the pity they clearly felt. Reluctantly, he agreed to take her up to the apartment. Damn that McCain. What a cowardly bastard. Why not just tell the poor woman and not have her hear it from a stranger? Why humiliate her? And why saddle him with the task of delivering the news?

He thought about McCain. He was polite enough, didn't complain about anything or make any unreasonable demands. He had been businesslike and matter-of-fact when he signed the three-month lease. The length of his lease was probably a detail he shouldn't share with the young lady who was now in the elevator with him.

The doors slid open and he accompanied Maribeth through the empty rooms. She insisted on examining each one, looking in cabinets and closets as if searching for some trace of something he might have left behind.

"The cleaning service was here earlier today," he told her.

She slammed the medicine cabinet door and marched back toward the elevator. He tried not to look at her—to give her some privacy—on their way down.

♦♦♦

Victoria almost didn't recognize the woman at her door. Dirty blonde strings of hair hung in her face. Her cheeks were crimson—from the wind or fever; Victoria wasn't sure which. Her bloodshot eyes bulged. And she was shivering violently.

"Oh my God, honey, what happened?" She put her arm around Maribeth and led her in. She sat her on the sofa, wrapping a cashmere throw over her shoulders, and poured her a brandy.

For several minutes, Maribeth didn't say a word. She rocked back and forth, staring at the snifter as though mesmerized, the amber liquid forming waves against the glass with her motion. Victoria tried a few times to get her to talk, but finally gave up. She leaned forward, her own glass cupped in her hands, waiting until Maribeth was ready.

Maribeth's first words were a whisper. "He's gone." She gulped her drink. "He's gone," she repeated, as though forcing herself, as well as Victoria, to understand. "It was all an act. He didn't love me. It was a game for him." She spoke in a monotone as if under a spell, telling Victoria about the unanswered calls, the empty apartment. "He just disappeared. I saw him yesterday for coffee. We were supposed to have dinner, but I never saw him again. He actually moved out without telling me! Right after we had coffee, I guess. I keep going over it again and again, wondering what happened—what I did wrong. I can't figure it out.

"I've been driving for the last three hours—with all the windows open—trying to freeze. Trying to stop feeling. I drove back and forth across the bridge. Four times, I think. I drove to Stinson. I drove to the top of Mount Tam. I can't remember where else I drove. I should have known it was too good to be true. A guy like that ..."

Victoria poured her another drink. Maybe it had nothing to do with her, she offered. Maybe something unexpected came up and he had to leave quickly. He would probably call her as soon as he had a chance.

"No. He moved out. All his furniture's gone. He obviously has been planning to leave for a while. He's been playing me this whole time. Once again, I've proven I'm an idiot—a naïve idiot."

"Maybe there's some kind of explanation," Victoria offered.

"Yeah. There's an explanation. He dumped me. Just like Charlie," she spat the words out. "And when I stop and think about it, I realize I really didn't know him at all. He never liked talking about himself. He said as little as possible about his past and his family. I tried to get him to open up, but the more I tried, the more he pushed me away. Whenever I wanted to talk about his business, he got really mad and clammed up. I was so thrilled to think he liked me—maybe even loved me. Hah! What an idiot! I didn't want to risk ruining it by asking him a lot of questions. I didn't want him to think I was chasing him. Now I've lost him and also ..." She stopped and took another gulp of the brandy.

Victoria waited, but the sentence wasn't completed. Should she pursue it? It wouldn't seem right not to. "And also what?"

"Nothing." Maribeth gripped her glass with such force that her fingertips were white.

Victoria thought the glass might shatter. "What is it, hon?"

Maribeth shook her head. "Nothing," she repeated. "It's personal." She took a drink of her brandy, brushed her eyes and looked straight at Victoria. "I've decided to move back to Kansas City. I've got a job lead there. A start-up wants me to interview with them, so I'm going to do it. And even if that doesn't work out, the market's a lot better out there for someone like me." She jutted her chin out defiantly as though daring Victoria to talk her out of it.

"Do you really think you should make a big decision like that now? I mean, you've just had a huge shock. Why not give yourself some time?"

"The only thing keeping me here was Rufus," she said flatly. "And of course, our friendship," she added. Even under severe stress, Victoria noticed, Maribeth was polite to a fault.

"Hon, why don't you spend the night here? I'll order in some dinner. You shouldn't be alone now."

"Thanks, Victoria. It's nice of you to offer. You've been a good friend—my only friend here, as it turns out." She gave a harsh laugh. "I really appreciate everything you've done for me. You got me through a horrible bad patch. I wouldn't have met Rufus if it weren't for you."

Victoria blinked. "What? I had nothing to do—"

"I would never have gone to that wine-tasting event where I met him if you hadn't taken me there. But more than that, I would never have had the confidence to start dating him. You did that for me. You helped me see that there could be life after Charlie, that I could be happy again. I owe you a lot for that.

"But it's clear that it was all a game for him. This place

will always remind me of him—and Charlie. I want a fresh start. So, I'm leaving tomorrow night. I decided. I just have to confirm my moving arrangements and then do one more thing and I'll be on the plane. I'm sorry to dump all this drama on you. I just had to talk to someone about what happened. You're the only person who really knows me here, the only one I can really talk to. I thought it was only fair to tell you in person that I was leaving." She reached for a fresh tissue. "Sorry, it seems like you always get the brunt of my breakdowns."

Victoria tried again to convince her to delay her decision, or at least to stay the night, but Maribeth had made up her mind.

"I do hope we can stay in touch," she told Victoria as they stood at the door. "Maybe you can come and visit me once I get settled?"

Victoria nodded. Maribeth gave her a hug, then left.

Victoria pulled out her red cell phone. She smiled broadly as she punched in the numbers. Disappointed that he didn't answer, she waited for the tone. "You cad," she said with a giggle. "Up and left the poor thing without even saying goodbye. Is that how your sister brought you up? Damn right! Anyway, Dorothy's off to Kansas City tomorrow. So, it's game, set and match!

"On to the future now. When are you going back to Geneva? I need to see you lots before you go. And we have to plan our vacation getaway! I'm thinking maybe we can meet in Australia in a couple of months? Oh, and we have to get together with Teta Vera to celebrate. So much to talk about. Call me. Call me!"

♦♦♦

Vera could hear the agitated voice getting louder as it approached her office. "I don't care if I don't have an appointment," it was shouting.

"Please wait a moment, Ms. Simmons." Cynthia was in quick pursuit, trying to stop her. "I'll see if Ms. Peterlin is available."

"She'd better be available. She ruined my life." Maribeth swung Vera's door open.

Vera, of course, had expected that Maribeth might return to see her. Two former victims had come back after they had lost Theo and their money. They had been distraught and panicked—and angry. But not as much as Maribeth; she was in far worse shape than either of them. Normally composed and well-groomed, Maribeth looked like she hadn't used a hairbrush or showered in days. She wore a stained sweatshirt, zipped halfway up, revealing what looked like an oversized sleeping T-shirt underneath. Her face was raw anger, eyes slit with venom directed straight at Vera.

"I'm sorry, I tried to—" Cynthia began.

"Don't worry, Cynthia, you can leave us," Vera interjected.

Maribeth stepped into Vera's office and slammed the door behind her. "It's you who should worry," she spat out. "Everything you told me was wrong. I followed your advice and lost my money and my boyfriend. I want you to explain yourself. And to fix it." Her whole body shook with the words.

FORTY TWO

THE SLAVIC ACCENT ON THE VOICEMAIL message took her back to her high school days. "Vera Peterlin! How wonderful to hear of you again, even though not directly. I trust you are doing well. It has been too many years since we have seen each other. This is Henry Drobnick, by the way. You referred a young man to me—Wyatt Slade. His father, Nick Slade, brought him in a few days ago. The young man has one of the most severe cases of Adner's-type ADD that I've ever seen. But the good news is, I am sure I can help him. His father seemed very grateful. I wanted to thank you for the referral. I will be able to use his case in my research. But equally importantly, I wanted to say hello. Maybe one of these years we can get together and talk about the old days in Ljubljana. That would be nice.

"Again, I hope you are well. Please call me when you can. I would love to talk with you in person and hear what you are doing." He left his number.

◆◆◆

Leticia Dubois from the FBI was in the reception room waiting for Vera. Earlier that day, Ms. Dubois had called Vera's office, asking to see her as soon as possible. When Cynthia told Vera about the call, a stab of worry took root in the pit of Vera's stomach. It had spread throughout her body. A solid chunk now lodged in her throat.

While the Bureau's behavioral-science expert did seek her out from time to time for help with cases, it was not he who had asked to see her this time. And generally, when he wanted her help with a specific case, he would say so when setting up the meeting.

Vera could think of only one other reason that the FBI might want to see her. Her insides lurched at the thought. Maybe she was wrong, though, she tried to reassure herself. Until now, all of the victims of Victoria's schemes had been too embarrassed to go to the authorities. While Maribeth had certainly been livid when she burst in to see her, she had given no indication that she thought Vera had done anything illegal, just that she had been totally wrong in everything she had predicted. Vera chewed the inside of her lip, smoothed her skirt and told Cynthia to let Ms. Dubois in.

The woman who entered did not look at all as Vera had pictured her. Vera chided herself inwardly. How could she herself have fallen for the same stereotypic thinking that others applied to her own profession? She had pictured Ms. Dubois as a brusque, mannish type, but she was actually a very attractive woman—probably a few years younger than Vera. She had flawless dark-brown skin, which seemed to glow from within. Her straight, bluntly cut hair skimmed her chin. Bangs were swept to the side, revealing the most luminous amber eyes Vera had ever seen. She was tall and carried herself with an air of confidence that emphasized her stature.

Used to being in charge, Leticia got straight to the point. "I'm here to talk about Nick Slade."

Vera savored an exquisite wave of relief, ensuring that not an ounce of it registered on her face.

"I understand that you are the one who blew the whistle on him," Ms. Dubois continued. "I'd like you to tell me everything you know about how he was able to siphon money from Bottom Line. How long, exactly, has he been doing it? Were there others involved, or was he acting on his own? Has he ever done this at other companies?"

Vera shifted in her chair, stifling a smile. It was always the same. Law-enforcement officers approached her ability to give them information as though they were accessing an Internet search engine. She had to explain that it didn't work that way. She proceeded to do the same with Leticia Dubois.

"When I am in the presence of people, things come to me. Usually, they come in no particular order, and they are generally not concrete, but abstract. For instance, it may start with a name—someone the person knows who is having a significant impact on that person's life at the moment. And then that name may develop into a type of energy that is being created by the two people together. I may then see how that energy is likely to progress and what the ultimate outcome may be. But notice, I've said 'may' all along. Sometimes my understanding of what is taking place—and why it is taking place and how it will end—is very clear. At other times, it can be quite murky, either because the subject is frightened of what they might hear, or because for whatever reason, they don't want me to delve into certain aspects of their life. Or sometimes my energy is simply tuned to a different frequency than my client's." *Like my experience with Maribeth Simmons*, she thought. She shuddered, remembering Maribeth's most recent visit.

Ms. Dubois' brows knitted as her analytical mind struggled with the intuition-based data being given to her. Vera turned to the specific subject her visitor had come to discuss. Going to her desk, she extracted a file and returned to her seat. She opened the folder and studied the notes from her session with Nick Slade.

For almost an hour, Vera took Leticia Dubois through the details of what she had been able to glean of Slade's scheme and how it was executed. She explained to Ms. Dubois that she couldn't give her any additional information about Slade or speculate about what he might have done in the past without seeing him again. She could report only on knowledge that had come to her from their face-to-face session.

Leticia Dubois made some further notes, then closed her black-leather portfolio. Vera started to get up, assuming the meeting had ended, when her visitor said, "Can I ask you about something else?"

Surprised, Vera sat back down, the wave of worry making itself known again. Her guest's demeanor had changed, she noticed. No longer the self-assured professional, the woman was blushing slightly, her formerly straight back losing its tautness, as though it had suffered a blow. "It's about a personal matter," she confessed.

Vera relaxed again, but was puzzled. Law-enforcement types had never asked her for personal advice before. Usually, the fact-driven mindset required for their profession was at exact odds with the need for an intuitive interpretation of what was taking place in their private lives. But here was an exception.

Ms. Dubois was clearly having trouble articulating whatever personal problem she wanted to bring up with Vera. "You see," she said, then stopped. She tried again. "A few weeks ago …" but again lost her footing.

Finally, it came spilling out. Her husband had recently

left her. He had fallen in love with someone else—younger, she assumed, though he hadn't been willing to share the details. He was an executive with one of the biggest wine distributors in the country, based in Napa Valley. She and her husband had built up a comfortable nest egg, which they were now in the process of dividing up in the course of the split.

"There are a couple of things I'd like to know," Leticia said. "First, who is she? What is she like?"

There it was again, that inevitable question. Uncanny how regardless of the type of relationship that had existed between the couple—whether they had been a close, loving couple or one that slept in separate bedrooms and led disparate lives, the question was always the same.

"Ms. Dubois, I'm so sorry to hear that this has happened to you."

"Please call me Leticia. And please, tell me anything you can about this woman."

Vera closed her eyes and focused. "Eva," she said. "Her name is Eva Stahl. She works in the valley, also in the wine business, like your husband. That's how they met." She let the images float forward. "You are right. She is younger than you—by about twenty years." She didn't disguise the disdain in her voice. "I'm sorry to have to confirm this. Does that help?" she asked, opening her eyes.

"I want to know more about her. What does she look like? What is her personality? I bet she follows him around like a puppy and waits on him hand and foot like I never did, right?" A mixture of pain, anger and hatred hissed in her voice. Vera barely recognized the dignified, almost regal, Leticia Dubois she had met an hour earlier.

Reluctantly returning to her trance, Vera described the dark-haired, brown-eyed beauty. Unfortunately for Leticia, Eva was not the bimbo type. That news would have been easier to take—and to deliver. Instead, she portrayed a very sharp, well-traveled businesswoman who earned more than Leticia's husband.

Upon hearing this, Leticia's spine crumpled a couple of inches further. Then she seemed to get a hold of herself and it straightened again. "Okay. So, what's going to happen to me after this? Am I going to meet someone, or am I going to be alone from now on?"

Her visitor was back to the direct, logical approach she had used for the initial subject of her consultation. Vera thought it unusual, though, that someone in her situation had moved on so quickly to focusing on the future. Carolina's reaction was more typical—dwelling on what had happened and needing time before being able to move forward. Vera returned to her reverie. There would not be anyone special for quite a few years, she told Leticia reluctantly. She would meet men, go out with them a few times, but nothing lasting would come of it. She would find that many of them would be intimidated by her job, her self-sufficiency and toughness. There would be one, finally, who would be worth the wait—a writer, journalist—something like that. The two would be together until the end, she told her.

Leticia nodded slowly, as though taking it in. "What about financially?" she asked. "I don't know much about investing and that sort of thing. Everett took care of all that."

"It looks like you will be fine," Vera said. "I don't see any difficulties in that area."

"But are there specific things I should invest in?" she asked pointedly.

Taken aback, Vera opened her eyes and frowned. "Leticia, I don't give financial advice."

"Oh, I just thought maybe ..." Leticia's voice trailed off, seemingly embarrassed. "You know, since you can see what's going to happen, I figured you'd know about those kinds of things, too."

Vera didn't buy her client's attempt at naiveté. There was something alarming about the direction the session was taking. She looked at her watch. "I'm very sorry, but I have an appointment with another client in a few minutes."

Immediately reverting to her professional persona, Leticia thanked Vera for her assistance in the Slade matter, and for helping her with her personal issues. She asked Vera to bill her separately for the second part of their session.

Vera closed the door behind her and went to her desk. She withdrew a cigarette from the hiding place in the drawer and opened the window. She noticed her hand was quivering slightly as she lit the end. Someone had gotten wind of something. Or thought they had. She reminded herself, as she had so many times in the last few weeks, that this was the last time for her. Assuming it wasn't already too late.

She went over to the bookcase, extracted the picture book of Postojnska Jama and removed the two pictures of Victoria and Theo that she had kept from Carolina's last visit. She knew what she had to do next.

◆◆◆

Victoria's red cell phone rang. Her aunt got straight to the point. Though she spoke slowly and without emotion, there was no mistaking the fury behind her words. And something else, too, something she had never heard in her aunt's voice. Panic.

"Victoria, you must meet me immediately. Theodore, too—the Sheraton, Chinatown. I've made Theodore a reservation there for tonight. I will see you both in his room at eight o'clock this evening. I am calling him as soon as I hang up with you."

"But, Teta Vera, I have plans for tonight."

"You certainly do. You are meeting me at the hotel at eight o'clock." The icy crispness hung in the air after she hung up.

FORTY THREE

SUDDENLY, A FEW MINUTES AFTER THE CALL was over, Victoria felt it. That odd, disoriented sensation, as though she had left her body and the present time and was hovering above, viewing the scene from another perspective, another sphere. The vision played out like an old film, frame by frame, the motions jerky and somewhat out of focus. Horses racing around a track, then a zoom in on a majestic stallion, taut muscles moving smoothly, lustrous mane shimmering in the wind, hoofs pounding in a rhythmic gallop as it approached the fence, sailing into the air, first the front limbs, then the hind ones, easily clearing the top, then returning to the ground, but at the last instant—a catch, the right hind hoof brushing the edge, throwing off the graceful balance, pitching the glorious frame awkwardly forward, the front legs buckling, the body meeting the ground with an awful thud, an unearthly wail coming from the stallion's throat.

FORTY FOUR

CHINATOWN WAS BUSTLING THAT NIGHT, as usual. Produce shopkeepers and butchers locked up their businesses and scurried to their small apartments up the stairs off garbage-can-lined alleyways. Groups of loud men—out-of-towners there for a sales convention, no doubt—traipsed raucously through the neighborhood, headed for the peep shows on Broadway. Everyday tourists, with more family-style fare in mind, wandered through the emporiums selecting cheap souvenirs, or settled around tables to sample Chinese food the locals wouldn't touch.

Nobody paid any attention to the pizza delivery guy carrying his thermal warmer box. He walked at a good clip, hoodie over his head and plastic money belt around his waist. He entered the Sheraton, saluted the desk clerk and pushed the "Up" button for the elevator. One would have had to look very closely to notice the French manicured nails wrapped around the plastic warmer handle.

Not ten minutes later, a fit-looking woman in a black running suit and wearing bright blue ear pods pushed the same "Up" button. She was flushed from her workout, but perfectly dry wisps of ash-blonde hair floated out from under her Nike baseball cap.

She took off the cap as soon as she entered the room. Victoria and Theo had already started on the pizza. She could tell they were nervous. They knew she was normally ultra-cautious about being seen with them in the Bay Area, so for her to have insisted on this meeting with only a few hours' notice meant something unpleasant was up. She knew that they would be totally unprepared for what she was about to tell them.

"The FBI is on to us." Her voice shook.

They stared at her. She could tell they were each beginning to formulate a question, but she broke in. In the same agitated voice she had used earlier in the day when she phoned them, she told them about Leticia Dubois' visit.

"What? She asked you for investment advice?" Victoria moved to the edge of her chair.

"Of course, I acted shocked and offended that she should ask such a question, and she quickly backed off."

"Good!" Victoria slid back.

"But then, just before she left, she told me she was investigating another matter and asked if I would mind if she showed me a couple of pictures. I was a little taken aback, but I said sure. Then she showed me these photos and asked if I knew the people in them. Of course, I said I didn't."

Vera whisked the pictures from the pocket of her jacket and handed them to Victoria. Victoria saw a fury she had never seen before in her aunt's eyes. She focused on the images and her blood froze. For several seconds, she thought she was going to pass out. A cold sweat broke out on her forehead. Her mind raced. *What? Who? When did ...?* And finally, *how could you have been so stupid?* She noticed that the hand holding the prints was shaking. Then she realized it was her own hand. She had lost all feeling in her extremities.

Theo was watching his sister with increasing concern. He reached over to take the pictures from her. When he saw them, a visible jolt went through his body, as though from an electric current. "Bloody hell. How did this happen? We were being watched?" He looked first at his aunt, then at Victoria for an answer.

But Victoria was using all of her energy to remain conscious. The room was tipping drunkenly to the left. She gripped both sides of her armchair and forced herself to inhale and exhale. She saw the bottle of wine Theo had brought for their meeting and asked him to pour her a glass. She downed it in successive gulps without pausing. Placing the glass to the side, she tried to collect herself and concentrate on how the pictures could possibly have made their way to the FBI.

The photographer she had hired had taken them. She was pretty sure of that. He had called her a couple weeks ago to confirm he had finished his assignment and asked what she wanted him to do next. She caught her breath as she recalled their quick exchange over the phone. He had taken about fifty pictures and was about to mail them to Carolina—did Victoria want to look at them first? She said no.

She was slipping. No, she had already slipped—badly. She was done. A year ago, this would never have happened. Here was yet another enormous mistake in a string of blunders over the last couple of months. But this one was fatal. For five times in a row now, she had executed things perfectly, without even a minor misstep. But now, one screwup after another culminated in a huge, spectacular, glaring error. Allowing this to get into the hands of the FBI was unforgivable, she thought, looking at the pictures that showed Theo and her, at her front door, smiling broadly, his suitcase in tow—then leaving the next morning. *You monumental, colossal fuck-up!*

Her voice trembling badly, she explained to Vera and Theo about the photographer—her way of breaking up with Josh. The photos had been taken by him, no doubt.

"But how did the FBI get them?" Theo asked.

"That's the part I can't figure out," Victoria said. She was biting the cuticle of the little finger on her left hand so hard that it started bleeding badly. "I know Josh's wife was very upset by the pictures—well, the ones with Josh, obviously. And Josh was out of his mind when he saw them. But I can't think why either of them would have a reason to go to the FBI." Then something occurred to her. "Wait a minute. Teta Vera, you saw Carolina. Did she mention anything about the pictures?"

"She said she had received photographs—but of course she was focused on the ones of Josh and you. She said there were several more of you with other men, but nothing more specific. She had no reason to care about those, really. She figured out that they were sent mainly for Josh's benefit— and, of course, she made sure he saw them." Vera paused for a moment, appearing to give the matter more thought. "When Josh came over to your house that last time, did he bring the pictures with him, or ask you who the men were?"

"No. He didn't bring the pictures or ask who the men were. He was just so upset that I was seeing other men when he apparently thought we had a future together."

Vera continued, "We have to consider the possibility that it wasn't your photographer who took these two particular shots, but the FBI itself. Maybe one of our former victims went to the police after all. Maybe they put two and two together. Maybe they've been following us all along on this one." Vera felt a shiver as she recounted this possibility. Of course, she knew Victoria's photographer had actually taken the pictures and that he had sent them to Carolina. There was no reason to believe that the FBI knew of the photos' existence. On the other hand, that didn't mean that the FBI *hadn't* been watching them. After all, they had sent Leticia Dubois to try to trap her. They must know something.

"Well, I'm leaving tomorrow morning anyway," Theo said. "But Vic ..." his voice trailed off.

"I have to leave right away, too. I have no choice." Victoria said numbly. She played with the Buddha centerpiece of her necklace, the one Maribeth had given her.

"Where will you go?" he asked.

"Travel for a while. Get some rest. I've got to get myself together. I'll call you both next week to let you know my plans."

"Yes. You definitely must leave. And quickly," Vera agreed. "Do let me know once you decide where you're going and what you're going to do." She shifted in her seat. "I will be out of the country for the next couple of weeks, though."

The surprise announcement jarred Victoria from her own preoccupied state. Vera hadn't mentioned anything about a trip the last few times they spoke. "Where are you going?"

There was an awkward pause. Vera cleared her throat. "Jake and I are going to Tuscany." She delivered the statement in a controlled, matter-of-fact way, as though she were reading from a business report. But Victoria and Theo instantly knew the importance of the news.

Their aunt had always been very private about her personal life. She avoided discussing it, even with them, the only close family she had left. Whenever they spoke, she was quick to focus the conversation on them: how they were doing, what they were up to, and so on. When pressed about what was happening in her own life, she always reverted to the topic of her work. Ever the professional, she rarely mentioned individual client names, but talked in general about business transactions she was working on or ways she was trying to help individual clients.

Victoria knew who Jake was, because Vera had mentioned his name a few times as a longtime and valued client. This fact alone was out of the ordinary enough that Victoria had wondered why her aunt had allowed this slip. Now that she thought about it, she could recall only a couple of other men's names that her aunt had ever mentioned.

Under normal circumstances, hearing about her aunt's upcoming trip with Jake would have caused Victoria to jump up, hug her and generally make a big deal about the revelation. But she was still physically sick from the shock of her life and so could barely muster a lukewarm, "That's fantastic, Teta! I'm so, so happy for you!"

Theo chimed in with his congratulations and did manage to embrace her, albeit stiffly.

"It's just a trip, my dears," Vera brushed it off. "And in view of our larger problem, very inconsequential."

They went on to discuss when they might see each other again and agreed they would just have to play it by ear, depending on the FBI's next move—if any.

"I just hope I can get out in time," Victoria said in a small voice.

"I do, too, my dear." Vera didn't sound confident. She zipped up the jacket of her tracksuit, pulled the hood over her head and inserted her bright blue ear pods.

They gave each other lingering hugs before they left—not knowing how long it would be before they were together again. All three wondered if they would soon be behind bars.

The woman with the black tracksuit went out of the side door of the hotel, adjusting the ear pod in her right ear. She began with a light trot. Soon she was up to a vigorous run, a smug grin on her face.

FORTY FIVE

FOUR PEOPLE FACED EACH OTHER around the oval table in the sitting room of suite 305 at the Omni Hotel in downtown San Francisco. For almost two hours, Agent Bethany Foster had recapped the events of the last few months, ending with her final visit to Vera Peterlin just a few days earlier.

"Her explanation was perfectly logical," Bethany said. "She pointed out that she had actually never advised me to do anything. She had just predicted events she saw in the future—which, in fact, ended up happening. During our first session, she said I had recently met a man with whom I would have a romantic relationship and described him. It was McCain. She didn't tell me to hook up with him. She just implied that I would. During our second session, she said she saw me investing $2 million, which also came to be. She didn't tell me to do it."

"I thought she told you that the investment was a good one, that it would be profitable, and that more would follow," FBI Field Supervisor Russ Claypack pressed.

"The first time I met with her, she told me that I would learn about an investment through this man whom I recently met. Her exact words were, 'The investment looks very lucrative.' Then, later, she said, 'It looks like a superb investment.' Both statements could be taken to mean it looks like it will be a great investment, but it isn't.

"The second time I met with her, she made a similar comment. She said that I was expecting significant returns from the investment I was considering. Again, you could take that two ways. It's all on tape, of course. You can listen to my visits word for word, if you like."

"I will most certainly do that," said Claypack dryly. "And what about you and McCain living happily ever after in Kansas City?"

"I haven't moved to Kansas City yet," she said with an almost imperceptible smirk.

"It sounds like you're defending Peterlin, Bethany," Claypack observed.

"No. I'm just stating the facts."

"So, let me see if I understand this correctly," Claypack said. "Steeplechase Enterprises was essentially a bank account set up by a C corporation, whose CEO was McCain. Bethany—or Maribeth's—contact for purchasing shares of Steeplechase was Jonathan Winslow of Smythe and Barnes, the private equity firm. Smythe and Barnes' clients do not include anyone named Rufus McCain, even though a printout of McCain's investments through the company were in his copier tray. Smythe and Barnes also never heard of a Jonathan Winslow, even though a Smythe and Barnes business card with Jonathan Winslow's name on it was on McCain's desk. The address on the Smythe and Barnes business card was a p.o. box opened by McCain. The phone number on the fake business card is also linked to a phone in McCain's name. Right so far?"

Bethany nodded.

Claypack continued, "The same day that McCain moved out of his penthouse, that number and his own personal number were disconnected." Presumably, the numbers had to remain operational long enough for Maribeth's check to clear. Then they, along with McCain, could cease to be.

"As soon as Maribeth's funds were deposited into the Steeplechase account, the money was immediately trans-ferred out to an untraceable account in Switzerland and the Steeplechase account was closed. End of story."

"It played out just like it did for Pamela Greenwald and Jennifer Lynche," Leticia Dubois, case agent for the operation, spoke up.

Ms. Greenwald had contacted the FBI office in Little Rock, Arkansas, almost five months ago, at the urging of her brother, who was a police officer there. Reluctantly, and with a great deal of embarrassment, Ms. Greenwald had related her story of having invested $2.5 million in Lightning Fiber-Optics, which turned out to be a non-existent company.

Her story mirrored Maribeth Simmons'. Pamela had lived in Ross, an exclusive neighborhood in Marin County. She was in the process of divorcing her husband, who had already moved out of the house.

Victoria Clifford, from the local Barnaby Wells real estate office, had handled the sale of her property. While her house was on the market, Pamela and Clifford had become friends. Clifford introduced her to a lifestyle she had never known, even though she and her husband were wealthy. Before Clifford, Pamela's life had centered on volunteering with organizations that provided services for homeless and abused children. She and her husband did not have any children of their own. They spent their free time quietly, devoting considerable time to the two horses they owned.

Under Clifford's influence, Pamela Greenwald had

dropped thirty pounds, and started wearing designer clothes and frequenting five-star restaurants. Several attractive eligible men had also begun to take an interest in her at around the same time as her house went on the market. Her volunteer work had fallen by the wayside.

Clifford had also taken Pamela to see Vera Peterlin. Peterlin told Pamela that she would fall in love with a handsome Australian. Indeed, Pamela fell hard for Adam Gossford, who—from Pamela's description—was a dark-haired version of Rufus McCain. Like Maribeth, Pamela had heard her new boyfriend talking on the phone to someone at Smythe and Barnes. He had left financial statements showing Lightning Fiber-Optics stock values on his desk, as well as a summary of the rest of his substantial portfolio, all recorded on stationery with the Smythe and Barnes logo.

Pamela had also found Jonathan Winslow's Smythe and Barnes business card smack in the middle of Adam's desk, where she couldn't miss it. The rest had followed in the same pattern as Claypack had described moments ago. Only the names had changed. Pamela had retreated back home to Arkansas when she realized she had been bilked.

What happened to Jennifer Lynche, the other known victim, had come to the FBI through more tragic circumstances. Her parents had contacted the FBI office in Cleveland, Ohio, after their daughter was killed in an auto accident a few months earlier. In tying up her financial affairs, they noticed that there was no trace of the proceeds from the sale of her former home in Belvedere, California, which had taken place two years previously. As best they could determine, the sale had yielded a profit of $3 million and the title company had deposited that sum into Jennifer's account. A couple of days later, however, Jennifer had written a check for that amount to Crater Technologies. Upon doing some research on the company, her parents had determined that such a company didn't exist—and, in fact, had never existed.

When the FBI's Cleveland office looked into the sale of the Lynche home, they had identified Victoria Clifford of Barnaby Wells as the selling agent. A search of the FBI database revealed that Clifford's name had also come up in the report filed by Pamela Greenwald in Little Rock. It seemed probable that the two cases were connected. Russ Claypack of the FBI's San Francisco office, the office of origin for the case, had been assigned the task of investigating the matter further.

"None of the information McCain gave to rent his penthouse tells us anything?" Claypack asked his team.

Agent Dubois responded. Step by step, she recapped all the actions McCain had taken to set up his identity in San Francisco. "On his applications and paperwork, he identified his employer as, of course, Steeplechase Enterprises and his boss—Jonathan Winslow—with the Winslow phone number for reference purposes. He listed a fake Paris address as his previous residence, which the leasing agent didn't bother to confirm. He paid first and last month's rent with a check drawn on his new account."

The team spent an hour dissecting each element of these transactions for anything they had missed that might give some clue as to McCain's real identity.

Claypack turned to Agent Foster. "Again, at no point when you were with him did he encourage you to invest in Steeplechase?"

"No. Quite the opposite. I tried over and over again to get him to talk about his business and his investments. He absolutely refused. The only way I found out about Steeplechase was from overhearing 'Winslow's' messages and from listening to Rufus talking to him on the phone when he thought I was out of earshot. Or, I guess, when he was sure I was within earshot."

"It was exactly the same for Pamela," Special Agent Mike Garcia interjected.

"And what about ties to Vera Peterlin? Nothing there either?"

Bethany shook her head. "No." She took a breath as if to continue, then stopped.

Claypack caught it. "Yes?"

"Nothing."

"Bethany, we are paying you for your observations."

"Peterlin *is* psychic," Bethany said flatly. "She knew my real name. She knew details about the house where I grew up, my family. If I hadn't spent all that time being trained by Aaron Norris, Peterlin would have easily known I was FBI, too."

Aaron Norris was the FBI's in-house behavioral-science expert. At least, that was the way the payroll roster reflected his title. In reality, he was a psychic, as well. While few in the Bureau would admit to this particular aspect of his expertise, the truth was that Norris was called in frequently to give "his professional advice and counsel" on difficult cases. Norris, in fact, was the FBI representative who occasionally contacted Vera to get any insights she might have on particularly perplexing cases. Norris had worked with Bethany for several weeks to prepare her for her sessions with Peterlin. The Bureau had a good indication from Pamela Greenwald that Peterlin might be involved. They were pretty sure that with respect to her sessions with Pamela, Peterlin was just relaying information that Clifford and Adam Grossman, Pamela's "boyfriend," had given her.

On the other hand, the Bureau recognized that Peterlin had been in business as a psychic for years and actually had psychic powers. They themselves had consulted her from time to time when traditional investigative methods—and even their own Aaron Norris—had failed to shed light on a case. So, it was very likely that when Bethany would be led to visit Vera Peterlin, as they expected she would, Peterlin would actually be able to see Bethany's past and, of greatest concern, her FBI-agent status. Training Bethany how to block Peterlin from "reading" her would be a difficult and tricky task.

Aaron Norris had been brought in to work with Bethany on this. For weeks, through a form of hypnosis, he had taught Bethany how to block her FBI status from Peterlin. Luckily, it had worked. But there hadn't been enough time to work on blocking techniques for other parts of her real identity.

"Really, Vera Peterlin *is* psychic," Bethany repeated. "You know we've used her ourselves for that exact reason."

Mike Garcia was having trouble hiding his smirk.

Leticia shot him a disapproving glance. "I can vouch for her psychic ability, too," she said. She shifted subtly in her chair and looked intently at the glass of water in front of her. "She knew a lot of details about me that she had no way of knowing." A tinge of bitterness curled at the edge of her voice.

Claypack's eyebrows went up, but he looked down at his notepad and flipped some pages. "Okay, let's move on. We can't establish a connection between Victoria Clifford and McCain, either?"

"She brought me to the event where I met Rufus—I mean McCain. That's it," Bethany said.

Garcia spoke up. "I searched her place—no family albums, no personal papers—and her computer was clean."

"What about Anthony Schurer?" Claypack consulted his notes. "That woman at the restaurant who happened to sit next to McCain on the plane from Zurich. She called him Anthony Schurer. Did we find anything on anyone by that name?"

Garcia answered. "Schurer was a university professor in

Zurich. He was an American in his mid-thirties, about McCain's age, when he died two years ago. But someone traveled on a passport under his name a couple of months ago—just happened to fly in to San Francisco from Zurich. And no, no one by that name has used that passport in the last couple of weeks," he ended smugly.

"Of course not," Claypack snapped.

Garcia continued more cautiously. "I spent a couple of hours interviewing Tess Chaplin, the woman who sat next to him on the plane from Zurich. She couldn't really tell me much. She tried to engage him in conversation, but he took a sleeping pill and was out until the next morning. She did say that he looked very uncomfortable when she surprised him at the restaurant. But that was it."

Claypack leafed through his notepad, then slammed it shut.

Thinking he was voicing his boss' thoughts, Garcia piped up. "I can't believe this. We have no hard evidence of a crime here. We don't have anything solid we can pin on any of them. We still don't even know McCain's real name and we can't link him, Victoria Clifford and Vera Peterlin to each other in any way, except circumstantially."

Claypack corrected him. "Impersonating a Smythe and Barnes rep is a crime, as is creating dummy stock statements on their letterhead, as is conspiracy to defraud. So is snorting cocaine, if memory serves. Unfortunately, the calls from Winslow were made from a phone that's nowhere to be found. We can't prove who developed the reports. We did confirm the coke, right, Bethany?"

Bethany nodded. "Yes, from her bag that night at the club."

"But I didn't find any in her townhouse—no rejuvenator jars," said Garcia. "She must have carried it all with her."

"No leads on Victoria Clifford's whereabouts yet?"

Claypack asked.

Garcia shook his head. "She hasn't shown up at Barnaby Wells. She didn't formally quit, just hasn't gone in to work since last Tuesday, which interestingly, is the day Leticia visited Peterlin. Don't know if there's any connection there."

"Of course there is," said Claypack.

With only a slight pause to recover from the shot, Garcia went on. "She went in to Barnaby Wells on Tuesday. The next day, she didn't go to work. We checked her accounts. There has been no activity since the Tuesday. There's about $160,000 total in her checking and savings accounts. We're monitoring them so we'll know when she tries to withdraw or transfer it."

"Won't happen," said Claypack.

Garcia's face reddened. "And no one using a passport under her name has left the country since the Tuesday."

"And I presume Peterlin's accounts are exemplary?"

"Yes." Garcia was finding it best to stick to short answers.

"No phone records connecting the three in any way?" Claypack couldn't hide the exasperation in his voice.

"If they did speak ..." Garcia caught his boss' look. "*When* they spoke," he corrected himself, "they must have used one of those prepaid phones with no contracts."

There were several seconds of silence. Claypack leaned forward, face flushed. "How many times have they pulled this? We still can't get any of the others to come forward?"

Agent Dubois spoke up. "During her time with Barnaby Wells, Victoria has had three other clients, besides Pamela Greenwald and Jennifer Lynche, who fit the Pamela/Jennifer/Maribeth profile. I've contacted each of them—more than once—and none says they've lost any large sums on phony investments. I've asked them if they know Peterlin. I've told them that information they give us may help other women—no dice." Her hands flew up in exasperation.

"I don't get it," said Garcia. "Losing all that money—why didn't they come forward?"

"Embarrassment," Dubois answered. "They were duped by some good-looking guy who paid attention to them, something their own husbands hadn't done in years. He was romantic, took them out to nice places, bought them presents. None of them had a real job. Their husbands made all the money and managed it. I mean, they could spend whatever they wanted, but they were dependent. Finally, because of McCain, or whatever he called himself, they thought they had figured out a way to make a lot of money themselves—to show their exes they could do it on their own. Their husbands left them, but they finally had a chance to get even: have a hunky, sophisticated, rich boyfriend and a fat portfolio to boot. So there!" Leticia delivered the explanation with a just a little too much emotion.

Recovering quickly, she added, "We've tried to check Peterlin's records to see if any of them scheduled appointments with her, but it seems there are no records. Peterlin's assistant tracks Peterlin's appointment calendar manually and the schedule is shredded at the end of each day. Peterlin apparently insists that clients pay her by money order only, for confidentiality reasons."

For several seconds, no one spoke. Then Claypack shook his head. "Talk about being embarrassed and taken for fools." In his 25-year career with the Bureau, Russ Claypack had been outwitted only a couple of times, and it stung.

For the third time in as many hours, Bethany apologized. "I really thought he was going to be around for a few more days. I should have been watching more closely. I was totally played."

Claypack ended the meeting, asking them to mull the case over for a few more days. Then they would regroup again, go over everything step by step one more time and see if anything new came to light.

He also asked Bethany to stay.

When Dubois and Garcia had gone, Claypack moved to the chair next to hers and swiveled around to face her. He was stocky in an athletic way. His square face was topped by thick gray hair. A loosened tie hung from his open collar, looking depleted. While typically curt and abrupt when discussing department operations, Russ was known to be kind and understanding when the occasion called for it. He leaned forward so barely two feet separated them. Intense, solid brown eyes bore through his steel-rimmed glasses and locked onto hers. "Bethany, you said that Peterlin was psychic and the only thing you were able to hide from her was your identity as an agent. Does that mean she was right about your falling in love with McCain?"

"Of course not," Bethany said without hesitation, meeting his gaze head on.

"And for the record, how did you manage to spend that week together in Mexico and not sleep with him?" he asked. FBI regulations prohibited agents from becoming intimate with criminals under investigation.

"Incredible self-control," she joked, then saw that he wasn't smiling. "Unfortunately, as soon as I got to Mexico, I developed a nasty bout of gynecological problems with some very unsavory symptoms, like vaginal drainage, heavy bleeding ... Rufus wasn't pleased, to say the least."

♦ ♦ ♦

A few weeks later, Bethany sat in the same conference room, in the same seat. Claypack was across the table from her this time. He looked at her curiously. She had called the day before, saying there was an urgent matter she needed to discuss with him as soon as possible.

"I'd like another chance with Clifford and McCain—or whatever his real name is."

"We had a wrap-up meeting over a month ago. I thought we agreed we had no leads and that there's nothing else we could do."

"Well, that's changed."

"What do you mean?"

"I know where they are."

"What!" he said, almost rising from his seat. "Why didn't you say so sooner?" He was almost shouting.

"Because I just found out."

"How?"

She went on to explain. They then spent the next couple of hours working out how the sting would take place. And this time, they wouldn't be foiled.

FORTY SIX

It WAS LATE JANUARY—a typically warm summer day. The outdoor art show in Sydney's trendiest shopping area was jammed with the usual assortment of tourists, middle-class locals and the inconspicuously very rich. The main street had been sealed off from traffic, allowing pedestrians to amble freely among the exhibits. White-canvas tents shielded the art, artists and visitors from the heavy noon sun.

Two women wandered through the bustling street, engaged, it appeared, in animated conversation. They could not have been more different. One looked like she had just come from a fashion shoot. She was slim, auburn-haired and held herself with a regal, self-assured posture. She wore a simple but elegant tangerine linen dress and an unusual necklace with a Buddha pendant rested on her neck. The other could have been her personal trainer. She was a stocky type, with cropped, brush-and-go strawberry-blonde hair. Her bright white sneakers made it easy to follow her in the crowd.

The pair approached the most popular exhibit, the one

featuring Australia's most acclaimed abstract artist. The shorter woman entered the tent. The other made her way to the row of port-a-potties at the end of the block. Several minutes later, the first woman exited the tent. A man with a beard and long ponytail stood at the entrance holding a glass of wine. Without looking where he was going, he turned sharply into the path of the stoutish woman, spilling his drink on her. Immediately, he began gesturing in apology, using a napkin to try to dry her off, then reached for his handkerchief to finish the job. He continued his conversation with her, leading her to the wine booth, where he bought them each a glass. They returned to the entrance of the tent where he had bumped into her and seemed to be chatting amiably when the taller, auburn-haired woman returned. The stoutish woman greeted her friend, then gestured toward the man, seeming to introduce the two.

From a restaurant terrace six stories above, Agent Bethany Foster surveyed the scene through her binoculars. A smirk spread across her face as she watched the familiar sequence of events play out. When she'd first caught sight of the man standing outside the tent, a shadow of sadness had passed through her eyes, but only for an instant.

She reached into her red Louis Vuitton bag for her cell phone and typed out "McCain just surfaced—'bumped into' Agent McKensie. This time we'll get them!"

Picking up her binoculars, Bethany focused on the trio again. The sun slid over the rooftops and shone directly on the restaurant terrace where she sat. Its rays caught the perfect sphere of the pearl, nestled in its shell, as it dangled from her necklace, giving it an ethereal glow. On the street below, the auburn-haired woman turned slightly, strengthening the GPS signal from the Buddha pendant on her neck. The sun illuminated the Buddha's face—it seemed to wink at the woman on the terrace who had created it.

◆

ACKNOWLEDGMENTS

Many thanks to Rick W. Smith, former FBI Special Agent and current Principal of Cannon Street, Inc., who kept me on the straight and narrow regarding FBI procedures and tactics and for explaining the difference between what is and isn't a crime. Also, thanks to my friend and editor, Sharon George, real estate broker, for her relentlessness in ensuring consistency of the plot's timeline and accuracy of real estate transaction details. And to my friend, Jill Hill, Coldwell Banker Residential real estate broker, for confirming the veracity, albeit not necessarily the proper ethics, of real estate dealings described.

I would also like to thank Laurie King and Jim Shubin, the "Book Alchemist," without whom this book would have its final resting place in the bottom drawer of my desk. Thanks also to Deke Castleman for his eagle eye. And special thanks to my talented graphic designer nephew, Alex Roberts, AJR Designs, for the cover design and chapter graphics.

The biggest thanks go to my husband, muse and best friend, Greg, for his unwavering support and faith in me. And for spending a good portion of his life reading, re-reading and giving me notes on all my writing endeavors. You're the best thing that ever happened to me.

Made in the USA
Middletown, DE
17 January 2022